Pauline McLynn grew up in Galway and started acting while studying History of Art in Dublin. She has played many stage roles, but shot to fame as the inimitable Mrs Doyle in *Father Ted*. Her other television work includes *Aristocrats* and *Bremner, Bird and Fortune*. Pauline has read several *Books at Bedtime* and her appearances on cinema screens include *Angela's Ashes*, *Quills, Gypo, Heidi* and *An Everlasting Piece*. Pauline has contributed to *Girl's Night In*, in aid of War Child, *Magic*, in aid of One Parent Families, *Moments*, in aid of Tsunami Relief, and the serial Irish novel *Yeats Is Dead*, in aid of Amnesty International. She has written three extremely successful comic novels featuring Dublin private detective Leo Street, *Something for the Weekend, Better than a Rest* and *Right on Time*, and the highly acclaimed novel *The Woman on the Bus*.

Visit Pauline's website at paulinemclynn.com.

Praise for *Summer in the City*:

'If *The Woman on the Bus* showed an altogether more serious side to McLynn, her latest book continues that trend and establishes her as an accomplished writer of popular fiction . . . She artfully analyses themes of marriage, grief, self-loathing and friendship . . . A warm novel . . . full of engaging characters' *Sunday Tribune*

'Pauline McLynn . . . deals compassionately and realistically with sensitive, complex issues' *Ireland on Sunday*

'A warm, witty and humorous tale that you can't put down' *Sunday World, Ireland*

D1321949

Summer in the City

Pauline McLynn

headline
review

First published in 2005 by HEADLINE REVIEW
An imprint of HEADLINE BOOK PUBLISHING

First published in paperback in 2006 by HEADLINE REVIEW
An imprint of HEADLINE BOOK PUBLISHING

A HEADLINE REVIEW paperback

2

ISBN 0 7553 2635 0

Typeset in New Caledonia by Palimpsest Book Production Ltd,
Polmont, Stirlingshire

Printed and bound in Great Britain by Clays Ltd, St Ives plc

Headline's policy is to use papers that are natural, renewable and
recyclable products and made from wood grown in sustainable
forests. The logging and manufacturing processes are expected
to conform to the environmental regulations of the country of origin.

HEADLINE BOOK PUBLISHING
A division of Hodder Headline
338 Euston Road
London NW1 3BH

www.reviewbooks.co.uk
www.hodderheadline.com

For Ger Norman,
friends always

ONE

It's just as well I don't have kids, Lucy thought as she stirred in the seat. I'd never be able to rear them in a Nissan Micra. A slogan mocked her. You can with a Nissan, it whispered, oiling her with sly malice. 'With one, perhaps,' she said aloud, 'but hardly in one.' Her back ached from its unnatural night-time posture and one of her feet was numb. She wiggled it and relished the darting pins and needles of a returning blood flow. Not quite Uma Thurman in *Kill Bill*, but she just might get there if things didn't improve.

She lay on the back seat looking at the padded ceiling of the car, wondering if she should go back to reclining in the front seat again. More leg and body room. She wasn't a long woman but this seat wasn't suitable for anyone beyond three foot six. Why don't I know that in metric? she wondered, the tiny miscellanies of life reintroducing themselves as a new day began. Her back continued to hum and her foot to gently stab. How had it come to this?

She held her hand aloft to check her watch for the time. Seven o'clock and already the sun warmed the interior of her metal home. It was going to be another scorcher. She gave a yawn and tried to keep her mood light. The first five minutes of every day were usually manageable, before her brain got hold of her properly and reminded her that she had never been so low. Tick, tick, three, two, one, and . . .

Good morning, Lucy, and welcome to your no-hope life. Today we'll be taking you on yet another tour of despair and you'll wonder all over again how you could have been so stupid as to lose everything you ever had. Except your car, a two-bit job and a small bank account perilously close to empty.

Lucy covered her eyes and steadied her breath. She needed a workout and a wash. At least her gym membership would not forsake her for another month. After that she'd consider jumping in the Thames, without planning to resurface. Come to think of it, that was an option at any time.

She kicked off her sheet but became tangled in the material as usual. Why she bothered with it was a mystery, but she seemed to need the normalcy of using it so the early morning tangle it was. It wasn't even as if anyone could see into the car, as she had the sunblinds pulled down over all the windows most of the time and all through the night. Thank goodness for the folly of 'raising the spec' when she'd bought it. At least I never succumbed to driving gloves, she reminded herself, and hadn't been the total idiot then that I later became.

She sighed and reached for the sheet corners, folded it

neatly into a small rectangle and stowed it in the footwell. Then she wriggled into a singlet and track bottoms, socks and trainers. Well, I'm supple, she thought, though it was scant comfort. She opened the back door of the car, swung her legs out and stretched into the day. She grabbed a backpack with clean-ish daywear and slung it on. She'd need to run fast to Bodybase if she was to make the loo in time. She hated having to duck behind hedges in daylight. You never knew who would see you or what you might find. And there was always the Crazy Lady to navigate. Not that she ever said anything or even acknowledged Lucy. It was rough to know that the only person on the earth who knew where to find her was a loony bag lady who talked to herself and couldn't give a damn that Lucy was alive.

Sure enough, Crazy Lady was stationed at the top of the road from the cul-de-sac onto the main thoroughfare, staring at the traffic roaring by in the distance. Hard to read her expression. She was frowning, sure, but then she always did as far as Lucy could tell. She didn't seem to register anything much and certainly didn't even glance in Lucy's direction as she began her jog. Feet thudding on concrete led to a limp and Lucy was forced to slip into a hollow by a tree and squat to relieve herself. She didn't look back as she resumed her journey but was certain she heard a mild cackle behind her. Perfect. Even the homeless were mocking her now.

You *are* the homeless, she told herself. That bag lady is a jury of your peers. She broke into a gut-busting, lung-popping sprint.

*   *   *

3

Helen stood dividing her attention between the morning traffic and the woman from the car. Resentment simmered in her veins. The stranger had arrived ten days ago and taken up residence without so much as a by-your-leave. This was Helen's place not hers, and it was most certainly not for sharing. What did she want here? And why here, of all places? This woman had disturbed the delicate system Helen had developed as her routine and the intrusion was causing her anguish. She had more to deal with than the annoyance of seeing off this stranger. But see her off she would. There was no room here for anyone but herself. She had been too patient and should have acted sooner on this matter. But she had been surprised by the situation being, as it was, so unexpected. Initially there was no way of knowing how long it would last. She had assumed that the arrangement would be temporary, that the woman would be gone the day after her arrival. But one day followed another and she was still here.

She hated that car too; red, an awful colour, the worst. The thought occurred to her that the stranger might leave if she wrecked it, although that would mean touching the vile thing, which was unacceptable. She might try throwing some stones at it in the hope of breaking a window, or better still the windscreen. She decided to think about it later when she had time. Now that the intruder had left she would probably be gone until dark, if her usual movements were anything to go by. That meant Helen could get back to the business of her own day. She hunkered down to let sorrow guide her, as it did constantly now.

Jack Smith reached out to thump his radio alarm into submission. He could never figure out why he didn't just switch it off when he woke, as he always did, an hour before it was scheduled to annoy him. Another of life's habits. Another bad one. The sun was beating in through the muslin, picking out the mirror of the dressing table, the glass perfume bottles on the mantel above the seldom-used marble fireplace and glinting off the silver candlesticks. This room had far too much wife in it. He was going to have to put his stamp on the place.

He swung out of bed and padded to the en suite where he savaged himself under a cold shower. It made him yelp and he found that pleasing. His skin stung afterwards as he shaved, a shake in his hand adding some danger. It might have been the wash or the hangover, each was a valid choice these days. Finished and miraculously without a nick, he stood back to admire what could be admired and was amazed once again how misery could hone a body to such good shape. Losing weight suited him, though he still felt like shit from dawn to dusk and beyond. His face had a chiselled definition now and his hair was a little longer than usual which gave him a foppish elegance. His ribs were toned and the tan from the expensive holiday in Florida some months earlier lingered to keep him on the right side of healthy. If his innards were on show the story might be different. But that was one of life's great anomalies; no matter how awful you felt on the inside, the exterior could be buffed into an acceptable version of survival.

In fact, he hadn't looked this good in years, or felt so bad. Go figure.

He shrugged into an ugly bathrobe he'd been given last Christmas, padded to the kitchen and fired up the espresso machine. He contemplated the rows of mueslis and health supplements and opted to pop some vitamins with his caffeine. Food was no longer as important to him as it once had been. His appetite had absconded around the same time as his wife. He missed both in a vague, angry way, when he could be bothered to feel anything at all. Now his head began to throb and he was grateful of the distraction. He went in search of aspirin. The kitchen drawers were full of stainless-steel items that looked unused. Hadn't he heard one of Laura's friends say they resembled nothing more than gynaecological instruments of torture? He had got the impression that all such instruments were torture, the greatest of which was their temperature – cold to freezing – and apparently this was a painful but hilarious observation if the drunken shrieks of delight afterwards were anything to go by. Then again, what women said and what they meant were often two very different things. The cutlery drawer clattered shut with the force of his shove but the tea towels hushed open in the very sound of extremely expensive kitchen units. No drugs. The cupboards held dishes to cater for an army. The wine rack was half empty. Oh, to finish it off right now and spend the next twenty-four hours anaesthetised. He returned to the bathroom and found a battered sachet of something fizzy that tasted foul and promised the earth. I'll take it, he thought, and I'll be grateful for small mercies.

His mobile began to chime Big Ben. He still didn't know who'd programmed it to do that. 8.02 a.m. Who in God's name would call at this hour? There could only be one answer, a client. The caption read, 'Jodie Taylor Jones.' Jack Smith heaved a reluctant sigh and pressed green.

'Jodie,' he chirruped. 'My favourite wake-up call.' If only she could see my face, he thought, my nose must have doubled in length.

Lucy pounded the pavement of South Lambeth Road in a slow but regular rhythm and arrived at Bodybase in a sheen of perspiration and mild panic. No need to do a warm-up on the treadmill, she decided, my heart rate is well fired up and my pulse feels like it's completely off the scale. She nodded breathlessly at the receptionist as she signed in. The youngster smiled and muttered something inane about the weather. The gym was already busy and Lucy recognised a few faces so she snagged her swimsuit from her backpack and made for the pool. It, too, was full of busy office workers getting into competitive gear by tearing up and down the lengths. The tension was palpable in the misty air, the fluoride tang of the early morning rat race. I am just so weary of all of this, Lucy thought, and in spite of my present predicament I probably would like to live a little longer, and well. She turned her back on the churning pool and waded into the Jacuzzi by its side. She climbed into the underwater metal frame, pushed the appropriate buttons and lay back to let the water pummel her aching muscles. If only it could reach into my heart, she thought wistfully, it could do with a right rigorous session.

The inhabitants of number 5 Farewell Square were on the move. Ulrika Henning sat wincing over a grapefruit half and longing for toast and marmalade. To begin, she had gulped back a litre of warm water with a squeeze of lemon juice, confident that this would help flush out any toxins and hopeful that it would stanch her appetite. She had lost eleven pounds in the first twenty-one days of her regime and was hoping to be a size twelve by the end of the month. She thought about how her days were counted as just that now, rather than rounded into weeks. Everything revolved around the diet. Whoever had remarked that diet was in fact 'die' with a 't' on the end was so spot on. She was famished. Still, it had to be done and it would be worth it, even if it did kill her as promised.

Her hair was neatly pinned into a bun at the nape of her neck and she had chosen a muted blouse and flowing skirt ensemble for the day. She was going through a concerted schoolmarm phase, which was appropriate, as she was a teacher at the local college on Larkspur Lane. Even her students had remarked on her diminishing size, which was both gratifying and encouraging. The staffroom ignored it but then they would.

She heard the Scissor Sisters begin to blare from Colin's room, followed by the sound of the groans of more than one person. She braced herself to meet the latest in a long line of his conquests. If she hadn't had any at all lately, Colin made up the numbers with plenty, and very few repeats. She grinned in anticipation, then grimaced again as that latest sour segment hit home.

Lucy was towelling off and feeling moderately refreshed when she heard the 'Cooee' of Loretta Hunter entering the women's changing area. This was the downside of having to use Bodybase as her early morning body base. And Loretta was the lowest point of that downside. Lucy steeled herself for the inevitable barrage of questions.

'A little birdie tells me that you and Pete have dropped off the edge of the social universe, darling. Tell me all.' Loretta planted herself on the bench by Lucy's side and stared at her hard as Lucy tried to wriggle into her civvies with some elegance and decorum. Already Loretta's nasal whine was hurting her head. Sometimes she thought she'd be able to tell what the woman was saying or asking simply by hearing the sounds of her annoying voice rather than the words.

'Well, you know how it is when you're moving house, everything is upside down for an age, Loretta.' She was amazed at how smoothly she could evade a proper answer without her voice wavering to the tune of her shattered life. 'I sometimes think it will never end.' At least that much was true, though there was still no telltale quiver.

9

'Darling, I hear you,' Loretta assured her. 'I have vowed never to move again after the last debacle.' Loretta, Lucy knew, bored easily and was in the habit of moving every five years or so, after spending much of her husband's fortune on redecorating whatever mansion they had moved to on her latest whim. These were rarely debacles or even mild disasters and Loretta often made a tidy profit on the refits. 'But surely you could do with help. Shouldn't I call round and add a pair of hands to your efforts?'

This was exactly what Lucy had been trying to avoid.

'You really are too good to offer, Loretta,' she told her. 'But what with the builders turning the new place into the seventh ring of hell and Pete and myself worked off our feet, I think we'd do well to put all visits on hold until we have something decent to show for ourselves, not to mention a functional plumbing system.' She added a little laugh, which she hoped sounded resigned but happy at the situation. Before Loretta had a chance to argue her case further she spotted more interesting company and excused herself with, 'You let me know when you need me, darling, and I'll be there toot sweet.'

Another minefield safely negotiated. Only twelve more hours of the same to endure, Lucy reminded herself, cheerlessly.

Famke K was already hard at work. She stood naked in front of her latest painting and wondered what was wrong with it. Today was a looking day and she found these the hardest to bear. She was not allowed to touch or alter the work in any way, just contemplate its awfulness (as she now saw it). She paced to the right, stopped and lingered. It gave nothing away. She tried going to the left and for the briefest whisper felt she was close to grasping what it wanted to tell her. Then the opportunity vanished. She knew better than to gripe. It would yield its secret eventually, she hoped. And if it did not, she would destroy the painting, for that was another rule; the work had a limited time to happen or find itself, then it was either released into the public domain or dispatched to art hell. That was the rule and she abided by it. Many tears had been shed over the years in that studio but at least it wasn't full of damaged pets. She sat in the wicker chair and let it trace its weave onto her body, then laughed as she remembered Colin once declaring he was hungry enough to 'eat a farmer's arse through a hedge'. She decided to get dressed and join the household for breakfast. She would function better on a full stomach. And she would save washing as another chore for later. Pace was everything on these days. She took one last look at the painting. It refused to speak.

'Have it your own way,' she told it. 'I'll be back.'

Colin stretched long and hard in his bed. He liked to start his day with a good rousing tune or a fuck, whichever was handier. Today he was spoiled for choice. Behind him he felt the timid stirrings of some guy called Tony who was engaged to be married in two months' time and experimenting for all he was worth in between. He'd picked him up in a bar in Pimlico last night, though funnily enough he hadn't gone out to pull. Generally he liked Sunday night to himself because he hated Monday mornings and the certainty of another week of mind-numbing accountancy so much. But Tony was cute in the smoky light and so he took seven seconds to convince himself that he'd only be young and energetic once, and then he pounced. It had been laughably easy. It usually was for 'our wee Colin', as his family in Belfast called him.

He thought about his choices, then decided to shower and get rid of Tony, who was a sad sack, actually, he now thought. He loved these spur-of-the-moment decisions and sometimes wondered if he should live by throwing dice some days. It would suit his temperament.

'See you?' he said in the heavy Northern Irish accent he kept for his campest moments. 'Time for you to piss away off. I have work, a career, and maybe you do too. Have a nice life. Be gone when I return.' He gave the last bit extra welly, and would have liked to do a finger wiggle but he was still lying down and facing away from his quarry. He pranced out of bed, letting Tony have a full view of his magnificent erection. Then just before he went through the door, he let his hand stray to his penis and left Tony in no doubt as to the pleasure he would enjoy with his shower. I am good, he told himself, and a *total* bitch. Satisfied with this, he bounded down the corridor to the bathroom, singing along with the Sisters. Gonna take your momma out all night, indeed.

❈ ❈ ❈

Lucy got her things together in indecent haste, but Loretta was deep in gossip heaven by then and oblivious of her escape. Lucy had once told Pete about the horror of being caught in Loretta's sights and unable to get away. 'The hunter and the hunted,' he had remarked. At the time she'd thought it another fine example of his wit and laughed girlishly in appreciation. What a mug. She would love to have other people to share the blame with, those who hadn't warned her about him, but there was no one because everyone had felt the same about Pete Kingston: everyone loved him. She often thought that maybe she still did too, just a little. That made her despair even more for the day. Her stomach rumbled loudly and she relished the hint, the opportunity to concentrate on something else – the sheer mundanity of feeding herself. She waved at Loretta and left. It took the other woman fifteen minutes to realise she'd gone.

Colin's room was empty on his return and he stretched again in celebration. Sunlight kissed his slim frame and he sighed with joy. God, it was good to be him. He threw open the window and leaned out to breathe in the summer air. He could see Helen on duty at the square end of the cul-de-sac. Poor bitch. Something would have to be done there. The traffic roared past as usual. Beyond, the rooftops of Vauxhall backed onto Kennington and further on to Stockwell, Brixton and beyond. Millions of people gearing up for another day at the coal face. Millions of people with the possibility of living, or dying, or winning

13

the lottery. 'It could be you-hoo,' he sang, pointing out at the city.

He chose a light blue suit and teamed it up with a white linen shirt and yellow polka-dotted tie. 'And the top of the morning to you too,' he said to his wardrobe mirror. Then he slipped his Italian suede loafers over pink cotton socks and wondered who would notice his outrageous choice at the office. He hoped for Jonny, the trainee, a sallow-skinned beauty from Cornwall and fabulously heterosexual and green. He ran some gel through his spiky red hair, clicked off the stereo and headed down to breakfast, stopping at the door of the kitchen to clock Tony sipping a cup of weak tea.

'Shame,' he said aloud, twisted on his continental heels and left.

He met Famke coming up the garden from her studio and kissed her on both cheeks. 'Can't stay, oh most wonderful of landladies. Ulrika is nursing the latest of my pathetic cast-offs. Inspect and reject,' he ordered. 'Later,' he promised and left Famke wearing an indulgent smile. He stepped into the cul-de-sac and greeted Helen who did not acknowledge him.

Something will have to be done, he thought again.

Bill Richards lay in bed looking at his ceiling. I can't do it today, he thought. I just cannot do it. Tears began to roll off his face and pool under his head, then seep into his pillow. I don't think I can do any of this any more.

TWO

There were lots of things to be grateful for, Lucy reasoned, as she made her way along the river walk. For instance, the Thames was looking fabulous as it winked at the day, sunshine sparkling on its surface, enough to gladden any dull heart. Even some of the suited passersby were paying it attention. Lucy stopped to lean on a warm rampart, close her eyes and breathe a little of its joy. Instead she became painfully aware of her exaggerated heartbeat. It pounded her chest against the stone and pushed her back again and again. She jerked away and collided with a group of Japanese tourists taking their leisure along the embankment. After mimed and spoken apologies and a lot of bowing from the Japanese she resumed her journey, pretending to be a tourist herself for a moment. She looked along the river to the London Eye slowly rotating up and over. She'd never been on it, like many natives, always believing there was still time for everything and sometimes finding that there was all too much time and most of it wasted. Behind and beyond to the right the

Gherkin glinted amongst the other buildings of the City. So strange to think of all the little ant-people busy over there, unseen, turning the wheels of commerce. What must it feel like to be important? To be needed or essential?

Time to move her mind on again. It was no good to stay for any length anywhere right now, physically or mentally, for fear of rediscovering the full extent of her problems and uselessness. And anyway, she was hungry and needed caffeine badly. A day had not truly begun until a double-shot latte hit her stomach. Although she habitually bemoaned her lack of a decent job, she was thoroughly relieved to be working at Mario's now. It meant she got fed and watered for free, and was very busy all the time. Just what her karma ordered.

She stalled at the door of Fifi's Flowers and waved at the proprietress. A hand waggled over a display of gerberas and a voice said, 'Morning. Can't stop. I'm in the middle of a massive apology bouquet to a certain individual's mistress and of course the even more expensive guilt bunch to his wife. See you later.' Fifi's frizzy blonde hair seemed suspended on invisible wire above the flowers, wildly careering in all directions. This was often all Lucy saw of her on a visit, as Fi's voice chatted ninety-five to the dozen and order after order appeared on the counter. A slow girl called Martha sat glumly by the till eating her fingernails and waiting for life to produce either excitement or death to relieve her apparent tedium.

Lucy moved on to Mario's next door and slid by the row of juniors filling the takeaway orders for the neighbouring office elevenses. 'No, no. Six apple Danish and four cinnamon and raisin.' The aroma of ground coffee made her smile and that didn't hurt too much. Life in the old gal yet.

Famke lay back in the froth of the lavender bubble bath and thought about the work she had just made. For a while now she had been painting what she termed her urban landscapes. They showed the mini wildernesses growing in the cracks of pavements and on the edges of the streets and roads of London. They were vibrant and teeming with grasses, flowers and plants, largely ignored by the busy passing population. She felt these places were every bit as beautiful as the landscapes chased by city dwellers as they dashed to the country for the weekend to live a more bucolic life. The longed-for euphoria could never cancel the amount of stress encountered in travelling and the tiny amount of time spent in the sought-after nirvana. Everyone was searching for a lost idea of what they thought the Good Life was. Maybe a little of what they wanted was right under their noses all along?

But lately bits of people had started to appear in the work. Her most recent painting had a shoe, and not just any shoe; this one belonged to Helen, the woman roaming the cul-de-sac each day. Famke hadn't expected it but was accepting when her brush and her uninhibited mind placed the shoe beside a clump of dandelions at the top of the narrow laneway. Now she had to figure out what it wanted to tell her. She felt the stirrings of excitement. The series was moving forward, taking on a life of its own as all of her best work did. The answer was outside her studio, just a few short steps away; all she had to do was to figure out the question, and she would have her theme.

'Simple as that,' she said wryly before disappearing into the water.

Lucy sipped her latte and sighed. I'm a simple woman really, she thought. Simple things make me happy. So what did I ask for in life that was so complicated I got dumped on from a height? Granted, for an English bird, latte and crostini for breakfast aren't *so* usual, she mused. She crunched into the bread and listened to the sibilant hissing of the espresso machine and the throaty gurgle of the milk frother. There were times when she regretted that mankind had moved on from the animals, not very far some might say, but enough to experience heartache when all anybody wanted was a rounded life of eating and reproduction. In mitigation, however, it had to be admitted that life would be a lot harder without Lycra, coffee makers and hair conditioner so there were a few pluses out there yet. She breathed in the dark, nutty aroma of the roasted grounds and, still munching, made her way to the changing area. Here she plugged in her mobile phone, shucked out of her civvies and into the café uniform. The black T-shirt and trousers were nicely slimming, even on Mario, and topped with a crisp white apron embroidered with the café name. All were laundered by Vida, a Slovenian cousin of Mario's wife, famous for bursts of temper and wisdom, one more frightening than the other. She was also a devout communist who rated Marshal Tito as her top dictator of the twentieth century; there were others she thought stopped a long way short of the mark. And she was one hell of a housekeeper to the company. Formidable would be the word invented for her if it were not for the existence of Mario's spouse, Maria. The husband and wife team was referred to as the M'n'Ms, but always out of their earshot.

Maria was a short wiry Italian who clung to her roots and refused to be anglicised. Fair enough, all thought, but there were times when they were certain she was just testing them for spirit and guts. She had a way with malapropisms that bordered on the completely ridiculous and as she was by no means a stupid woman they began to think that after forty-five years of London, she was just having the world on. She started small, telling stories of the price of cooking oil going 'to high sky', then put up signs pointing out the 'fire distinguishers', before moving on to referring to her foot fingers, at which point Lucy bit her tongue and tried not to let suppressed laughter show in her eyes. Maria pierced her with her own black dots and raised an eyebrow. From then on Lucy was sure that Maria knew that she knew that she knew, and on towards the infinite with that.

Mario stuck his head round the chrome partition and

smiled. His glorious white hair was sculpted into a quiff worthy of Elvis and his cheeks were rosy enough to take a bite out of. He was every inch the playboy and, even after all of his time living in England, still had the magical rhythms of his native Italy. He charmed her every time, the old dog. 'You're on,' he burred. The breakfast rush segued into the elevenses rush and on into lunchtime, so there was barely a moment for the staff to slacken. Mario and his nephew, Vida's son Ivan, did the earliest shift, then Lucy took over with whoever was rostered. 'My empire is yours,' Mario told her, expansively. 'Have a nice day.'

Lucy gulped back the last of the latte and shoved the crostini into her mouth. 'You got it, boss,' she said through crumbs and froth.

He wiped her chin as she passed, whispering, 'Such a messy girl. I pray to God above that we don't have a visit from the Health and Safety.' She was lifted by the twinkle in his eyes. Her good humour was dashed when she saw that Danny Brock was working with her, as mean-spirited a crank as could be found in a day's trawl of the area. She switched on a warning smile, brushed past him and set to serving customers.

'Same to you,' she was sure she heard him mutter.

Colin blinked twice to clear his eyes. The figures on the computer screen were beginning to blur and his brain was on the fast track to a boredom coma. He stretched his neck in every direction possible and settled on looking

west towards the kitchenette which was full of more interesting activity. The gorgeous Jonny had his oh-so-cute butt
perched on the counter and was chatting happily with a
busty brunette from the Legal department. Time to put a
homo stamp on proceedings, Colin decided, springing into
action and rushing at the snackers. As he passed his best
pal's desk she smirked and said, 'Wasting your sweet gay
time, precious.'

'Oh, we'll see,' he trilled. 'I have a lot of success with
my hetero brethren, as you know. They're just so curious
about what us fairies get up to. And I've not met one yet
who didn't like a *little* cock up his arse.'

'I was right all along, you do have a tiny wiener.'

'*Au contraire, liebling.* I just put it *in* a little bit. Most
of them can't take all of what I've got. I am a force of
nature, let me assure you.'

'What you are is the worst, do you know that?'

'But you love me,' he cooed, then sighed. 'Well, who
wouldn't?'

'Mind if I tag along?'

'Oh, the more the merrier.' Colin rose to his full height.
'Look and learn, angel cakes.' He began to walk towards
his prey, glancing back once to say, 'Let's see some mincing.'
He led off by example.

Jack Smith pushed the last of the press release through
the fax machine, watching it disappear into one end and
emerge out of the other. Shit was hard to get rid of. He
wondered about his latest spin on the facts available to

21

him. His highest profile client had been implicated in a nasty story of Class A drugs and underage hookers. The fact that Jodie Taylor Jones was a woman added undeniable spice to the tabloid claims. In spite of her protests to the contrary, Jack was sure she was in this present mess up to her neck and playing it for what it was worth. Her latest wheeze was to suggest that she marry a long-term family friend with a similarly complicated moniker, which would leave her with a quadruple surname if family traditions were followed. He should really start charging per word, he thought. It was a worrying sign of how far he'd come that it took him an hour or so to wonder about any of the morality attached to dealing with this sort of sleaze. His usual argument that, like criminals, all alphabetically rated social stars deserved the best representation that money could buy till proven too guilty to prop up any more was ringing particularly hollow this morning. But he was a top PR guru and his time and experience cost the vast packet he needed to maintain his lifestyle. Or should that be the lifestyle his wife, Laura, demanded. Even now.

'I am actually a complete pushover,' he told himself aloud. He wondered what his clients would make of that if they knew. Chances were they already did. London was a goldfish bowl at the level he operated on and everyone knew everyone else's business. And he should have heeded the rumour that the woman known as Laura Wilcox had a fitting name. He'd put all that down to puerile innuendo and jealousy on the part of other social wannabes. As the truth began to emerge he made allowances, even tried a stab at reform. Why did anyone in love think they could change a leopard's spots? Or the habits of a thirty-year lifetime that had never known monogamy before he stumbled into her orbit?

'And just who are you fucking now?' he asked his absent wife.

He sank into a chair as the self-administered blow struck home. After all that had passed between them she could still wind him, and worse than that; he still wanted her so badly he could taste her on his tongue. It had the salt edge of despair to it. And it would not go away.

Ulrika had coffee in the canteen with the students and some of the staff. The number of people moving around the university meant a person need never get bored of any one batch of company. It also encouraged alienation which the staff were all versed in staving off, in the students that is. There didn't seem to be a course for the lecturers themselves to help deal with the flux of a changing and transient population. Her tummy rumbled and a wave of light-headedness passed over her. She gripped the table and panted till the nausea passed. She needed something solid as ballast for her digestive system. A scone might help ease off the hunger pangs. After all, she'd had no real calories so far today. What harm could a few carbohydrates and a little sugar do? She'd have the energy for her next session then. She got to her feet and wove a slightly drunken route to the serving counter. She chose a brown lump that

looked as unappetising as it tasted and she felt sure that
would be that. The disappointment in the eating would
cancel out any harm to her diet. She sat back feeling over-
full and uncomfortable. This will settle, she thought.

Suddenly she knew it had all gone horribly wrong as
a cramp ripped through her and her stomach heaved.
She clutched her midriff and dashed for the ladies' where
she retched the sinful mouthfuls back up. A trickle of
sweat ran down her spine and a violent shiver racked her.
She spread a hand on each of the cubicle walls and
gulped in a few deep breaths, then went trembling to
the handbasin where she drenched her face with tepid
water from the cold tap. Nothing in this place was an
extreme when you wanted it to be, she realised. She wiped
her face dry and checked herself in the mirror. Was she
imagining it or was there a new definition there? This
was pleasing in spite of how bad she felt. The light was
industrial and cruel to her skin tone but that was fluo-
rescence for you. She longed for a toothbrush and paste
to clear the acrid burn and rancid smell from her mouth.
Instead, she rinsed and spat a couple of times and straight-
ened once again.

'Sounded nasty,' remarked a fresh-faced teen to her
side.

'Yes. I think there's some sort of bug going round.
Probably just a twenty-four-hour thing.'

'Well, if you need anything for a little extra pep in your
step you just let me know,' the girl said, winking.

She should have hauled her ass to a disciplinary monitor

for that, but Ulrika was oddly comforted that the young-ster had mistaken her for a student. Ridiculous, she told herself, but it made her smile all the same.

Helen could not get her mind off the intruder and it was upsetting her routine. She had re-created her world and now this woman and her red Nissan Micra were threat-ening to take it away, to wrest it from her control. She couldn't allow that, of course. It would take a lot more than that slip of a thing to pull off that stroke. It was another hell-hot day and she was sticky and uncomfort-able sitting here. The loneliness was as bad as ever. But she didn't want company either. She wondered how Nicholas Farewell was doing out front, imagining his statue covered in pigeons' droppings, his grey stone uniform streaked with their scorn. But she would not visit to see the mess piled onto poor Nicholas. He was custodian of the front of the square; she needed to keep watch out back. When the rain finally came he would be rehabili-tated, though rain, even in a deluge, would hardly help her own predicament.

Helen had to formulate a plan to get rid of her unwanted visitor. The others living on the square knew better than to interfere with her now, so they were not a problem. But this stranger was. What had brought her here? Not that she ever intended to find out. She didn't need to know and, more crucially, she didn't want to know. She had her own concerns and they were more than enough to be getting along with. I have my own impossibilities to deal with, she thought, shuddering to admit it. She gasped, clutching at the air. It was so hard to breathe when the memories came, when the fullness of the loss pushed forward. It hurt on so many levels that she felt like an open wound, weeping. And yet her stupid and untrustworthy body persisted with the in and out of life, the awful inevitability of the next breath. She tried to resist sometimes but at last a gasp would wrench itself through her and tug in the air that kept her here.

She used to fancy that she would drift away if she closed her eyes tightly enough, but no matter how hard she squeezed them shut the weight of her heart hanging heavy in her chest was so real and painful it ground out the possibility of relief. Each time she thought she could no longer go on, her mind would churn over, torturing her, and her body continued to breathe. There was no escape.

Bill Richards finally summoned the will to get out of bed. The phone had been ringing all morning and his answering machine chided him as he passed it in the hallway. 'Piss off,' he told it. Out of habit he went to the front door and took post from the mailbox. He flipped through the junk and bills and threw the lot onto another ignored pile on the sideboard. 'You can fuck off and all,' he said. He stopped and ran a hand through his unruly and unwashed hair. I'm a lot of 'un' everything, he thought. Uncertain. Unhappy. Unloved? He leaned against the wall and let his body slide down it until he was curled in a ball on the polished marble floor. It was cool but hardly merciful. He began to cry again. When will this end? he implored of the ceiling, and the stairs, and the banisters and anything else that would listen. I want my life back. I want whatever I can still have of that back. Silence echoed around him.

Unanswered.

THREE

Colin sighed happily and dunked his Jaffa Cake. 'A total result,' he declared.

'It's just a Jaffa Cake,' Stella pointed out.

'One,' Colin raised an elegant finger, 'I didn't mean the Jaffa Cake. And two,' another digit went up, 'a Jaffa Cake is not *just* a Jaffa Cake, as you well know.'

'OK, back to basics. We have a result. For me,' she reminded him.

'Whatever.' He waved a fey hand to ward off annoying details.

'Jonny asked me out, not you.'

'Yesyesyes, but if you don't turn up he's all mine.'

'And I would not turn up *why*?' she asked slowly.

'Loyalty to me. Fear. Et cetera, et cetera, et cetera.'

'Yul Brynner, *The King and I*,' Stella said without inflection and by rote. 'But no way, buster. I fancy a date with this guy.'

'Well, so do I, so boo hoo.'

'No, boo hoo to you.'

'You.'

'You!'

'Stella, Stella, Stella,' Colin said, pityingly, 'it's obvious he's just doing it to grab my attention.'

'You are such a fantasist.'

'And I deliver the fantasies too, dear, unlike so many others. I am every man's fairy godmother.' He threw both hands in the air. 'I am she.'

Stella crossed her eyes. 'I have work to finish. And so do you.' As she went to her desk she heard a 'You' directed at her back. She spun round. 'No, you.'

'You!'

Famke looked at the painting and made some notes. She was placing layer upon layer of paint on the canvas, slowly building texture and life. The thick oils took time to dry and presented new possibilities with their finished surfaces. Here she glazed, there she scraped, inching to the ideal time of abandonment, when both she and the painting let the other know it was time to part. She was close with this one. It was hell not to be allowed to alter anything but today was only for looking and plotting progress. Helen's shoe needed more expression, though she was unsure how that would be achieved. It had emerged as an awkward shape, slightly too large for the foot and all the more vulnerable for it. The flat grey concrete beneath was uncompromising, hard against the softness of that tattered shoe. The wispy greenery of some scutch grass reached out to touch this symbol of humanity. To touch it? Or to soothe it? To rescue?

But could Helen be rescued?

Was that what the series wanted to ask?

Famke felt her limbs tingle and her nose twitched. She was close to understanding the nature of the work. She turned and walked away from it, breathing steadily. This was a delicate moment and to rush it would mean disaster.

Lunch hour was a bitch and a lie. First up, it was never just an hour and secondly, with Mario and Ivan back on duty and all hands on deck, the area behind the counter got tight and the staff were left looking like kids after an elaborate bun fight. Lucy sat at the staff table and picked egg mayonnaise and a bit of something that looked like a mashed prawn from her hair. She drew the line at tasting it to ascertain its origin, wiped a greasy hand on her now less than pristine apron and reached for her double espresso. A tabloid lay open before her showing a socialite stumbling from a Soho club in a sheath so short it left nothing to the imagination. On her feet a pair of ridiculously beautiful sandals sparkled in the photographers' flashes. Some multiple-barrelled gal getting into trouble for having too much money and very little sense. Lucy would have happily swapped at that moment. Her neck was so tense it hurt and no amount of head-turning eased it.

Pete had loved clubbing and no matter how she protested that they didn't have the money he always assured her that times were good and they needed to reward themselves. She wanted to believe that. She wanted him to be happy and in love with her, and he was. Then. She had loved him taking charge, deciding on a night out or a shopping trip or simply a beer in their local. He took care of it all. And how.

'Dream on,' a voice behind her encouraged, without conviction.

She didn't need to check to see that it was Danny Brock come to mock her. The only surprise was that he had taken as long as he had, some five to six minutes. All of a sudden she lost the will to keep a firm lid on her emotions. She wheeled round.

'Danny, as you are well aware, I don't like you, so why don't you fuck right off and leave me alone?'

Brock could have no idea that she was lashing out at the nearest target available, but as she really did not like him the message struck home and instead of arguing, as he might have, he did indeed slink off, leaving Lucy amazed and shaking at her outburst. That's not like me at all, she thought. Well, maybe it is now, she conceded. A new rude and selfish Lucy. And not before time?

Bill finally made it to his kitchen. The clock said midday, which was outrageously late to be starting the day. He looked desperately for signs of his lost life but didn't find any. He was alone. The room was vast to accommodate an eight-place table by the large folding glass doors, an island for food preparation and behind it a six-ring gas hob and oven with cupboards and smooth surfaces left and right. What it lacked was a family. He filled the kettle and flicked a switch. He was so exhausted with grieving for all that was gone he felt there was nothing left of him any more. Nothing of the man people had found worth in. And yet there was still a little hope, out there, within reach. So tiny a hook to hang on to. That worn-out cliché that while there's life there's hope. Almost as worn out as he was himself now.

He made a bitter cup of instant coffee and took it into the garden. His heart went out to the parched plants and greenery. He felt the rough scrape of the withered grass beneath his bare feet. The place was a disgrace, he decided, and something needed to be done. He abandoned the coffee and made for the hose. Moments later he was carefully watering pots and the areas in shade beneath the shrubs and small trees. He didn't want to scorch the leaves, mindful that this would harm the plants. A little of the weight in his soul was lifted temporarily and for the first time in a long while he thought about tackling work again. He decided to sit on the idea until he was totally rational again. Whenever that would be. That was, of course, if anyone could ever be accused of being 'totally' rational. There had been a time when he would have let his mind go off within itself to consider this notion and follow it where it wandered. But he had given up such fripperies. He'd given up most things, to be honest.

He reached the boundary wall and leaned against the wooden door that led to the cul-de-sac. He stood listening for the sounds, hardly breathing for fear of alerting anyone to his presence, but heard nothing. He turned to the large tree which hung its boughs over the garden on one side and beyond the wall on the other. He placed the hose at its foot and reached in to kiss its trunk. Then he walked back to the house, not caring about how much water he was squandering. It was time to get washed and dressed. That would be some sort of declaration of normality.

Famke climbed onto the tiny roof terrace above her studio. She loved this view. Right now it was also her inspiration. She looked down into the gardens of the rear of Farewell Square on its south side. Only three of them actually had access to the cul-de-sac: her own house and those of Bill Richards and Jack Smith. Three gates led to the top of a t-shaped area from which a short, inclined slip road emerged onto a busy main road. The furthest garden had been made over Japanese style just weeks before Jack's wife had run off with some smoothie from the BBC. It was a beautiful job, no doubt about it, and just about feng shui-ed out of existence. She grinned; must have all but wiped out his money corner. Last year Laura had had it done out in a Baroque style with vulgar fountain and ornate gazebo, folly in the extreme. That had all exited in a skip when the mood had taken her, though several expensive pieces were salvaged by strangers under cover of darkness.

Bill Richards was making his way up the overgrown

path of his eighth of an acre with a bit more purpose than she'd seen in a while. His plot was taking its own course with vigorous weeds flowering and seeding like there was no tomorrow. Bill usually looked like that was the case.

What Famke really wanted to check on was Helen. In the cul-de-sac, a figure sat sheltered by the wall of Bill's house under the canopy of his tree's leaves. She was in a flowing orange frock today and had her feet tucked under the skirt. Her arms were wrapped around her legs and her chin rested on her knees as she gazed down the little alleyway to the traffic roaring by on the main road. She was so still that the glance of a casual passerby would not have spotted her, but Famke could read the pent-up energy in the hunched shape. Poor Helen. How could they help her? Or did she have to help herself?

Again the idea of rescue came forward. Was this her theme? Can we be rescued from our lives, by ourselves or by others? And is it more difficult for the city dweller, beset by the daily stresses of modern life or, in Helen's case, something a lot worse? It was enough to move on with, Famke decided, hurrying back to her studio. As she reached the door she began to wonder about the car she'd seen. It had been there for over a week now and there was obviously someone sleeping in it at night. Was it to be a part of her ideological scheme? She needed to consult a brand-new canvas. She felt the flutter of excitement. To hell with the looking day, she thought, I'll burst if I don't paint something. And surely it wasn't cheating if it was a new canvas. She pulled a large white square from a selection stacked against the wall and propped it against her easel. Then she set to work and it was dusk by the time she paused again.

Jack sat in traffic in his sporty two-seater Mercedes. The soft top was down and fumes surrounded him. He had decided to visit his city centre office not because he didn't trust his people but because he needed to get out of that house. Mothers and au pairs dragged schoolchildren in yellow and grey uniforms home along the path with promises of play and treats. For a moment he saw Nigella Lawson but her shout of 'joshrubyellie' and all that followed made him realise she was not the particular domestic goddess he'd pegged her for. Goddess all the same, his inner man said. He threw her a smile but she didn't seem to notice. She might be ignoring me, of course: some strange bloke giving her the come-on from a flash motor. What do I look like? he wondered. Some fly-by-night yuppie, though a little old for that now surely. She'd probably taken the car and his forty years as a cry for help, thinking he had a big motorbike at home and a new tattoo somewhere on his body, testament to the passing of a significant and unwelcome birthday. God, how depressing: I am a social type, it seems, a stereotype. Then he pulled himself together, reminding himself that he didn't have a Harley or a tattoo and didn't intend to get either.

'What I do need is to get out more,' he said.

Horns barped and the line of cars edged forward. The Gherkin twinkled in the distance. London calling.

'Good idea,' he told the air, slipping in the disc and letting the Clash take control.

In the rear mirror he saw his Nigella turn round and laugh. He smiled sheepishly and raised a forty-year-old hand in acknowledgement.

Lucy checked her mobile phone; two missed calls, two messages received. They were both from her mother. Before she called her mailbox to hear them, Mario arrived to say, 'Your mother called to remind you that you are to hang an exhibition with her and serve at the opening.'

'How many times did she ask you to pass on that information?'

'Only three. She must be learning to trust you.'

Or she's too busy with her latest young squeeze, Lucy thought meanly.

'No need to listen to these then,' Lucy indicated the phone.

'Oh you must, they may be different.'

'Mario, you are one of life's optimists.'

'And so are you, lovely Lucy.'

Vida slid in, a small dark blob. Without looking at them she said, 'No, she very, very unhappy. I know.' She poked a claw into her own chest. 'Vida know.'

Vida is a witch, Lucy thought, not for the first time. To avoid getting into an argument about the rights and wrongs of Vida's feelings and premonitions, Lucy dialled in and listened as her mother's light voice twittered about her latest assault on the art market. Evie ran the White Rooms, a small gallery in Mayfair, and changed exhibits every six weeks from a rotating base of new and established artists. Her latest venture involved collaboration between a musician, a graphic artist and a painter. Lucy had no idea what to expect but her hopes weren't high as to the calibre of what would be on offer. Her mother was waxing about the profundity of the pieces, which made Lucy even more nervous. Her mother's taste was mostly decorative and she tended to follow the latest trends a little too slavishly for Lucy's liking. In fact, this was sound business sense as the work generally sold to the fashionistas desperate to be seen to be in tune with current fads but Lucy longed for a time when her mother let her choose more of the work. She wanted to encourage some of the newer artists languishing in group shows who deserved a wider audience. Her mother pointed out that the success of what Lucy thought ridiculous funded the more serious endeavours. For all her apparent woolly-headedness, Evie White hadn't survived forty years as a dealer without learning a few tricks.

Lucy gathered up her share of the tips and said her goodbyes for the evening. Mario's closed late afternoon after the gentle coffee drinking of passing tourists and preparation of the next day's essentials. To the eyes of all, Lucy was on her way home to her husband and she was the only one who knew this was not the case. Today she decided on an amble along the embankment then on to a

cinema for one of the cheaper early evening shows, courtesy of the extra money from her day's work. She was living
on chump change.

She stepped into the light and paused to adjust. The
heat felt tropical compared with Mario's air-conditioned
climate. After a few breaths and the initial pleasure of sun
on skin she set off at a leisurely pace, having learned not
to rush. All around her people dashed from one point in
town to another. Lucy had no reason to. This had been
one of the unexpected problems at the beginning of her
abandonment; she had far too much time on her hands.
She too had been in a hurry to get around but realised
very soon that she had no need to. She had nowhere to
be, no one to meet. She was human driftwood now. As
she walked towards the South Bank Centre she realised
that the time was coming closer when she would have to
tell someone about her situation. She was not looking
forward to the prospect. How could she admit that the
man she had fallen in love with and married had ditched
her and run away?

Colin's brain had seized up with the jumble of inane facts
and numbers that invaded his mind at work. He hardly
engaged with them now, just juggled, processed and moved
on. All he could think about was a swift pint then home.
He hadn't had a quiet night in for ages and Monday was
just the time for hibernation; the start of another week of
drudgery. He'd get naked on his bed, switch on the electric fan and TV and veg out. Very, very nice.

He dispersed his particular wisdom amongst the pubbites then headed for the Tube, smelling of smoke and booze, and whacked if he was to be honest. Some weirdo tried to talk to him but he put on his sunglasses and tuned out. He could practically feel his duvet beneath his back and taste the microwaved chicken korma from Sainsbury's as his television flickered mindless nonsense at him. Lovely. An early rejuvenating night then on to pastures nouveau for the rest of the week.

But his rapture was interrupted when he entered the communal kitchen of 5 Farewell Square. Sitting at the table and looking both nervous and at home was whatshis-name from last night. This was his worst nightmare: one of the Smitten come to haunt.

'I hope you're not here to see me,' he told him, sweeping by and wondering how he would extricate his meal and zap it without getting involved.

Ulrika appeared from behind a cupboard door saying, 'I thought it would be nice for Tony to join us for a bite to eat.'

'Your funeral, dear,' Colin said without breaking stride. He went seething to his room, hungry, annoyed and not knowing how to deal with Ulrika's latest fuck-up. He threw himself on his bed and kicked his heels again and again on the mattress, colouring the air with a stream of inventive expletives. When he was spent he turned on his stereo and decided to kill off all alien presence through noise. He was ripping though, no doubt about that, so he picked Mozart's Requiem and turned the volume knob up high.

They won't be expecting that, he told himself, delighted with his apparent unpredictability. It's a pity this one doesn't go to eleven, that'd really lift them right out of it. Stella would have guessed the Spinal Tap reference but he was alone and his delight at his own fabulousness fell on deaf air.

FOUR

Famke K had made her name in the art world through controversy and that suited her fine. She had trained in Wimbledon and was spat out into the market wanting to be a painter. But by then even she knew that to be a successful artist in Britain she was going to have to be able to talk a good piece whatever about being able to produce one. It seemed like a strange sport to want a visual artist to justify their work in words. Surely the deal should be to communicate it through the visual experience? she would argue. To move the audience to a response should be the goal. Not entirely, she learned. Talking, waffle, bullshit, whatever you wanted to call it, was just as important. And actually to be discovered by a patron of some sort would be handy too. It was exhausting. And that was before that elusive lady, Luck, came into the equation. Famke had seen many wonderful artists flounder by coming round the wrong corner at the wrong time, or even the right corner at the wrong time. It was a minefield and there was no map or sure course to follow.

She had initial and relatively modest success with a series of studies of politicians depicted in odd situations. These pieces were beautifully produced but left her hollow and unfulfilled. She felt they were gimmicky. Worse, they were bought mostly by the politicians themselves on whom their irony was all but lost. To her horror she realised she was pandering to their vanity. It was a badge of honour and trendy vogue to be chosen as a subject by Famke K and this was contrary to all she'd hoped for. The irony had turned round and taken a large chunk out of her behind. When she began to drift into what she felt was cartoon and caricature she abandoned the theme.

What shocked her most was that now, all these years later, the price of this old work when changing hands was at a premium. She was making other people a lot of money, as usual, and most of them were political hacks who really didn't need it. From time to time she considered returning to the style and content, if only to plunge the market value of this early work into the doldrums and stop the profiteering. But deep down she knew she just hadn't the heart for that. And it would be a giant waste of time.

She moved on to civic installations, almost to try to cancel out her unwitting encouragement of what she saw as the charlatans running the country. She worked hard to make sculptures and outdoor murals that would challenge the public but again found herself drifting into simplistic and sometimes condescending hectoring. She might as well be working for a Soviet Politburo forcing Party sentiment on an unsuspecting public (who didn't give a shit anyway). Later, she realised that her work from this time was in fact not quite as bad or morally repugnant as all that, and the public didn't ignore it even a quarter as much as she'd originally thought. In rare moments of what she generally dismissed as sentiment she would even admit to liking some of it. A fantastical windmill she'd built near Cardiff gave great pleasure and was mentioned in several guidebooks as a 'must see' for visitors and natives alike. It also now looked as if it had always been part of the landscape it inhabited. She had stood beside a child once who'd pointed excitedly and said to his parent, 'Oh, Mummy, look at the magic thing!' This had delighted her. She couldn't now remember exactly what the massively overwrought theory behind the construction was and it didn't matter. What did matter was that it was magical, at least to one person out there. And so she always referred to it as the Magic Thing and told interviewers that this was what she always intended it to be, though its formal title was Worldwind 2. Or 'hot air' as some long-forgotten lover had called it, not altogether unkindly.

As she drove home from a session overseeing the installation of the windmill, Famke saw something that would change her life and catapult her to the top of Brit Brat Art. Or perhaps it would be more accurate to say that she noticed something properly. It was a simple shrine at the side of the road, the aftermath of a car accident. Some bunches of flowers were placed by a fence with cards that read, 'Goodbye to my beloved husband, all my love forever,

Natasha,' and, 'We miss you, Brian. Love, your broken-hearted Mum and Dad,' and lastly a worn teddy bear with a note in blue crayon saying, 'Daddy, Ted will look after you now. I love you, Molly.' Famke had found her new theme and it was to cause a furore.

She began with a replica of the M4 shrine and soon her take on the Art of Road Death was shocking and exhilarating the nation. It was installed as part of a summer show in a new Docklands gallery that was hoping to be edgy and hip. It was, now. The first reviews singled out 'the disturbing realism of Famke K's frank evocation of a modern human tragedy'. Calls came through from other galleries wanting similar work, to which she agreed because she was engaged totally with her theme. She travelled the island visiting the new, impromptu graveyards of Britain. Each was more moving than the next, and each unique. Then people began to send her items from the shrines as they were being replaced so that she could have a little of the real experience to incorporate in her installations. It was, they explained, their way of immortalising their loved ones. At one stage a whole votive piece was to be destroyed when a motorway was widened so the family asked Famke to come and take the entire memorial away to put on show. She did and the work automatically escalated in breadth and depth. But there was further to go.

Critics referred to Famke K's 'wake-up call', praising her for 'moving, heart-rending images of man's destruction of mankind' and 'sensitive exploration of a country losing touch with humanity'. Best of all, for the galleries at least, there was a backlash as she was accused of 'raiding the nation's grief' and 'elevating carnage as Art with her particular brand of neurotic realism'.

In one daring solo show, Famke incorporated real shrines, but also created replicas of others and (crucially) installed live video feeds from cameras placed by the actual roadsides to relay images to the exhibition. One week in, a camera on a road to Southampton showed a real crash and the death of a young motorcyclist. An audience of twenty in the gallery watched in shocked awe as the mysteries of life and death unfolded before their eyes and they too became part of Art History. This piece was now in the Saatchi Collection complete with the CCTV footage of the viewers present at the moment of the incident. It is widely regarded as one of the seminal British works of the early twenty-first century and features in all textbooks and study manuals of UK art.

Her final piece on this theme was 'The Ho-Ho House' for which she reconstructed the façade of a two-storey house alive with flashing outdoor lights of Santa and reindeer and icicles and baubles. Beside it, forlorn, is a pavement strewn with the floral tributes to all who stalled to admire it on foot or in their cars, and perished in the process. Its sly wit and tragic story made the nation laugh and cry, and was nominated for the Turner Prize. It was destroyed in a warehouse fire in North London along with works by the Chapman brothers and Tracy Emin and so remains forever immortal.

Famke could now choose to do what she wanted, when

she wanted and for as much money as she wanted. Her reputation was unassailable, and rather than be dictated to by fashion she could now choose to work to her own prescription. She returned to her first love, painting. She sat on the floor of her studio contemplating the emerging study of Helen in the cul-de-sac. Her crouched figure screamed in oils slashed and dragged across the canvas. Shadows sucked at edges of the figure, threatening to swallow her. Despair and hopelessness were palpable and disturbing to the eye. Famke was exhausted but happy. She decided it was time to let that image settle itself before the next onslaught.

She went to the roof again to watch the tiny world of her preoccupation and let it talk to her in its own language. London twinkled its coloured lights in the early darkness of the night. The smell of charcoaled meat filled the air and somewhere close by an outdoor dinner party was in full swing. Famke heard laughter and the soft pluck of corks pulled from wine bottles. She stretched towards the sky. Her arms ached from work and her back throbbed from all of the strange, unpredictable movements the painting insisted on. She had twisted and pounced on specks, angles, surfaces all afternoon. No wonder she didn't need a gym.

The red car was still in the cul-de-sac and seemed not to have moved an inch since it had appeared. Why not? And deep in some hidden fibre of intuition Famke was certain it would be included in the series. Well, if that was to be the way, she was not going to argue. She had learned over the years not to interfere too much at this crucial early stage. Sometimes it was best not to argue at all.

Jack Smith spent the large part of his afternoon chasing Jodie Taylor Jones and fielding media queries as to her whereabouts. She was splayed across most of the tabloids, though had been bumped off the front page of one by a minor royal who had worn, shock and horror, a Dolce gown with Dolcis shoes. Next week the glossies would be hailing it as the latest in fashion statements; Top Shop with Manolos, Oasis with Jimmy Choos. Jack could feel the inklings of a conscience trying to rear up on him about the suffering and dying beyond their world of comparative fluff. Reality was trying to get him every day now and he didn't know how to accommodate it. So he did what he was best at and launched into some highly paid work (a few phone calls), doing everything he could not to scotch rumours that Jodie might be holing up in a shack at the end of Bono's garden in Dublin. As far as he knew, the closest Jodie had got to the U2 frontman was to buy the latest album (and promptly lose it in Stringfellow's). The call of a real life was not assuaged, however, and he knew that he was just postponing a big heart-to-heart with himself. Perhaps I am having that midlife crisis after all, he thought while shredding a photograph of his missing wife that had popped out of a desk diary. Even that failed to give him any satisfaction.

He glanced at the planner for the following day. He had

the chance to waste another morning at home but decided to punish himself instead by arranging a game of golf with a business contact. He would have to lose, as usual, in order to flatter his associate. He caught his reflection looking at him from a designed-to-death chrome wall section by his desk. It didn't look too impressed with what it saw. I am such a bullshitter. You're also in a dead end, his conscience reminded him, one of life's great cul-de-sacs. Thanks for that, he muttered. He had a press conference at 2 p.m. with an up-and-coming star who had an uneasy relationship with the media and was getting unhappily drunk even now, by all reports, in preparation for his gruelling. Jack would be paid a handsome fee for either shielding the youngster through the ordeal or offering him up to the hounds of Wapping, whichever the film company decided was most useful on the day.

Clara, his assistant, knocked on the open door and invited herself in.

'You look like shit, boss. Wanna come for a drink later?'

'Thanks. You're fired. And yes, I'd love to.'

Even as he reached for his coat, he knew he would end up in her bed that night. It was the way his life was going. And it was a bad road to be on.

Helen's dinner was ready for collection, as always. And, as always, she was surprised to be able to eat a thing. In the beginning she was sure she would never eat again and that sheer starvation would take her out of this agony but, as with the breathing, her body went onto automatic and kept her here to suffer. It was one of her favourites tonight, chicken in a white wine sauce. She did not eat red meat any more. It had lost its appeal, naturally enough. She took the plate and cutlery and headed out again. To say that she didn't want company would have been too much of an understatement to dignify with utterance and she dreaded the return of the car woman. It was getting crowded around here since she'd arrived. Happily there was no sign of her. She wasn't usually home early, which was no surprise. It's not as if she had much housekeeping to do in her Nissan Micra. And Helen had seen no evidence of in-car entertainment.

Beyond her seclusion the traffic went on by, an unending state of affairs really. She had never truly noticed that until she'd had to. Day and night it screamed by, always busy, always people going somewhere, or perhaps nowhere for all she knew. They may just like driving around, she thought. Well, if they do they shouldn't. It's dangerous out there.

She lived by the sun now. That's how she measured time. When the sun came up, Helen did too. When it disappeared, she lay down to sleep. And she often did sleep and that was another thing that surprised her, something she thought no longer possible. Aside from that she had no idea of regular time and no interest in it either. Why should she? What had it ever done for her? Except bring on a fate that no one would ever wish for, even upon an enemy of the highest calibre.

❖ ❖ ❖

Lucy wandered back along the river, annoyed. Why was it that every movie she saw now and every song she heard was about lost love? Heartache didn't need to be rubbed in like that. It was misery enough to have to go through it without constant reminders of how awful life is when you've been betrayed and left for emotional road kill. She'd stuck out the latest film simply because it filled in time but it had been a trial. Beautiful and talented woman falls in love with a handsome no-hoper and is put through the wringer before emerging stronger and happier with, of course, a new and even more handsome potential problem on her arm. Lucy was hacked off that she wasn't seeing her own experience of snot-hoppingly tedious crying and wretchedness and ugly contortions of face and heart. And there was no Prince Charming waiting in the wings to offer comfort or indeed any idea of a future happiness. Hollywood knew nothing. And while she was about it, she was sick and tired of being manipulated too.

The tang of an ebbing Thames stank up the London air. At least it had an honesty to it. She strolled past the brutalism of the Hayward Gallery and decided that it was an honest brutality of a thing too. It had not aged well and was almost beautiful in its dull grey condition. This was more like it. All she really needed now was to be mugged to top off the need to feel short-changed by life. Bring it all on, she dared. Physical pain might have been gratifying and a way back into the world of regular mortality but no one obliged her and all she suffered was a vague sense of disappointment. Expectant dads sat smoking outside St Thomas's and she almost felt sorry for some of them. She hardened her heart and limped on. It took an age to get to Bodybase where she ignored an evening of gospel music aqua-aerobics with Gloria, showering instead and grumbling to herself some more about the callousness of city life. It was an ideal time to phone her mother whose answering machine kicked in with a badly recorded message. She waited for the beep.

'Hi, Mum, it's Lucy.'

She could have kicked herself there and then. Pete had always teased her for announcing herself to everyone. 'Who else would it be?' he wanted to know. 'There's only one you.' It was just a habit, she explained, charmed all the same by his observation and taking it for ultimate affection and, disastrously for her, loyalty.

'I haven't forgotten about tomorrow night,' she continued, then heard her mother lift the receiver at her end.

'Darling, we were screening calls.'

We? Great, that meant the latest young cretin was still in residence. He had some weirdly impossible name like Fantorio or Macklerick.

'What's wrong?' her mother demanded.

'Nothing,' Lucy spluttered, caught in the surprise of the moment.

'Something's up. I can hear it in your voice. I'm your mother, you know, you can't fool me. It's Pete, isn't it?'

Lucy pulled on the vast reserves of her inner lying tank

and laughed. 'Don't be ridiculous, Mum. I'm fine. We're fine. I'm just a bit distracted with something else at the moment.'

'Mmm,' came the unconvinced reply. 'I'll see you tomorrow and we'll deal with it then.'

It was hard to predict how this could get worse, but knowing that it was best to expect the unexpected these days Lucy rapidly signed off with an airy 'Whatever' and kisses. Christ, that was close, she thought as a single large bead of perspiration trickled down her back. She looked at her watch, willing time away. It was still only eight o'clock so with heavy feet she headed to a Portuguese place near Stockwell for a chow-down before bed, aka the front seat of her car. Life's tatty tapestry was unravelling fast and it was not a pretty sight.

Colin was so hungry he could have eaten his own hand, but there was less than no way he was going back to that kitchen with that creature in it. Tony. He didn't even like the sound of the name now. To be honest he usually didn't even ask names these days. What was the point when he was *so* not seeing them again? He could smell the maddeningly enticing odours of cooked food and his stomach pleaded with him to get some. More laughter now, and Famke's voice. Shite. There was always fun and badness when Famke appeared. Fuckedyfuck deluxe. He was going to kill Ulrika when he got a chance. He said a silent prayer that her latest diet failed. He had no idea why she bothered any more. And besides, she was the only one who thought she was fat. He was just about to give in when a timid knock came on his door.

'Enter,' he announced, lightly. His tummy gave a thunderous roar, which he covered with a cough.

The vile Tony peeped in. 'May I?' he asked.

Colin looked at his bedside table and brushed off an imaginary speck. 'If you must,' he conceded without meeting the man's eye.

'I thought you might be hungry so I brought you some tikka masala.'

Colin gave the theatrical sigh of the much put upon. 'As it happens I'm not in the least bit hungry and I may as well mention that I do not appreciate you meddling in my life.' He mustered another even more tremendous sigh. 'However, I cannot abide waste so I'll try to do it some justice.'

'Famke was wondering if you wanted to join us or should we bring the party to you?'

'Oh, bring it in here, for Christ's sake. My evening's ruined anyhow.'

Tony went for the others and Colin dived into his curry. Oh God, it was good and, weirdly, it tasted homemade. He shovelled it all in as quickly as possible and set to lighting candles and throwing his dirty smalls under the bed, all Armani now so there was no disgrace in having them seen really, just seemed more hygienic. He could always fish them out if they were stuck for conversation later. That Tony had quite a cute tush, as it happened. Perhaps he'd let him stay, though he didn't want to give any impression of stability. Two nights in a row was practically unheard of for Colin; it was tantamount to a relationship for him. Still, never look a gift horse and all that. It was great to be young, free and single and he was all of the above, so why not? Finally he gave Mozart a rest and let Robbie Williams sail forth. Time to boogie.

Bill Richards stood at the kitchen sink washing dinner dishes. There was no need to use the dishwasher these days. In fact it was one of the early sad lessons for him, as he struggled to have enough of a load to warrant a wash and a detergent tablet. The most he'd managed, before the smell from the machine was too rank to ignore, was a load every three days or so and that was mostly cups and the plastic containers of microwaved dinners, getting washed before their journey to the recycling bank. A waste of natural resources right there given the amount of water involved. Not to mention the trip in the car using up precious fossil fuel, polluting the air and clogging the traffic system. He was becoming aware of a lot of the nonsense of city life now.

He'd also let the cleaner go. With no one but himself making a mess there was no need for her to come every week, not even once a month actually. And she brought with her the image of a house lived in and noisy and happy too; a house with love in it and lots of chaos and dirt. She had cried when he'd told her, but she understood. The mere sight of her was enough to set him off and as he was proficient at doing that to himself it was best to let her go. He'd given her an enormous severance package even though it wasn't ever part of any deal. All bets were off now so he figured she deserved it. And besides, she had been affected by events too, made unhappy at the way life had turned on itself. There were few enough people in the area that hadn't been touched somehow. There was no comfort in that thought, however.

He missed the noise and the mayhem of his family. He missed the smell of other people. He was entirely fed up with his own company. His heart was broken, torn asunder. His eye fell on a dusty bottle of Armagnac, long ago abandoned as too strong a drink and likely to send a man mad. He turned away and left it to its own devices. He had enough to drive him mad without the help of alcohol. Not that he hadn't tried it as a cure-all initially. Oh, he had. It hadn't worked. He suspected that nothing ever would in spite of all the platitudes about time's healing ways.

Why had Lucy not confided in anyone? It was not as if she didn't have friends. In fact, she had plenty. The trouble was they were the mutual friends shared in a partnership, the marriage having even diluted arrangements she had with people she had known solo for a lifetime. There was also the fact that she had wanted to indulge in Pete alone, not to have to share him beyond what was absolutely necessary. Sure, they had friends to dinner and revisited them in their homes, but given the choice, Lucy always preferred having Pete to herself even on a night out. She began to let her married life become autonomous, opting to stay away from his business parties and narrowing their activities as a couple to some social outings with mutual types who were also mostly in pairs. She now regarded that as an awfully smug way to live, but she could think of worse words for it too.

She was so ashamed of what had happened that she could not face any of her contemporaries with the shreds of what was her present situation. Lord knows, it had taken her long enough to admit to herself that it was happening. It was difficult to see how much longer she could keep up the charade. Someone, somewhere, soon was going to get through to the truth. How could she explain it to another person when she could hardly explain it to herself? And she was wary of analysis too. She had a suspicion she would turn into a word junkie if she headed along that path; someone addicted to comforting but meaningless waffle. But the moment was coming when she would have to be honest with herself. The truth was she didn't trust herself enough or at all any more and so could not be sure that the honesty would be plain or good or even ugly, or some new hotchpotch of half-truths and deliberately crafted misunderstandings designed to see her through another day.

Lucy turned the corner into the cul-de-sac, walking past a faded green ribbon tied to some broken fencing and looking as battered as she felt. The Crazy Lady was sitting on a kerb.

'Hi,' Lucy tried, brightly. 'Another gorgeous evening.' She wasn't surprised at the silence but decided to go for broke. 'It's almost boring at this stage, isn't it?'

Did she see a flicker of interest, or plain annoyance?

She reached her car. 'Home sweet home,' she muttered as she put the key in the lock. When she looked to say goodnight to the woman she was gone.

Helen watched her from her vantage point. She's wondering where I am now, she thought. Serves her right for disturbing me like that. And making a joke. She'd nearly made her smile, which was unforgivable. Why did she not just go away? Helen had let her get too comfortable, that was the problem. Now this creature was getting into her head and taking up space. Look at her, glancing this way and that. Helen felt like going 'Yoohoo' to scare the living daylights out of her, but then she would work out where she was and Helen wanted that less than frightening the bitch.

Lucy looked around in astonishment. How could the Crazy Lady have disappeared like that? She had only looked away for a nanosecond. The woman must still be close by, unless she'd been imagining this other woman all along and nothing was too outlandish to contemplate at this stage. She turned a full circle then said, 'My name is Lucy, by the way. Pleased to meet you.'

That settles it, Helen thought, she'll have to go.

FIVE

Ulrika woke fully clothed on her bed. Her stomach cramped tightly and her right arm was numb under her torso. Her neck had come to rest at an awkward angle and promised a day of agony if she so much as tried to look to the right or left, however vaguely. Her clothes were sticky and her hair wet against her skin. She felt like shit. Suddenly her body heaved and tried its best to be sick, but there was nothing to expel. Even the white wine she'd unwisely agreed to drink last night was trapped by dehydration in her thinning body and she had nothing left to give. She heaved a dozen times more, leaning unnecessarily over the side of the bed, before heading to the bathroom where she stood on the scales and noted with satisfaction that her weight was at least static. This beat adding the pounds although it fell short of shedding them. She wondered if she should be thinking in kilos and if it wouldn't be easier to shed those? She stepped under a cold shower and watched as her skin tightened and perked. She might feel terrible, she thought, but she was certainly looking better.

❧ ❧ ❧

Jack came to with a start. He sat up, rudely pushing aside the woman's head between his legs. He immediately began to apologise.

'I'm so sorry,' he said, fumbling with the bedlinen to cover his embarrassment. 'You frightened me.'

Clara laughed. 'That's not what you said last night. Boss.'

He wished she wouldn't call him that, off duty anyway. He was disgusted with himself for not sneaking away during the night, and more disgusted with himself for even considering that an option. But he liked to wake up at home and didn't want to give this affair any footing. In fact the very thought that Clara might regard it as an affair appalled him. Yet what else would she think? He had spent two to three nights of several weeks in her bed. Well, he had never brought her to his place, he reasoned, and surely that was a sign that he was in no way committed. He hated the very language he had to think with to reason this situation, resented its presumption designed to trap him.

Clara had exited the bed, which was a minor relief. 'Coffee?' She didn't need to add 'boss' to that, it was so implicit. Oh God! He watched her toned and sheer body make its virtually hairless way to the door. The maintenance alone must cost a fortune. Actually he knew it did because he had paid for all of his wife's treatments, probably still did, he realised with distaste. The one he had finally tried to draw the line on was the Brazilian wax. He hated the child-like labia staring at him, making him feel like a pervert, but Laura insisted that it made arousal much better (for her) so that battle was lost. In fact it was all he could do to persuade her that he would not benefit *at all* from waxing his 'sack and crack', as she had so eloquently put it. He didn't care if all of London was doing it, he would not and he was happy to remain a sexual yeti. Looking back, it was clear that Laura had already embarked on her affair with the television producer she had left him for because although she liked to keep up with all of the fads that urban beautification required, she was also well able to lapse. He had now decided that any surge of dedicated body care in a marriage spelled trouble and was a prelude to extramarital activity. No extra in the marriage, he reflected, extra beyond it. Clara had a neatly trimmed bush, probably waxed at the sides, and any perversion involved was adult and allowed. And she had never commented on his pubic hair, which he took to be good manners and satisfaction. She threw on a silk kimono, too beautifully pressed to be an accident, and left to fix him breakfast. He wanted to flee but knew that this was too bad-mannered for words. He sat sweating against a pillow instead.

He looked at the garments strewn across the floor. Clara's underwear was expensive and matching and she favoured stockings. He could smell her scent on him still, a Jo Malone that must have cost a fair chunk of one week's wages. Recent too, so it must be for his benefit. These were the instruments of her seduction. He groaned. Clara was a good-looking, intelligent young woman. Was it so hard to meet someone in London that she had to make do with seconds? Another woman's cast-off? She deserved better and he tried to tell her as much but when it emerged, the speech sounded like a cry for reassurance and he ended up with an elaborate pat on the head and another energetic bout of intercourse. He felt a fool.

Helen was up and washed with the dawn. She stood in some shade breathing in the cooler morning air, relishing its depth before the heat dissipated any of the good in it. Agitation prickled her. So, the woman's name was Lucy. This was bad. Helen didn't want to know her name. Now she was *someone* and not an *anyone* that she could ignore. Well, obviously, she would continue to ignore her but it was bad to have a name to attach that to. She could see the red car begin to rock slightly as the woman tried to stretch herself awake. She had those snazzy sunblinds on the thing but if you got right up close you could see inside. She had slept in the front seat last night, after an unsatisfactory spell in the back. To look at her you wouldn't think she'd need to live in a car, Helen mused, but no doubt thereby hangs a tale, as the cliché will have it. Was that a cliché? Or just a pathetic saying? Is there a difference? She was becoming distracted by minutiae. She needed to focus on the now. Now as it became then and time did its definitive version of inexorable, thrusting the world forward till suddenly we find ourselves halfway through another day.

She realised that a 'we' had crept into her thinking and hated it, blaming the car woman. I am not an inclusive person any more, Helen reasoned. Well, occasionally she was but that was with someone special, someone who had shared so much with her and who respected her need to be alone here to deal with her demons. And now *she* had barged in and Helen didn't like it, not one bit. It was intolerable, in fact. She was going to have to see her off.

She saw that Lucy was out of the car and leaning back in to tidy the tiny space. Now she was upright and looking uncomfortable, probably bursting to go to the loo. Helen had to start her campaign if she was ever to be rid of this unwanted presence. She inched forward, making certain that she could be seen, sure this would make the other woman self-conscious enough not to go behind the chunky electrical substation for relief.

It didn't work.

She was beginning to really goad her now. Helen was not in control any more.

Lucy couldn't help it. There would be no sprint to Bodybase this morning. She was so careful to stay hydrated in her mini-home that her bladder was under intolerable pressure. She slunk behind the metal closet and hunkered down. The Crazy Lady didn't seem to notice but, just in case, Lucy breezed a 'Sorry about that' in her direction. 'I guess that's one of the hazards of mobile living. And yes, I know I didn't wash my hands but I will, I promise.' She even hazarded a wry chuckle.

How dare she try to implicate me in her life? Helen fumed. She needn't wash her hands ever again for all I care. Just fuck off, she wanted to scream. She coiled up tight at the sound of the voice.

'Are you all right?' The woman was close beside her.

Helen could bear it no longer. 'Just fuck off,' she screamed.

Lucy backed away, uncertain what to do. For a moment she reached out to comfort the shaking woman, then thought better of it. 'I'm sorry,' she said. 'I didn't mean to upset you.'

There was a note of tender defeat in her voice that provoked Helen further though she could not figure out why. 'Just leave me alone,' she hissed.

As Lucy rounded the corner, Helen began to cry, lightly at first then huge choking sobs. It was a brief episode but dense and exhausting. She gulped the tears to a halt, wiped her eyes and face in her skirt and walked towards the car. She wanted to kick it hard on a soft area of door but that would have involved touching it. She picked up a stone, checked it for weight and hurled it at the vehicle. It made a hollow thunk sound and left a small dent which she found so gratifying she went at it again. And again. And once more. The blood-red paint cracked to reveal the pale and naked metal underneath, a small criss-cross of scars mapping the door. As she walked away she realised that this was the closest she had been to a car in over three months. It left her feeling confused but outraged too. I hope that this 'Lucy' will be as upset as I am, she thought. She deserves all she gets.

Bill put a bachelor load of dirty clothes into the machine. Some other items were drying on the washing line outside and he wandered out to check on them. He heard an altercation in the cul-de-sac and rushed to the garden door to listen. He heard crying now but knew better than to interfere. His fist wrenched at the handle but he resisted opening the door. Then clanging sounds rang through the air, stone against metal. The car must be getting a going over. What to make of this? He looked up and saw Famke on the roof of her studio. She shrugged slightly, made a face and suggested a thumbs up. Could Helen be on her return? His instinct was to rush out and help her, perhaps even congratulate her but he knew better. If Helen wanted him she knew where he was.

He retreated, buoyed at the thought that Helen had engaged with some outside force beyond her control. It sparked an energy in him that nagged at his psyche. He needed to let off steam. He paced the floor. This house was hemming him in, high ceilings or not, and he decided to take the action outside as a sign that life was on the move again and normality needed a visit. This is as good a time as any to try to get back into the swing of things, he thought, as he picked up the phone and started to dial.

*　　*　　*

Now that was extraordinary, Famke thought as she watched the exchange between the two women. Helen had given up speaking weeks ago and before that could not exactly be called communicative in any meaningful way. Now she was shouting and attacking cars. Was it progress? Did it mean she might say and do more? The car and its inhabitant were assured of a place in the series now so Famke went back down to her studio and studied the canvases to see if it should be included in what was in progress. One painting from last week rested against a wall. It was pavement as a cracked fresco: flat and formal as an ancient Greek mural. Beside it was another that showed Helen's hand on the chain fence by the green ribbon. Her fingers gripped the metal, veins standing in relief against the strained skin and flesh. It occurred to Famke that this was not unlike the entrance, in reality, to the cul-de-sac and perhaps that was the way to grade the work as it built; the layers according to the lives taking place at the back of the square. And in spite of the vibrant sunshine lighting up the colours and objects as she saw them, so far the feeling from the canvases was a sorrowful one.

Her stomach groaned in hope of food. She walked up the path to the kitchen to refuse lemony water from Ulrika and dive into strong coffee and fresh croissants from the hand of Tony, Colin's latest and a good laugh. Colin had not yet put in an appearance but they could hear him singing in the shower.

'It's a pity he hasn't one note in his head that could

follow another musically,' Famke said. 'Or even plausibly.'

The others nodded sadly.

'I'm not the biggest Barbra Streisand fan,' she admitted, 'but she does do a lot more justice to that song.'

'We all have our crosses to bear,' Tony said. He laughed self-consciously. 'Look at me, I'm supposed to be getting married soon. What's all that about?'

After a brief and uncomfortable silence, punctuated by Colin's insistence that people who needed people were the luckiest people in the world, Famke said, 'You might want to think about that one, Tony.'

Honesty had cut the conversation down and they experienced an impasse. Colin clearly had no such trouble and continued to give his tribute to Babs socks. This only highlighted the social horror in the kitchen.

Ulrika finally cleared her throat. 'I wondered if you might need me to pose for you this week, Famke?'

'Thanks, but no.' She saw the dismay and added, 'It's just that the series has taken off and it's not about what I thought at all. Thanks for the offer, Ulrika. I will take you up on it sometime. You're looking great, by the way.'

This was untrue. Ulrika looked like death warmed up but it elicited a smile and that was a good start to anyone's day. Colin swept in swirling Eau Sauvage for all to smell. 'Because I am one,' as he explained.

'I thought you were a socialist now,' Famke said.

'Only in my leisure hours, dearest FK. It's a completely unworkable way of life, after all, but tremendously useful as a hobby. Ask New Labour if you don't believe me.' He stuffed his mouth with croissant and bolted a coffee. 'I'm off. See you all. Have nice lives.'

Famke sighed. 'Ladies and gentleman, Elvis has left the building.'

Lucy shouted 'Hello' at the back of Fi's head. Martha looked like she hadn't left her post at the till of Fifi's Flowers since Lucy had last seen her. She was gently tugging on one of her chins and sniffing loudly.

'You're going to have to deal with that coke habit of yours,' Lucy said brightly.

Martha yelped and reddened alarmingly.

'Relax,' Fi said. 'She's only joking.' She turned to Lucy. 'The heroin is what's bothering me. I think I may be paying her too much.'

No amount of chivvying was going to engage Martha so they gave up. I don't know how she does it, Lucy thought, but she's now made me feel like the ultimate bitch and bully, and I was only trying to make contact and put her at ease. Fi met her eyes and rolled them in agreement.

'Busy again this morning, I see.'

'Yes, a certain individual must be in terrible trouble on both fronts because it's a repeat of yesterday's order, but bigger and more expensive.'

'Ooh, don't love hurt.' How trippingly it rolled off her tongue, as if it didn't cost her a thought.

'You said it, sister. Long may it last.'

Lucy was putting on her apron next door when she made a decision. She took off her wedding ring and put it in her purse. She looked at the pale crescent of white, indented flesh that had signified her marriage and felt her heart stop a moment. She tried to imagine a girder of mental steel for protection. I don't need to be mocked every moment of the day, she thought, and that's all the ring stands for now: derision. If she was waiting for any feeling of liberation or relief she was disappointed because all she got was a loose sense of failure, far worse than any physical and localised pain.

From across the room Vida pierced her with a knowing look.

'It keeps getting caught in things, snagging,' Lucy said, knowing that even to stoop to an explanation was a wrong move. It also made her acutely aware that she had never had an engagement ring. Diamonds were the real snaggers of this world.

Vida grunted.

'What? That's all you've got to say?'

'You dig a hole, you lie in it.'

'Thanks a lot. That's a great help.'

And then out of nowhere, Vida smiled.

Stella was stunned. 'You gave him a return match?'

'Hardly a return fixture if he came back to mine again,' Colin opined as he fanned himself with a spreadsheet. 'I should never have brought him home in the first place. Now he knows where I live. And I couldn't help myself last night. I was weak with hunger and couldn't think straight.'

'What'll you do if he goes ahead and gets married?'

'Let him. Nothing to do with me, dear. Mind you, he is sweet, in a totally pathetic way. Marriage should suit him.'

'He can cook.'

'Yes, imagine. And that, in itself, is a mark against him. I'd put on weight eating Indian and croissants every day. I congratulate myself with the knowledge that he is now corrupt and will forever remember the time before his wedding as the happiest and most fulfilled of his life. Plus, he's not my type.'

'Your type is anything in pants with a cock, a pulse and the ability to look good in a Village People outfit.'

Colin sighed. 'You have such narrow parameters to your Gaydar, my sweet prejudiced Stella.'

'Eh, don't think so, not since you admitted trying to cottage in St Paul's Cathedral.'

'Point of fact, Madam Chairwoman, I *successfully* cottaged in St Paul's which some might find extraordinary and even tasteless but I offer by way of explanation the fact that I was deranged with grief following the death and subsequent funeral of Diana, Princess of Wales.'

'Point taken.'

Ulrika's working day began with a staff meeting at the college. Alexander Dount (pronounced 'don't' to the delight of all-comers) was chairing and doing his best with the crowd control the task involved.

'Bet he'd prefer to be taking a class,' one of the computer heads said. 'The pupils are far easier to manage.'

The contentious issue was the art department. Valerie Latchford, the senior lecturer, had allowed a display of life drawing along the corridors leading to the department and a cleaner had objected to this on religious grounds.

'The only offence, as far as I'm concerned,' Valerie was explaining, 'is that some of the drawings are very bad indeed. Beyond that I think it's ridiculous.'

Ulrika raised a hand. 'What religion is he?'

'Muslim.'

A groan went up.

'Religion du jour,' a commerce lecturer muttered.

'Now *that's* probably very offensive,' Ulrika whispered to the person sitting next to her.

Principal Dount decided to guide the meeting. 'Having discussed this with our Muslim colleagues on the teaching staff, it seems to me that we are headed into the impossible territory of *über* political correctness and so cannot win no matter what we do. With that in mind, I am going to suggest that this cleaner be gently rostered to other areas of the college. I would hate to offend him or to thwart the artistic impulses of Valerie's very fine department.' He simpered a smile in her direction and closed the meeting.

Ulrika made to get up but a wave of dizziness overcame her and she fell back onto her grey plastic chair with a rattle. She passed it off as clumsiness but waited a few moments before attempting to rise again.

She was walking slowly along corridor G in the South Wing when she saw the student from yesterday: the girl who had offered her something to give her a little lift. I wonder, she thought, then dismissed the idea. Once she got her weight to plateau at the right place on the scales she would be fine. No need to interfere with the usual teething problems of any diet. It wasn't getting any easier, however.

SIX

The letter was in a plain white envelope with an indecipherable postmark. It was propped against a sugar bowl on the small table in the staffroom at the back of the café. It looked so innocent, Lucy might have ripped it open and relished the contents had she not recognised the hand. Peter had writing like a doctor, almost unreadable, but somehow she felt she would be able to get the gist of this without needing to fully decode every word. It began, as all of these missives surely do, with him telling her that this was the hardest letter he had ever had to write in his whole life. That almost squeezed a laugh out of her. Was his suffering in some way supposed to reassure her? And how could something so serious be steeped in so much cliché? The words began to swim in a blah blah way on the first hurried reading so she surprised herself by putting it back in its cover and then into her handbag. It could wait, she decided; neither of them was going anywhere in a hurry. Besides which, Vida was loitering. To back up the correctness of her action Danny Brock appeared so she bolted for the front counter and began to serve the gathering customers.

The sound of Mario's sing-song accent soothed her as she chatted to the punters. There was a run on avocado today and they all wondered if some cookery or lifestyle programme had hailed it as the new wonder food the previous night. A local called Greta was bucking the trend and having prawn mayonnaise.

'Ah, *la dolce vita*, that is what you are living with this,' Mario told her. She was ninety if she was a day and Mario reckoned she came in for a chat as much as the food.

'She is lonely,' he told Lucy. 'Do you know that the supermarket told her to move on more than once when she tried to talk to the cash register person? So sad. This London.' He shrugged. 'I dunno no more.'

Lucy waved a hand at Greta who rewarded her with a smile so wide her heart jumped a little. That could be me, she thought, now at thirty-two years of age. Words from the letter began to flash in her mind. 'Dearest Lucy' was the first phrase to rankle. How bloody dare he call her that? He had forfeited any right to intimacy when he had run out on her. She was boiling now and hadn't got past the first two words.

Martha appeared to get lunch for all at Fifi's Flowers: two iced coffees, two avocado and bacon on ciabatta and a quick almond bun for herself while the order was being filled. Lucy wondered if this was the eaters' version of an alcoholic having a quick short at the bar while waiting for a round of drinks. As she handed over the food she said,

'Didn't mean to upset you about the cocaine remark earlier. I was just joking.'

'No problem,' the girl muttered. 'Wish I could afford drugs.'

Lucy smiled. Her apology had been accepted. And just wait till she told Fi that Martha had probably made a joke.

Then she remembered the phrase 'betrayed and hurt' from the letter. You have no idea how much, buddy. 'Next,' she barked.

He told no one he was coming so when he appeared on site in his hard hat and working clothes, more than a few mouths hung open. His second-in-command rushed forward to pump his hand, delight genuine upon his face.

'Bill,' he enthused. 'It's so good to see you.'

'It's been so long I'd say no one recognises me any more. How are things going?'

'Very well. We're on schedule and the show apartment is going down a storm. The order books are filling up.'

'I knew you'd be fine without me, Sean.' Bill meant it. Sean Harris was a great worker and an even better friend. 'I'll never be able to thank you enough.'

'Now, say no more. You'd do the same for me.'

I sincerely hope so, Bill thought. He looked up at the block under construction. Its glass and chrome shell was reaching skywards into a blue yonder. Top of the range two-bedroomed pads overlooking the river, built by Richards Construction Corporation. It would include a gymnasium and pool on the third floor, underground car parking and twenty-four-hour security. Bill now knew there was no such thing as safety all the livelong day, but it seemed to be what people wanted. And it was a long day to live through with dangers and pitfalls, many of which you could never predict, or at least not the most impactful ones.

'How about a tour?' Sean suggested. 'I'll introduce you to some of the new lads.'

As they set off in silence, Bill saw Sean steal a glance, obviously itching to ask the obvious question.

'Things are the same at home,' he said.

'Right. Right. Well, all in its own good time, I suppose.'

My Dearest Lucy,

This is the hardest letter I've ever had to write in my life. You must have been very confused at my disappearance. I am, myself, that it has come to this. I don't want to bother you with too many details but suffice to say I got myself into a bit of trouble and had to leave. I will pay back the money I took as soon as I can. I cannot believe that I have betrayed and hurt you as much as I have and be sure that I will never forgive myself for that.

I love you very much.

Yours, forever,

Pete.

Lies and excuses in the pathetic binding of a 'genuine' letter from his heart. In rage, she scrunched it up, threw the paper on the ground and danced on it. Tears sprang unbidden but the expletives she muttered were all her own and she'd had time to work on them recently. Finally she reached down, picked up the ball and sat on the public bench smoothing the sheet so that she could forensically dissect it, looking for traces of guilt or hope and always feeling that in there somewhere was the proof that everything was in fact her fault.

She ignored the naked plea for sympathy in the first sentence, moving on to the issue of confusion. What arse was this about him being confused? He was the one who left, without warning and with every penny from the only asset they had, the money from the sale of her apartment. When she married Pete she shared everything with him, assuming it was a two-way deal they had both signed up to. The dark maw of hopelessness threatened to consume her as her predicament tried to hijack the moment. She read on. Bother me with details, she wanted to scream. I have a right to be bothered with them even if they are merely blandishments. I want that effort and that respect. I am your wife, you fucking shit.

How could she not have noticed he was in trouble? Were the cops after him? If she just knew what was going on at least then she could make a proper decision about how to proceed, but there was nothing. No return address was given so she had no recourse to an answer, let alone seeing him face to face. She was livid at his cowardice.

Don't forgive yourself, she urged, you don't deserve forgiveness. As for love, you don't know the meaning of the word, you fucking shit.

'Would you like to talk about it?' asked a quavering voice. 'Only people are staring and maybe we should take things indoors.'

'Oh, Greta, I didn't see you there. Sorry. Was I shouting?'

The old lady from the café stood before her looking worried.

'Just a little, dear. Nothing more than some of the loonies around here, but you don't look the type and I think that is giving cause for concern to some of the populace. You are provoking comment, if I may say so.'

Lucy was now embarrassed as well as furious. She decided to add this further insult to the list of injuries perpetrated by Pete Kingston. The hurt was pounding through her now and one false thought or word would send her south. She took a deep breath.

'Greta, you are the sweetest woman to offer help, but I'm just not ready for that yet. When I am, I'd be delighted to tell you what's on my mind. It's just I've had a bit of bad news. Maddening too because I really should have seen it coming. And it's a very badly written letter.'

'I understand, dear. There is no excuse for poor penmanship or grammar. In time, when you're ready, I'll make us a lovely cup of tea and we'll figure it all out. Sometimes it's good for an outsider to have a look over a problem, a fresh perspective, you know.'

'Thank you, Greta.'

'And not all men are villains.'

'I'll try to remember that.'

They managed twelve holes without a mention of Laura. In spite of himself, Jack was playing well but even the smallest reminder of his errant wife took care of that. His score at the eighteenth was about to hit double figures before he managed to check himself.

'I didn't realise it was still such a sore subject,' his colleague said as they were handing in their cards. 'Sorry.'

That bitch will be the root cause of my losing my five handicap if I'm not careful, Jack thought. 'No need to apologise,' he said. 'It's just all tied up with details now, messy separation and so on.'

If he hoped this would be the end of the conversation he was disappointed. His companion was waxing lyrical now.

'You don't need to tell me. I've been divorced twice, after all. My advice is get a good lawyer and never walk down that aisle again. Second time out I thought I'd try a younger model and it was a complete disaster. She got the daddy she always longed for and I got a dysfunctional daughter I never wanted.'

Jack realised with a jolt that he hadn't thought this through. In some strange way he had written the whole thing off as something Laura had to get out of her system. He half expected her through the door at any moment, apologetic, desperate to be home and a wife again; his wife. He had shuttered out the notion of divorce, sugaring the split as a separation. He was going to have to make his mind up. Did he want her back and if so what did he intend to do about that? It was shit or get off the pot time, as his golfing partner had so finely described it.

He drove back to town like a zombie, his mind churning over the possibilities for nastiness associated with the train wreck that was his marriage. Kilburn High Road had been invaded by giant chickens. He thought they were protesting against battery farming, but the leaflet thrust at him announced another new branch of a fried chicken franchise. Just what the world needs now, his soured brain muttered. It made him hungry, though, and consequently ashamed.

And in the meantime his golf game was in tatters.

The girl had a good bedside manner, notwithstanding that they were on a bench in the college grounds. She listened to Ulrika and asked a few questions then recommended speed.

'It'll give you the extra energy you need and take the edge off your appetite,' she said, handing over the pills. 'I want you to eat sensibly still, though you'll find you won't need as much to get by. There's no need to worry about getting addicted to these babies, because you're only going to be using them to tide you over this difficult stage in your diet. And once you've reached your optimum weight you can stop altogether. Also I'll only give you a few to try initially, just to be sure that they suit you and that'll take away any urge you might have to overdo it. And I'll have plenty more for you when you need them.'

Ulrika gave her the money.

The girl handed back a fiver. 'Special introductory offer,' she smiled. 'Nice doing business with you.'

'How will I find you again?'

'I'll find you, Miss Henning. Don't worry, I'll know when you're ready for more. You're in the hands of a professional now.'

Ulrika felt a glow of gratitude towards the girl as she watched her lope back to the school building. She realised too late that she'd forgotten to ask her name. Never mind, she could do that next time. She popped a tablet and washed it down with a Diet Coke. Then she sat back and waited for the buzz.

Lucy chose one of Pete's single friends who she thought might be discreet. When he answered the phone he immediately said, 'He's done a bilk, hasn't he?'

'Pardon?'

'He's done a runner.'

Her surprise was evident. 'Well, yes. How did you know?'

'Simple, he hasn't borrowed any money from me in about a fortnight. Which means he's got it elsewhere or he's had to disappear because of his debts. Maybe both?'

Lucy had played loose with the truth for long enough now and it was liberating to be able to talk about the situation frankly.

'I don't suppose you have any idea where he is?'

'No. If I did I'd be chasing him for what he already owes me.' He paused. 'I'm sorry, Lucy, I thought it'd be different this time.'

'This time?' she squealed. 'There were other times?' Her throat was constricting, squeezing ever more improbable sounds out. The truth was harder to handle than she liked.

'Jeez, I can't believe I'm having to do this.' He gave a pained groan on the other end of the line. 'Pete has always been a bit flighty. And he has a problem with gambling, as I'm sure you know.'

She didn't. She felt her world falling away. How could she not have known something like that? It had never occurred to her. She had noticed nothing new in any of his apparent anxieties, it was just the bump and grind of London.

'He gets in over his head every so often and has to go to ground. I thought he had it under control this time. He swore to me he had. And he's daft about you, Lucy. I never saw him like that. He adores you. He married you, for God's sake.'

'He did me no favours, believe me.'

She thought of the small, hurried ceremony in the register office. Pete hadn't wanted fuss but he couldn't wait for the union to be official in the eyes of all. This was his big commitment to his future, their future. It had been the most romantic day of Lucy's life, poor fool that she was.

'For what it's worth, he always turns up again. I think

he goes off to work off his debts and get his head together.'

'Gee, that's great to know. But I don't think he will be back this time because he's made off with the proceeds of the sale of my apartment.'

'Aw shit, Lucy, no.'

'Yes, shit. A lovely new twist in the saga, I think you'll agree.'

She needed a punchbag. She wanted to scream and rant and to hit something very, very hard. Frustration threatened to strangle her. She began to run and kept going until her legs gave out and her chest was raw from heaving air. She would still have welcomed a punchbag even then. Instead she began her slow walk back to Mario's, wondering what to do next.

Helen's day was consumed by restlessness.

It's that Lucy's fault, she thought. She's rattling me around and I resent it. I am none of her business and she is none of mine but she has thrust herself on me and I don't know how to get rid of her.

She could call the police but what would she report her for? Vagrancy, perhaps? She could have her car towed. The police knew the area well and called regularly to clear out the junkies who liked to shoot up in the secrecy provided by this little out-of-the-way spot. In fact the law had been very successful and none of the addicts had yet returned after the last ousting. She dealt with the truants herself. They were usually entrenched by the time they noticed her still figure and it was easy to scare the further bejeepers out of them with a wall-eyed stare. None of the various groups returned after that. This was a different scenario. Any deliberate course of action meant asking strangers into the cul-de-sac and the last time it was full was such an unhappy one that Helen was in no hurry to repeat even the roughest semblance of it. It looked increasingly as if she was going to have to talk to her, this Lucy, and reason with or plain bully her if that didn't work.

The heat was worse than usual. It cloyed along her body and clothes, weighting her with uncomfortable moisture. She could zone out most of the time, moving very little and concentrating on the emotional churning inside, but not today. The air was too thin to breathe effectively and she had to stretch to pull in oxygen. She was wheezing and uncomfortable.

The strangest thing was that, for the first time since her vigil had begun, she was feeling bored. It amazed her. She still stood or sat sentry and felt time pass. It still whizzed by with each breath, no matter how busy or how idle she was. But somehow that wasn't enough any more. She was still gutted by misery but the magnificent torpor of her days divorced from any rat race was beginning to seem like an indulgence. What she had thought was a proper focus on life, rather than an escape from it, was now ringing hollow and she didn't know what to make of that. If this was a moving on, some sort of textbook progression, she was prepared to resent it. She refused to be categorised with the general. Her grief was particular and special.

She had memories to preserve and lives to remember and that was usually enough. But something had happened here that she could not grasp and she was troubled by it. I must hold my nerve, she thought. It will pass. Bigger things had, more's the pity. Then without warning she crumpled again and cried. Tears had been elusive this past while and now they had returned twice in a day, an unwelcome surprise like the unwanted visitor. She was drained. I'll go have a lie-down, she thought, and that will help me think with a clearer head later.

She would ask for a Greek salad tonight. She found herself wanting olives and feta cheese, like a craving.

Lucy had finally made a home: that was what marriage with Pete had meant. They were buying a house together. She had a companion and lover. She felt settled. She had never known a father or even a permanent father figure. Her mother was a bohemian spirit who always insisted that no one had ever had the manners to ask for her hand so she remained single. Although Lucy was well aware of other girls having dads, she also knew many who didn't. And she never wanted for male influences in her formative years. There were always lots of men around in the various circles in which she and Evie moved. The lack of a permanent father figure never bothered Lucy and it still didn't although it occurred to her more than once that she might be a psychotherapist's wet dream, particularly in the light of this latest fiasco with Pete.

As legend had it, Lucy's biological father was a painter

named Mason who died in the early seventies, leaving a small body of work and a lot of debts. One of his pastels of a pregnant Evie was all that she had held on to and even it was rarely on display as it provoked too much emotion in its appreciation. Evie always insisted that she had been more in lust than love and that the finest thing to come of the liaison was her daughter, in whom she thrilled. Lucy thought that this was an elaborate half-truth. She knew Evie was delighted to have a daughter and loved her very much, but she also felt she protested too much on the casual lust part of the story. This was her method of filing the emotion away for herself, and possibly from herself, in an effort to make the loss manageable. And in that strange, half-baked way Evie had, she probably thought it would help Lucy to come to terms with a dead father by exonerating her from the need to mourn or to miss him.

All through her growing up Lucy's mother had moved the two of them around. Home had become a boarding school or the weekend retreat of a rich man who wanted to be her mother's latest squeeze and another new uncle for Lucy. It had been exciting but transient, until the acquisition of the White Rooms in Mayfair; the gallery was at ground level, the first floor was her mother's small apartment. But that had been a mere ten years ago, by which time Lucy was a grown woman. Her nomadic childhood had remained just that and stability, late arriving, was not suited to keeping the two of them together when it presented itself. Lucy rented a room in a house full of wasters nominally studying art or crafts and, on one occasion, a stray that had wandered in from a TEFL course ate all the food in the cupboards for a month and disappeared without paying his rent. It was uncertain whose friend or acquaintance he had been and more than once a real tenant had posited the notion that he had just wandered in off the street and no one was cad enough to ask for his credentials.

Lucy was as aimless and idle as being broke would allow. Her great passion was the gallery. She had learned early on, during a spell at art school, that though she had a modest way with drawing it was not what could be described as talent. As her mother pointed out, the genes for creativity were on one side of Lucy's family tree but not Evie's.

'My talent is for getting by, dear,' she had told her. 'That is my gift to you. And you may thank me for it some day. Your father has obviously mucked things up by introducing a rogue creative side, but you'll harness that as needs be, I'm sure.'

Lucy's real talent was her 'eye'. She could spot an interesting artist at some distance and even though her mother did have to make ends meet she was always grateful for her daughter's input as it led to at least three interesting exhibitions a year. The rest was a cynical sell, sell, sell mode but that was the getting-by bit of life that Evie was so good at.

As Lucy crossed the cobbled street leading to the mews gallery her battered spirits sank. She saw the distinctive tweedy head of Finn Beaker, musician and bore. That meant the other two collaborators would be in attendance also. Sure enough, there were Rita Fuller, painter, and the half man, half lemon that was the writer Jez Anderton standing in front of a fan cooling themselves. This was going to be a long session.

Her mother clapped hands excitedly when she saw her, grateful of the rescue. 'Lucy's here. Marvellous. We can get down to brass tacks. Literally.'

Lucy muttered her hellos as the others laughed at her mother's little joke. Evie knew the evening was ripe for arguments and bad feeling and had chosen to haul them all above that with good humour and wine. Lucy cast a curdling look in the direction of Bartok, her mother's new, young, best 'friend'. He ignored her, poured himself a generous measure of claret and pointedly sat to observe the others breaking sweat.

'Tremendous news, Lucy,' Evie was warbling. 'Finn has had the most wonderful idea of playing the music that inspired the work, live, as people are viewing tomorrow evening. It will be a "happening".'

'Great.' Flat would best describe her response but it remained somewhere above the heads of the gathered artistes.

'Yes,' Finn agreed. 'Our process during creation was I would play and then Rita would paint and Jez add words to the picture to complete the statement.'

'Or sometimes I wrote words on a canvas and then Rita painted over or around them,' Jez added.

'How exciting,' Lucy managed, in more dull monotone. What bollocks, she thought. I hope this tosh sells.

She glanced at a pile of canvases stacked against the far wall. They were bright, that much was clear. And plenty of colour schemes. Surely there was something there for everyone in the audience who had a wall to cover and a sofa that needed matching. These were surely the cushions of the art world. Michelangelo, rest easy, she thought, no need to eat your heart out just yet.

'A cup of tea,' she suggested. 'Then we'll begin.'

SEVEN

Colin was appalled at the missive. He waved it at Stella as if it stank. 'They want to promote me.'

'Isn't that what you've been angling for, for ages?'

'Yeeees,' he sang, explaining the obvious to a cretin. 'But not a transfer too.'

'It's not the Paris office, then?'

'No. They have crossed the line.'

'Colin, you do not have a line,' Stella pointed out.

'I do now. It's fucking Belfast. They want me to head up a new division in fucking fuckedyfuck Belfast.' He threw himself across Stella's desk. 'It could *not* be worse.'

Stella remained placatory. 'Is there no currency in returning to your home town in triumph and wiping the eye of all who once knew you?'

'Tragically, even that would not be enough. God, I spent so long trying to get away from all that.'

'Was it the war?'

'Oh, don't be so fucking stupid, Stella. The war had nothing to do with me. I'm a privileged, upper middle-class

Protestant from off the Holywood Road. The war never came near us. No! It's the whole scene there. I'll never meet anyone again.' He began to hyperventilate. 'Do you know, when I was growing up I thought I had it bad as a homo until I heard there were only two lesbians in the whole of the town at the time. And they didn't fancy one another. How grim is that?'

'That was probably an urban myth, Colin. Belfast is really hip at the moment you know.'

'Yesyesyes. The point is my family lives there. Nearly every last one of them. I love them to bits, I do, because I can, because I am hundreds of miles away from them. If I go back there I'll have to see them regularly which is out of the question. My fragile love would not survive the strain. Besides all that, I couldn't listen to someone with my accent all day long: I'd go clinically insane. Do you know how sloooowly some of the people round our way speak? Thank the dear Jesus Lord God Our Saviour that my poor father is dead, or this would surely kill him; his ginger, faggot son come home to roost.' He took a calming breath. 'The money is fantastic, of course.'

'So, you'll consider it.'

'Yes.'

The afternoon flew by for Ulrika. She threw herself into educating her media studies students with a verve she hadn't felt in ages. Both students and staff took note and compliments were fulsome. She felt as though she was finally back in the place from where she had started as a rookie, when she had wanted to shape a new generation. For too long she had let herself languish in despair at the system and the students. It was almost romantic to be back.

'This latest diet is beginning to kick in,' she explained to the faculty secretary. 'It was like having the flu as my body was adjusting but now that I'm over that I'm on a roll. I feel great.'

And she did. She even took a trip to look at the offending life drawings on the corridor leading to the art department. They were fairly dire, as reported, and for that probably deserved banishing. In fact, it was hard to tell that they were taken from life at all for the most part. But in the time-old tradition of fair play and the democracy of free expression she would champion these pictures' right to exist and to fail. She felt it was indicative of her rediscovered passion for the job that she had bothered to look into another aspect of college life, to become involved again.

She felt light rather than light-headed and her appetite had vanished. And was it her or did the waistband on this skirt feel as if it was shifting around, no longer subsumed beneath and into her flesh? She bought a diet fizz from a vending machine and pressed the cold can against the back of her neck to cool it. Then she rolled it around the front and down her chest a little. By accident she brushed it against a nipple and received a jolt not entirely explained by the temperature of the tin. It was a surprise to feel sexual again and she found herself fantasising about being taken quickly and roughly in a toilet cubicle. She ached for a lover's touch but seeing no opportunity for such a union she popped the ring-pull on the can and slugged back a mouthful before marching in to her jaded second years and setting them a paper on morality in advertising.

Jack was pulling in behind a birdshit-streaked Nicholas Farewell in the front square when Bill passed by in his Saab. He raised a hand in acknowledgement, surprised to see the other man out. Bill parked, then waited by his front door to say hello.

Jack smiled as he approached his own. 'You went back to work?'

'Yes. I thought it was time to check on the empire. It's still ticking over. Any news from your neck of the woods?'

'No. I'm still hawking the usual lies and spin, old stories in new bindings. And my wife's still shacked up with the Telly Tubby type. Do you want to come in for a drink?'

'Just let me check on things here first and then I'll pop round.'

'I'll put the ice on to cook.'

'Yes, this weather is phenomenal, isn't it?'

'In a way I hate it.'

'Me too. Too much of a good thing.' He chuckled in spite of himself. 'You'd think I'd be the last person to complain about that, wouldn't you?'

Jack opened the several locks on the heavy front door and switched the blinking alarm off. The sounds of his feet on marble and keys clanging into a bowl echoed in the cathedral-cool hall. It was a big house for one man but that had never bothered him and he was determined not to let it now. For one thing, he had bought the house before meeting Laura. And the only mistake he made after that was to marry the bitch. Which could be remedied. And he was damned if she would do him out of his beautiful home. He loved it and once it was clear of her clutter and shitty art purchases he could get back to a normal way of living and become a proper human being again.

Puckish thinking for sure, particularly as he stared at the stairwell they had made love on so many times when they couldn't wait to go to the bedroom or just fancied experiencing a different location. The house was full of such sites. He tried not to let it defeat him, especially as it was sex he remembered not love. He needed to hang on to such thoughts and perspective.

He felt all too corporeal standing in his crumpled shirt and trousers, smelling of petrol fumes and sweat, so he dashed upstairs, threw himself quickly under the shower and grabbed a fresh T-shirt and trunks. When he answered the door, Bill gave a low whistle and said, 'If I'd known it was a date I'd have brought flowers.'

Jack laughed, delighted to hear his neighbour crack a joke. He clapped him across the back and welcomed him in. 'You're using me, you cheap son of a bitch, but I'll allow it this once,' he said.

They stood in front of the large open fridge enjoying the coolness and gazing at the beers. Jack felt a bit sheepish to see the mad array before them. He had had no idea till then that he was a collector and by the look of it a serious one.

'I think I must have a representative of most continental countries, which makes it a Eurovision festival really, and of course a few sundry continents and eastern nations are there too.'

'How shall we measure a man?' Bill intoned.

They each chose a beer and Jack flicked on the stereo. There was tacit agreement that they would not go into the garden, mindful of disturbing Helen in the cul-de-sac. Jack looked around the conservatory and didn't see too much of his wife, though the garden beyond the glass panels still bore all the signs of a bored housewife on a feng shui kick. It was beautiful in its spare way and he decided he could live with it. That and the fact that the gravel out there had been too rough on the skin to invite any al fresco sexual activity. They sat in comfortable silence, two abandoned men, not wanting to spoil some simple moments away from complications not entirely of their making.

'Sometimes I think she'll never come back,' Bill eventually said, for himself as much as his companion.

Jack heaved a sigh. 'Sometimes I don't want mine to,' he admitted.

They went back to their beers.

Helen listened to the music seeping over the wall from Jack's house: Steely Dan. She liked this album, very easy on the ear. It was a while since she'd bothered with music. It didn't seem very relevant any more. And she had grown sick of hymns, had never liked them anyhow, courtesy of an Irish convent education. Violence was what she remembered of a lot of them, blood gushing and poor old Jesus in the throes.

I'm not sure we were worth it in the end of all, she mused. Humans are an ungrateful bunch, in general, and they always think they know best.

She'd practically lost all religion by the time it was thrust on her again, at which time it was a bit late for God's intervention by way of help. If God had been as merciful as the nuns had insisted all those years ago He, She or It would have intervened earlier in Helen's life and spared her. God, should that Being exist, had a lot to answer for as far as she was concerned. I'm surprised I can be so light about all of this, she thought. Time was when she'd have started to shout and rant at the very notion of the Almighty. Perhaps she would take some time later to get angry about it. Right now she was drawn along by the Dans and wondering who *is* that gaucho? At least it wasn't one of Jack's mad jazz records. She smiled to think of his consideration. He knows I like a tune and can't stand the progressive stuff. She had been the same at school. She loved Latin because she could work it out; it had rules. Mathematics, on the other hand, eluded her. As it approached purity it seemed to get more and more vague and improvisational. Latin had a tune, maths did not. There go my thoughts, she realised, riffing along without me. Since her body was doing its own thing without her volition it was probably only natural that her mind would get in on the act too. She had wanted to die, after all, but no one listened to her, least of all herself in the form of her own organs. She had capitulated, gone on, though it had little to do with her real wishes.

Jack's nice, she thought. He deserved better than Laura but, as wives go, who was she to pass judgement? Laura was good fun, mind you, and a tremendous gossip. She'd run off with some fella who gave her the glad eye while she was pissed at a do and then followed the whole thing up when any normal hungover person would have forgotten the whole sorry incident or chosen to. Jack was away on business at the time; at least she hoped he had been or Laura was a lot bolder than she'd estimated. She would be back, of course, in spite of all the new devotion being lavished on her. Laura bored easily.

Helen was getting tired and there was no sign of Lady Muck yet so she decided to give up on her for the day. The Greek salad had been delivered as requested and after so long just shovelling grub in for the sake of it she had enjoyed it. It had been an odd day. The heat was particularly sapping and though sorrow was still lodged in her gut, her heart had finally tried to assert itself. 'I'm here all the time,' it seemed to say, 'big, fat and juicy, beating, beating.' There was no choice but to continue, and not just on her behalf alone.

She breathed and felt the beating.

Beating.

Beating.

❋　❋　❋

Colin and Famke sat at the old pine table gobsmacked at the new Ulrika dashing from stove to vegetable rack and back.

'She's out of focus,' Colin complained, his hands waving ineffectually. 'It's making me dizzy. And exhausted.'

'Shut up,' Famke instructed.

'You could probably do with some exercise,' Ulrika said.

'Are you right in the head, wee girl?' he exclaimed. 'I'm worn to a frazzle keeping up with the men of London town. Exercise, *mes amis*, is the last thing this poor shell needs. I am a shadow of my former self.'

'Drink your wine and belt up. You should be thrilled with yourself.'

'For why, oh loveliest of lovely landladies?'

'You are surrounded by the best company available on the terrace this evening and you've been offered a fab new position.'

Colin held up a hand. 'That guy is getting married in a few weeks' time. I shall be passing on his affianced delights.'

'I meant the job, actually.'

'Mmn. That is undeniably another matter and I'll keep you posted re same. Now I think it's time to celebrate.'

'Anything in particular?' Famke asked.

'It's Tuesday, which is cause enough, but also we applaud Ulrika for joining the rest of the household on our plateau of wonderfulness.'

'Bitch,' Ulrika commented. 'Make mine a large one. I'm feeling invincible tonight.'

'Fighting talk. What's brought all this on?'

'I've just found my personal velocity,' Ulrika explained.

The others whooped and toasted her.

'I wonder where he is,' Colin mused oh-so-nonchalantly, after a pause.

The ladies exchanged a glance.

'He left his phone number on the pad,' Ulrika offered.

Colin tutted.

'It's your turn,' Famke observed. 'If you want to see him, you have to call him.'

'*Moi?* I think not.'

'That's the deal in the real world, Colin.'

'The deal sucks.'

'Something you understand perfectly,' Ulrika laughed.

'To echo your recent sentiments, dear, "bitch".' He tossed his ginger fronds but knew it was not his finest moment.

It was dark and close when Lucy returned, the cul-de-sac deserted. Her clothes were like a second, unwelcome skin clinging damply to her body. She was unwilling to commit herself to the tin can just yet. Instead she opened all the doors to let some fresher air in and sat on the kerb beside it. She heard the distant tack-tack-tack of a helicopter and the pops of gunfire. Brixton, she presumed, perhaps unfairly. The little alleyway was clear but for her car and the urban flotsam and jetsam of sweet wrappers and crisp packets blown in on a phantom breeze. She felt the fine dust and pollution of the day settling on her and in her. Reluctantly she swallowed more water. Really, an en suite was a total necessity for the city car dweller. She must write to the car manufacturers and tell them that. In fairness, it would make more sense to live in a camper van if one was to go it rough and she'd know that for next time. A hollow laugh never made it past a dying synapse in her head. She hadn't the energy for it anyhow. She looked up at the sky beyond the orange haze of the city, hoping to see some stars, and the reassurance of a universe out there that was bigger than her human problems and would abide long after they or she was gone.

'You're probably wondering why I'm here,' she said aloud. 'I found this place by accident months ago when I took a wrong turn on the way to a friend's house. Good job I remembered it. My husband, Pete, has left with everything I own. Well, that's not quite true. Our stuff is in storage in the wilds of North Acton because we were supposed to be moving house. I have some clothes in the boot and some toiletries, just to tide us over while we were in rented accommodation between the sale of our old place and signing for the new one. Just a few weeks, that's all he said it would take. I even visited the new house, measured it for curtains and ordered some furniture. But it was an illusion, like my marriage, as it turns out. Anyhow, he's gone now with the money and I'm living here in my car and I don't know where he is or what to do or where I'm going. So, that's me. What's your story?'

She got no answer, nor did she expect one. As she got into the car she had the thought that she had never seen any of the Crazy Lady's bags. She didn't even have a shopping trolley to live out of. Where was she? And where was her stuff?

So now I know, Helen thought. Poor bitch. Mind you, it was not the worst story she'd ever heard. In fact, she could match it. I'll see your misery and raise you, she wanted to say, throwing in her hand of cards. She could certainly give Lucy a run for her money. Instead she answered the question, though she knew Lucy wouldn't hear her.

'My story?' she whispered. 'I killed my babies.'

EIGHT

Sleep proved elusive. Her mind would not let her rest. She damned and cursed Lucy, who had woken her and then engaged her mind with her problem. It heightened her own sense of alienation and made her wonder again why exactly she had found it necessary to divorce herself from the world. An opportunistic fox wandered in looking for a meal. Its musky scent floated on the air as it poked an elegant nose into bushes and under doors and gates and railings. As its auburn brush trailed out of sight, a ginger tomcat filed in, mooching from one animal marker to another, spraying his hormones to mask the visits of others. He eventually sniffed out the car and had a fine time rubbing up against it and stinking it out. It would reek to high heaven tomorrow when the sun burned the metal and released every last unsubtle hint of the aromas the cat had bestowed.

Beyond the rooftops Helen could hear the sky rumbling with the sound of jets returning from faraway destinations. Further out, satellites orbited, watching and recording, amid the space junk floating in zero gravity, man's litter tumbling in slow motion through the void. Why were we so anxious to conquer space when we hadn't yet figured out the earth? What vanity to want to thrust our chaos on the rest of the universe. It was the continuation of man's attempt to best whatever cosmic force might be out there, to float above the stuck-down world as a person approaching the light of death gazes down on the lives below.

The city sighed in a general sleep but, on the margins, the nocturnal comings and goings of unseen workers in their unfashionable or unsavoury jobs ticked on, ready to clear away the detritus of daytime lives. They were the shadow spooks. I am one of these Disappeared, Helen thought. She liked the idea of that, this brotherhood in which it was better as a member to be aloof. She was an echo of the city's women; a mirror image of a mother and wife. It hadn't always been so, of course.

Happiness was such a fleeting commodity. Had she grabbed at it too hard, or expected too much of it? For a while it seemed so ordinary, so unremarkable. There were no details sticking out, demanding attention, only a general feeling of content, it seemed. She hadn't seen the wood for the trees nor the ivy choking it.

Some days were knockout memories, of course, both good and bad. The good led by the boys' births. First came Stephen. She remembered their trepidation at the news; eyes held wide at first, not knowing how to react, then laughter followed by concern. Were they ready to be parents? How could one learn this strange new trick? Would they cope? What if there was anything wrong with the baby? She had adored her fecund body expanding in preparation for giving him his life. The thrill of feeling him move inside of her, his heartbeat thudding with her own. Often a little limb would poke out at her side and she would gently tease it back into the orb that sheltered him. Funny how she had to remind herself of the all-day sickness of the first trimester, it seemed so inconsequential a detail in the wider context.

Sitting here, now, she could still feel the massive throes of involuntary spasm as her body tried to push the little boy out into the world when his time came. The exquisite agony of each contraction, one more awe-inspiring than the next. And then the final thrust to release him. His purple body turning to red, held aloft, the scalded face creased in indignation, then a cross squall of complaint. Her flooding relief and the all-consuming love she felt for this small, glistening creature. It choked her with its intensity. She might have died happy there and then. Given a choice and knowing what she now did, she would have opted for that, she thought.

Having experienced childbirth, surely it was possible for a woman to shed her past life, like a snake losing skin, to emerge a new and better version of herself? It would have a cathartic healing power. That was what she needed, wanted: healing. Catharsis you could keep. It was over-rated and not worth its price.

It was ridiculous to say that the darkest hour is just

before the dawn. Physically that was no longer possible for the city, baking in its own greenhouse emissions and orange phosphorescence. Poor old London, wrecked with the daily effort of having to be one of the top cities in the world. It never got to take a break. Even in quieter moments acid rain ate at it, pollution blackened its skin and humans whittled at its core, leaving a worn-out husk encased by concrete and finished off in brick and slate, and darkened faddy glass shining on its face like the wrong shade of lipstick.

Stephen took to his mother's breast with gusto, deep-sucking and smacking of his satisfied lips dragging at her. When the initial pain abated she realised what a lot of time they would spend together. He was a regular feeder but also curiously paced with bursts of frenetic activity and little breathers throughout each session. She looked at his downy head and thought, I am in love, again.

He was taking drunken steps and trying words when they discovered he would have a sibling. Reaction on this occasion was sheer happiness. They were to be a bigger family. Archie came feet first with a flurry of anxiety and the midwife muttering 'Second children' in confirmation of their contrariness. He had insisted on attention from before his entrance and doubled his demands after it. Curly hair sprang from his head in a riot of activity and statement. I'm here, he bawled, whaddaya gonna do abouddit? Stephen looked alarmed but was obviously prepared to row in with the two people he trusted most in life, his parents. But there were glimpses, even then, that he thought they'd made a mistake and had bitten off more than anyone could chew. This baby was nine pounds nine ounces, after all. 'Mama, loudy baba,' he would say, pointing at his yowling brother. From then on all was mayhem.

'We're just servants now,' her husband would say.

'You better believe it,' she agreed. 'And we brought it all on ourselves.'

'I suppose we'd best be good to them. They'll take over the world some day and it would be nice to be remembered kindly.'

Were their lives measured before birth? Were every one of their childish breaths and heartbeats counted? Was every new experience numbered and finite? She would give her life for theirs in an instant, but it had only required an instant to snuff them out. She had taken to wondering if they had lived in Australia would the boys have had one day longer in their short lives? She would have had an extra twenty-four hours to love them. How could two such potent forces be removed when they deserved so much more? And what was the purpose of this extinction? How could it benefit those left behind? There was no sense to the carnage, especially as it had been by her hand.

Helen sat waiting for her punishment. As the time passed she realised that she was living it, every moment of every day, awake and asleep. It was fitting, though hardly enough for what she had let happen, she thought. She became agitated at the need to make proper reparation for her crime. She needed to lash out, too, at the world that had brought this sorrow to her doorstep. An early thin light peeked through the tree leaves and the birds redoubled their chorus. The cars and delivery vans of the new dawn passed and then she heard the sirens.

At first they were distant enough to block out, as she always did now. But increasingly it became obvious that they were approaching. She could identify the nee-naw of an ambulance and the more insistent clanging ring of the fire brigade. Their terrifying cavalcade was coming to claim more victims. She felt her pulse quicken and her head throbbed as if ready to take off. She could feel the vibrations of their approach through the tarmac and into her feet and steeled herself for the flashing lights to zoom by on the main thoroughfare. She shielded her ears and shook her head, trying to loosen the bells' grip. And then the cavalcade turned into the cul-de-sac and she started to scream and rage.

Famke looked out when the noise of the sirens drew closer. She saw Helen erupt. A fire chief was waving the main vehicle on its way. Then he turned his attention to the hysteric tearing out her hair. Famke took up the phone and dialled a number. A man's voice said, 'I'm on my way, I can hear her from here.' To see Helen lose it was in some ways a relief but Famke worried about the conse-quences for her. How would she deal with the aftermath? Famke saw Bill exit his garden through the gate of number seven and go to relieve the fireman.

✿　　✿　　✿

Lucy had been dreaming of Eden but finding no comfort in the vision. Finn Beaker, the musician, was playing some sort of lute, which barely covered his hirsute and naked body, while Rita Fuller painted something brown and unidentifiable on a book Jez Anderton was holding aloft. Evie was encouraging the group with gifts of wine and half-eaten apples, and her paramour, Bartok, leered from the sideline, lisping a split tongue in and out of his twisted mouth. Then Finn produced a bell and began to beat it, chasing away the birds and sundry bees of Paradise before running at Lucy with an evil grin across his sweaty face. Her mother began to shout and cry. Lucy awoke to find that the noise was now louder rather than gone and it was all around her home. She struggled into a T-shirt and track bottoms and opened the car door. In the excitement no one noticed where she had come from.

An ambulance was stalled at the mouth of the cul-de-sac, siren blaring and light flashing an intermittent blue-tinged hue on the air. A fireman leaned from a fire engine, waving at it and shouting, 'Wrong turning, it's the next one we want.' The ambulance moved on. As the red truck began its reversal, the Crazy Lady ran at it screeching and throwing air punches in its direction. Another man in a fire uniform went to comfort her and suddenly Lucy felt protective of her comrade.

She rushed him, shouting, 'You leave her alone.'

He stopped in his tracks, stunned to have to deal with two harpies. Just then a man emerged from number 7 and ran across to them.

'It's all right,' he said to the Crazy Woman. 'I'm here now.'

Incredibly she let him take hold of her. Her screaming turned to loud sobs and she remained inconsolable. He turned to the fire officer and said, 'I'll take it from here.'

'I'm so sorry about this, Mr Richards. The driver is new and got the wrong turning. We couldn't have picked a worse place to end up.' He looked ashen against his uniform and no longer a figure of authority.

'Don't worry about it,' Mr Richards told him. 'It wasn't anybody's fault. It was just a mistake.'

Lucy stood nervously by, feeling useless. The fireman left. She didn't know what to say or do now. A dark-haired, dark-skinned woman in a flowing green kaftan approached from another gate. Lucy recognised her and was weak with apprehension and heat. Suddenly the place was uncomfortably full and Lucy felt utterly exposed. The dark beauty approached the little group and addressed Lucy, saying, 'I'm Famke. You can come with me. Bill will look after Helen.'

The others seemed to accept that this would be so and Lucy found herself obediently following Famke, not knowing what to expect next. She was knocked for six to be in the company of Famke K. Ordinarily this would have put her on her professional mettle. But there was a lot more basic stuff at stake now. Would she get her marching orders from the cul-de-sac? she wondered. And where would she find so handy a parking space again? She was of fixed abode, for sure, but its address might be about to change. As they walked through the gate and on through the cottage garden to the rear of the house, Lucy suddenly wished she was wearing a bra and knickers. I'd feel so much more confident, she thought.

Famke pushed open the kitchen door and announced, 'I've brought our mystery car woman.' It was met with a small round of applause.

Jack was glad to stretch beneath his own sheets. It occurred to him that he quite liked being alone in the double bed. Not all of the time, of course, and it would be nice to have a choice in the matter within his marriage but this had been untimely ripped from him by his wife. She had been rubbish at keeping her end of the bargain whereas he was happy with the idea of being faithful to one another for as long as they both should live. This had never had to withstand the hoary test of time, since one half of the fellowship had absconded. He yawned and realised that he was growing accustomed to the new arrangement and not in an entirely unpleasant way. To celebrate this he decided the time had come to remove some of his wife's uglier ornaments from the bedroom, and throw her various beauty accoutrements in the bathroom bin. He felt a flutter of liberation.

His mobile rang. In fact it was never off: he was on twenty-four-hour call to clients. When he answered it a tabloid hack wanted to know why Jodie Taylor Jones was in hospital. This was news to Jack and as he shot upright in a start he managed to mumble, 'I'm losing you, the line is very bad,' and hit the red 'off' button.

'Shit, shit, shit,' he swore, shucking into some clothes and running to the kitchen to brew an espresso. Life was an endless run of woman trouble, it seemed. And there was no way a mere human male could face it alone and without stimulants.

He knocked back some black, scalding caffeine as he dialled Jodie's number and listened to her recorded voice asking him to leave a message. He did, terse and to the point. She was back on to him within seconds.

'Jack,' she gushed. Jodie always gushed unless she was unconscious. 'I haven't been admitted. I'm in hospital *visiting* the sick and the broken. It just seems that I have so much and others have so little and I thought it would be good for everyone if I started to give a little back. You know?'

'Jodie, it's eight forty-five in the morning. Isn't it just a tad early for good deeds, even in your world?'

'Oh, yes, I see what you mean. But not really, you know? It's quite late in my world actually.' She laughed. 'You see, I was on my way home from a party at Hugo Belleville's place and we were passing Hammersmith Hospital, at least I think that's where we are, and it just seemed the perfect thing to do. Should I go home, then, do you think?'

'Yes, I think that would be best, Jodie. Go home, get some sleep and sit tight until I call you later.'

Honestly, the woman was born out of time. She would be perfect in a P. G. Wodehouse novel, on acid. He wondered idly how she had gained admittance to the hospital in the first place but then decided that it was probably best never to know that. He toyed with the idea of letting MI5 know that she had skills ripe for spy training but worried that this course of action would put the entire world in danger.

Jack headed to the computer to put together a mini press release heralding Jodie's new angel status and reassuring the journalistic populace that she was most well, positively bursting with health and good deeds. He heard the first sirens of the day close by, on their way to collect the new fodder for the hospitals and jails of London. Oh sweet Lord, he thought, pitying the poor and disadvantaged; they had no idea what was still in store for them.

Lucy was surprised at how benign the inquisition was. She was probably in luck with the timing of the piece as Colin and Ulrika had to get to work and couldn't get into any sort of stride. She fobbed off the major query as to why she was living in her car, glossing over the temporary nature of the exercise and saying it was the result of a ridiculous mistake too complicated and boring to go into.

'Well, I for one will be prepared for utter boredom later,' the redhead said.

He was a handsome fellow and obviously gay so it was redundant of him to mention that he was a 'big, Northern Irish fairy'. The information explained his accent, however, which Lucy hadn't quite been able to pin down. Ulrika was a tall blonde with piercing violet eyes, an old-fashioned clothes sense and way too much energy. She said she worked in the local college but was originally from Purley via a Norwegian dad and a South London mum. Lucy was treated to a mini CV, bewildered that the woman felt the need to share all this with her. It did take the spotlight off her own situation, however, so she was grateful for the seed and breed of Ulrika's life and career. Throughout this Famke kept her silence and seemed to be studying her intently from all angles. When the workers had left in a whirl of bags and perfumes, a strange silence settled at the kitchen table. Lucy did not feel like breaking the resultant calm in case it meant spilling her soul but suddenly she realised why the other woman was looking her over so closely: it was her job to observe.

'You're Famke K,' she exclaimed. 'I recognise you.'

Famke smiled. 'I'm impressed. Not many of the public would be able to identify me without major hints and help.'

'My mother runs a gallery and I curate most of her exhibitions. I don't know if you've come across it? The White Rooms?' It babbled out of her and she felt stupid and awestruck all at once.

'Ah, yes, Evie. She's great fun and a bit of an icon in the art world.'

'Well.' Lucy shrugged, not really knowing what to say to this. She was more or less stuck to her seat with awkward wonder at where she found herself.

'I take it she doesn't know where you're shacked up at the moment. Evie may be eccentric but I doubt that she'd abandon her daughter to the streets.'

'Eh, no,' Lucy admitted. 'I've been too embarrassed to tell her, to be honest. I feel like enough of a failure without involving Mum in this whole sorry mess.'

They let that find its own space in the air around them. Lucy tried to continue with her coffee but her hands shook too much to make this work plausibly. She set to on a bowl of muesli Ulrika had put in front of her. At least it filled her mouth and precluded talk. Her jaw ached slightly from masticating the bran-heavy cereal.

'Who is the other woman from the cul-de-sac?' she finally asked.

'That's Helen.'

'What's her story?'

'You'll have to ask her that,' Famke said.

'She hasn't even grunted in my general direction since I got here so I doubt we'll be swapping stories over the camp fire.'

'I wouldn't count on it. Since you arrived she's been acting differently. That's a good thing, I think. But we'll have to wait and see.'

'I can't believe such a well-dressed woman can be living rough in this day and age.'

Famke smiled. 'You're hardly in any position to make that observation, are you?'

Lucy surprised herself by laughing. 'No,' she admitted. She shook her head. 'Get me, huh?'

Famke stretched and yawned. 'I'd better get to work myself.'

Lucy felt her blood race: a Famke K exhibition was

always a major event in the art world. 'You're working on something new?'

'Oh yes. You're in it, actually. I'm not sure why or how just yet but I'll know soon. Perhaps you'd like to pose for me sometime? That might be useful.'

Lucy nearly choked on the last half walnut from her bowl. 'Are you kidding? I'd love to.'

'Good. I'll let you know when I'm ready for you.'

'Great. You know where to find me.'

Lucy wandered out of the house and through the garden in a daze. As she put together a bag for the day she pinched herself several times to check that she was not dreaming. She was hard at work for an hour before she realised she had forgotten to put on underwear, so huge was the impact of meeting the artist.

It was only later in the day too that Famke admitted to herself that she should probably have offered the box room, but somehow it just hadn't come up as an option. She hadn't let it, selfish to the last and protective of her new series. After all, if Lucy was not in the cul-de-sac she would not be in the work. She could hear a phrase of Colin's tumble through her mind. 'I'm not so green I'm cabbage,' he liked to declare. Famke was looking after Number One.

Helen sat on a deckchair in the garden, shivering in spite of the heat. Bill brought tea, toast and Marmite, which she loved.

'Perhaps you should have a lie-down after this. You've had a bit of a shock.'

'I got so angry.'

'That can only be a good thing.'

'You think?'

'Yes.'

'How are you?'

'I went to the site yesterday. I thought it was time to get out. And I was pleasantly surprised.'

Helen nodded.

'You sleeping all right?'

'Yes. Except for last night. That other woman, the one in the car, she upset me a bit and I couldn't get off.'

'Would you like me to ask her to move on?'

'No. She has her problems too.' Helen finished her toast and wiped her fingers in a napkin. 'Will you go to work today?'

'I suppose so, unless you want company?' He was taking a chance here and hoped it wasn't too much too soon.

'You go on to the site. I'm sure they're delighted to have you back.'

He nodded, trying not to feel hurt, telling himself that she would come to him when she was ready. She had before and she would again. 'Fine. You'll be OK?'

'Yes.'

Bill Richards watched his wife walk back down the path. He sat on his hands and rooted his feet to the ground, afraid that he might run to her and throw his arms round her and declare the enduring love and passion for her that consumed him. She turned before the gate.

'The Greek salad was excellent,' she said. 'Thank you.'

119

NINE

Colin was itching to dial the number he had found on the pad by the telephone at home. However, it was not his custom to chase and he was choosy about who he let contact him. He was amazed that this guy had got under his skin, even minutely. Sure he was fun and could cook but Colin would expect that to be as read before ever seeing a guy a second time. Not that he did see people more than once as a rule. It was just better that way. No baggage. No mess. No sharing. No heartbreak.

Julio had been the last one he'd let in and he was not about to make the same mistake twice. Julio, the carpenter from Stockport with an unlikely name and a cruel and addictive personality. Colin had been happy to be used and pleasured and had convinced himself that he had found the One. But it was an infatuation and ended as everyone had predicted, messily. There was also the small matter of a black eye, cheek fracture and a broken wrist for Colin, but he was healed now. His joints could predict rain but he was otherwise unscathed and unscarred, he told himself.

Stella was the only one at work who knew he had not injured himself in a fall from a ladder while trying to attach Day-Glo stars to the bathroom ceiling (that had gone off a week before without incident). Colin had taken time off and cried like a baby but when that was done he never mentioned the 'J' word again and only ever wept at Judy Garland movies. 'I have to,' he would explain. 'I'm a poof.' He no longer believed in real-life romance but reasoned that was one less shackle to deal with in the rat race. A harsh lesson had been meted out but it was an important one and he was glad of it.

He had learned Tony's number off. If he had taken it with him or been seen to copy it he would never have lived the matter down. His fingers poised over the dial and he flexed them, ready for action. A 'Boo!' over the partition made him screech to a stand with his hand over his heart.

Stella had sidled up to check him out. 'I was right,' she crowed. 'I knew you were up to something. Spill it.'

'Fiddledidee,' he scoffed, heart racing and armpits wet. His mind clicked into overdrive. 'I was thinking of phoning Human Resources to ask more about the Belfast job. The devil is in the detail, as I have told you a zillion times.'

'So you're not phoning the wedding guy?' she asked, her voice dripping insincerity.

He had taught her too well and this accuracy was the price of his superior tutelage. 'I'll ask you again. Are you sure you're not a tranny who began life as a gay man, because you are the most suspicious woman I have ever met.'

'I'm going to allow you the very good recovery lie with the Human Resources schtick, so we'll move on.'

'And your hands are very large,' he pointed out.

She ignored this. 'Are you going to call him?'

'Not now I'm not.'

'I knew I was right. You really have trained me well.'

'I curse my own genius and generosity. To think I was once glad to have my very own hag. Now I am not so sure. Go away.'

'Done. And for your information *I* am not your hag, *you* are my fag, an accessory at most and disposable, so don't get uppity.'

'I have decided to issue you with a verbal warning,' Colin snarled. 'Now begone, you menace.'

'Let me know what he says.' She wafted off.

He counted to seven, because it was a prime number and he had room for his own made-up superstition, then dialled. He heard the phone ring twice in the distance followed by a tentative, 'Hello.'

'Oh, I seem to have a wrong number. That's not Tori?'

'No. Is that Colin?'

'Er, yes. Who are you?'

'It's Tony.'

'Tony . . . oh, *Tony*. I must have pressed the wrong button on the phone. Sorry about that.'

'Don't be. It's nice to hear from you. And even nicer to know I'm in your phone.'

'I'm sure it is.' Damn, Colin thought, that caught me on the hop. Now it looks like I could be bothered. I'm getting sloppy.

'How's work?'

'Boring,' he sing-songed. Then he went for his sucker punch. 'Actually, it looks like I'll have to relocate.'

'No.'

Gotcha, Colin thought.

'That would be awful. When will you have to go?'

'To be honest I'm not sure what to do. I suppose I could stay in London if there was something to keep me here, but there isn't. So!'

'Em, well, I guess while I have you I should pin you down to having a drink, maybe.'

Colin left him to figure out the details. He really should have let Stella stay for this master class but there were some things that an apprentice had to do the legwork on and this particular skill was one that she would have to acquire for herself. Years of trial and error were ahead of her before she could challenge for his title.

'How about meeting up after work?'

'I think I could do that.'

'What about the Duck and Cage in Clapham Old Town?'

'Yees . . .' He liked the open-ended sound he made and wrote a little 'tick VG' on the pad in front of him.

'I work in a garden centre in Tooting so I could get the Tube there. Is that convenient for you?'

'I can manage it this once,' he honeyed, making sure

Tony knew he was making an effort but magnanimous in his wonderfulness.

'So, let's say seven o'clock.'

'Let's.'

Colin hung up and resolved to be at least twenty minutes late that evening. But he could not deny that he was excited.

'What time and where?' Stella asked, upon him in an instant.

'I will go back to Northern Ireland if you don't leave me alone, bitchface.'

'Oh, so tempting,' she said. 'Don't push me.'

'That's my line, now piss off.'

She left, trilling, 'He likes him,' as tunelessly as any human should ever be allowed. Her inability to sing was simply another reason to love her.

Colin certainly couldn't go back to working now. He decided to go free range across the office floor in search of someone to toy with.

As Lucy passed the front counter where Ivan was serving, she decided that Vida must have stolen him from a stranger's pram when he was a baby. There was no way that she could have given birth to such a genetically different person. He was lovely, Vida was a nightmare. She saw yet again that, yes, he had similar dark eyes to his mother but his showed humanity whereas hers were cold and all-seeing. It made Lucy's viscera chill to catch Vida watching her. Which she did the moment she entered the back staffroom of Mario's. Then Lucy saw the reason. A bunch of flowers stood on the staff table with a card addressed to her.

She wanted to act nonchalant as if she knew who'd sent them and just as she ripped the envelope open she realised that she did but it was too late to back away now. 'Sorry' was supposed to make everything all right. She burned at the waste of money on this redundant gesture. She could more usefully employ it to rent a place to live. She fumed and hyperventilated, tapping her palm on the table again and again in a gesture that screamed to become violent but struggled to remain controlled. Vida left. She's had her fun, Lucy thought. She sat clutching her stomach as her body thrummed with despair. She hated her inability to remedy this state of affairs. Cruelly, her mind reminded her that she had relinquished any tenuous leverage she had when she gave her husband the run of their finances. She had invited this abuse.

The card read Fifi's Flowers so she stormed next door, stopping herself just short of an explosion. This was no place for a scene. After all, none of these people knew that she was anything but a happily married woman under stress because of a house move.

'I see my hubby is wasting money on your excellent product,' she said to the proud proprietress.

'Well, he got good value because the bouquet was for you.'

'When was he here?' The effort to keep her voice light nearly killed her.

'Oh no, no, he phoned it in,' Fiona explained.

Martha shrugged to reinforce this truth then went back to chewing off her split ends.

Lucy cursed herself for expecting anything else. Pete would never chance being caught in person. Not now. They were too far along their road for any true reasonableness. She would have strangled him and faced the consequences with the law without batting an eyelash. He would know that unless he had lost his mind completely, which would explain a lot. Yet, even though it was futile lunacy on her part, she found herself running around the piazza hoping to catch a glimpse of him. Surely there was a chance that he might be keeping an eye on her without wanting to be seen. She whirled this way then that, looking like a crazed dervish driven to distraction by London and the heat. Tears rimmed her eyes and her lungs burned. Her arms and legs trembled with excited tension. Passersby whispered and pointed. Glancing back at the café, she saw Vida looking through the window, her face cast in a knowing grimace, agate eyes flaming with interest. Lucy gulped back a painful breath and returned to work like a lamb walking on new legs. She felt foolish and disgusted. It was a terrible combination.

Vida watched her get into her apron and said, 'You will give you a heart boom if you not more careful.'

'I know,' was all Lucy could manage.

The cul-de-sac was empty so Famke used the opportunity to steal out and take some photographs. She liked to have a record of the tiny areas she could not see from her studio roof. The car cooked gently in the early heat and it didn't half pong. A tomcat had sprayed it and it hummed with a new, somewhat uncomfortable identity. She captured the green ribbon on the fencing, now joined by the catkins of tall grasses, all looking dusty and worn. She clicked on the trash blown in and the cars moving past. She sat on the kerb and tried to get Helen's usual perspective on the world. It was mesmerising to watch the movements in front of her and she found that a quarter of an hour had passed without her noticing. She took pictures of the canopy of leaves above the three gardens here at the rear of the square. She lay back on the concrete and let her eyes close, listening to the sound of the city. She felt invincible and invisible here in this spot. No one knew where she was in a city of so many millions. She was alone. It was hypnotic and so tempting to stay there cocooned against any ugliness that might be encountered abroad on the streets. But there was work to be done. And she didn't want to be in the way when Helen took up her sentinel duty.

She walked back to her house, and a ringing phone, and an agent wondering when her latest exhibition would be ready. It was not lost on her that she had not absconded for long and that Mammon awaited her efforts for commerce and other people their commission. So much for freedom of artistic expression; nowhere to run, nowhere to hide.

❋   ❋   ❋

Martha picked sandwich-making time to land in from the florist and strike up a conversation.

'Your husband has a lovely voice,' she opined across the top of the display case.

'Yeah.' Lucy was disinclined to elaborate and continued to pile egg mayonnaise into a baguette.

'He sounds dark.'

'Oh, he's that for sure. Lettuce? Cress?'

'No. Green eyes, I'd say.'

The girl's wistfulness was beginning to grate. 'Hazel actually. He's five foot ten but acts six two and his feet smell. Anything else?'

'Did you not like the flowers, then?' Martha was perplexed.

'They're gorgeous.'

'Only he especially said plenty of gerberas because they have a happy face like you do.'

She blinked back tears. 'I'm sorry, Martha, really I am. I don't mean to take anything out on you. It's just that I'm all over the place at the moment.'

'Fiona thinks you're pregnant.'

That jolted her. She took a quick look around. The others were pretending not to have heard this latest remark but were obviously on tenterhooks awaiting her response.

'I am not pregnant,' she said, very loudly.

Some of the customers tittered.

'So why have you given me yellow peppers instead of egg and all in a jumbo sausage roll?'

'It's good for you.' The gooey mess certainly didn't look too healthy.

Mario arrived to take over. 'Maybe you want to eat this?' he asked, holding up the concoction.

'I'm not pregnant,' she reiterated.

'Of course not,' he soothed.

Jack stayed at home that morning because it meant being away from Clara. She was a great girl and a wonderful worker but he didn't want to encourage her notions any more than was absolutely necessary. It smacked of a rear-guard action and his brain told him he should have dealt with it long before this. They had slipped into it so easily he was enmeshed before he realised how careless he'd been. A few drinks too many after work with a sympa-thetic ear, smelling Clara's delicious perfume, hearing her flattery and on into bed. She knew he was feeling pummelled and massaged him in all the right places. Clara obviously found him attractive and that had come as a surprise when he was sure he was a troll to womankind. He tried to pinpoint times when he'd noticed interest in their working day but couldn't locate any. She had been careful not to cross the lines of his marriage and their jobs. It had never occurred to him to do so until then, although he saw that she was an attractive, interesting woman. He was married, she was his PA: that was all there was to it.

It was simplistic to suggest that Clara made all of the running. He had to face up to responsibility for the situ-ation too. In mitigation he would cite his screwed-up emotions and desperate craving for physical comfort. He should have known better, however, and left well alone. An office affair was always a disaster, but what was done was done and it was now time for damage limitation, something he was well used to in his job. This was another symptom that was getting him down lately. It used to be that people initiated a campaign through him to woo the public. Now he was more likely to be brought in as a troubleshooter. He parried bad press as a retaliatory measure when a bad photograph or a journalistic disembowelling occurred. It was all response these days, so little was voluntary any more.

With Jodie, his most needy client, safe in her bed, the phone rang less and he could skive off a little. He sat in the garden tapping at his laptop and snoozing intermittently. He would have loved a beer but his watch advised against it. Jodie would have said, 'It's six o'clock somewhere, darling,' while snapping the cap off a Becks. He smiled to think of her airy and frivolous life and silently congratulated her for having such a good time while doing very little harm in the world.

He heard, 'Oi, you,' and looked up to see Famke standing on the roof of her studio wearing little more than a sheath. 'Wanna come over for a coffee?'

He could see her slim frame silhouetted against the sky and felt a stirring in his pants. God, he was rampant since his wife dumped him. Why couldn't he have been this aroused and attentive to her when she was here? He plopped the notebook on his groin, regardless of radiation and cancer scares. It was warm through the fabric and he didn't like the sensation so he put it on the wrought-iron table by his side.

'I'm a bit swamped,' he told the artist.

'You could throw an eye over my new work,' she suggested.

If that wasn't a blatant invitation to play he didn't know his ass from his elbow. Damn it, he thought, here I am hesitating, no less. What is wrong with me? I'm as good as single under this present circumstance and I'll regret this till the day I die, if that's the day I pass away wondering what it would have been like to shag Famke K. I am a man and therefore a dog, roll with it.

'OK, but don't let me stay too long. I have loads on.'

'Give yourself a break,' she laughed. 'It won't take forever.'

Later, as they lay on her bed, she said, 'See? That wasn't so bad, was it?'

Oh no, it certainly wasn't bad. At all.

'I liked your paintings,' he said, by the by.

'Just buy one when they're released into the community,' she laughed.

She was not pregnant, of that she was certain. It was the one thing Lucy was totally sure of then. She could have hocked her new house on it without the worry of losing it but for the other fact, which was that her husband had absconded with the funds for said notional house. But what a perfect scenario that would be, like a plot from a penny novel: husband abandons pregnant wife to penury and homelessness. The only time she had even been late, Pete had taken her to the pharmacy for a pregnancy testing kit so fast her neck had had mild whiplash for a week afterwards. When she had remarked on his unseemly haste he had broken into a speech about how he wanted her all to himself, that he was selfish and didn't want to share her even with a little person they might make between them. Actually she hadn't been thinking of children at that point and now she supposed wouldn't have to. Just as well, she thought, because that Nissan isn't big enough for even the smallest of crèches.

Her marriage was over. There was another fact for this list. It was mounting by the day, as were the attendant complications. She was not going to be able to keep her situation secret for much longer. It was time to make some decisions.

Like any life change, it was crucial to plan ahead and not to rush into anything. When starting a diet it was best to wait till after a weekend. Ditto for a new exercise regime. She would use the private view for the exhibition tonight as a metaphorical weekend. Tomorrow would be the day to tell relevant people about the change in her life circumstance. She should probably start with her mother but wondered if that would mean moving in with her. In a weird way, she was managing OK in the car, as long as her gym membership held out, which didn't leave her long. Perhaps the thing to do would be to borrow money from her mum, without telling her why, and use it to pay a deposit on a small flat somewhere. Though it was probably more realistic to think in terms of renting a room in someone's house initially. Whatever, she needed to check the evening paper. She could stave off admitting her shameful predicament till later, when she had figured out what the hell to tell everyone.

Her cheeks burned and her breath caught in little gasps in her throat. It was a positive thing to decide on a course of action she told herself, but it hurt. Her heart was broken. Try as she might, she found it impossible to be a detached onlooker gazing at this interesting problem from a sideline and then acting on it. She was involved to the core. And she dreaded facing her love for Pete and having to acknowledge it and its hopelessness or smash it into oblivion. Even if things were to take an extraordinary turn and he came back to her, she could never forgive him. She shook herself to even allow the idea of his return. That was finished now, those days were gone.

She sifted through the details of the chaos. She racked her brain trying to think if anyone had spotted a flaw in Pete, anything suspicious that would have suggested she steer clear of him, but there was nothing. Had there even been an innocuous bad habit that grated and might grow over decades into the stuff of divorce? Again with the popular novel scenario. It wasn't even as if he had been too perfect. He was, well, he was just Pete. And even if anyone had spoken up, she had been head over heels and they would not have been thanked for the warning.

No one would have dared venture a contentious opinion.

She began to detest thinking about him. He was taking up the bulk of her time and she now had too much of it to be taken up in this way. She had shed a lot to be exclusively with him, she realised, though it had hardly seemed so as it was happening. She had simply devoted herself to life with her husband, the person she would spend the rest of her time with. And he had turned out to be one of life's great con artists. Now it almost killed her to think of him breathing, let alone in the luxury he could afford from the sale money of her apartment. She had worked so hard for that little place and she had loved it. But in the grander scheme of things she had been glad to offer it as her half of the kitty for their new life together. What a mug.

He had arrived like an unexpected gift. He wandered into the gallery with a friend late one afternoon when she was filling for Evie. They had struck up a conversation about some sculpture on show and ended up going for a drink. His friend left, they continued to laugh, bond, flirt and he stayed the night at her place. It just developed organically from there in an unassuming and predictable way. But now she wondered had they been speaking different languages all that time? She scoured her memory for the tiny details of early betrayal but found none. They were an ordinary couple. Their pipes leaked on cue, bulbs and fuses blew when it was inconvenient and they probably spent beyond their collective means, but who in London didn't?

Lucy was becoming more involved in the gallery and its affairs and was only too glad to let Pete take charge of the mundanities of everyday home accounting. She kept a small personal bank account but they had a mutual one for bills and general spending. They operated separate credit cards because there was no romance in buying a treat for a spouse only to have them pay half in the long run and to know how much it cost at the end of the month. They needed more space and after a long trawl south of the river found a house in need of major repairs which would be their dream home after years of muck and drudgery. Pete handled the sale of her apartment and with it her independence finally vanished. She signed everything he put in front of her without question, and mostly without reading it. They packed their superfluous regalia into boxes for storage and she loaded her car with her necessities and he with his, each better able to guess for themselves what they would need for the interim between sale and acquisition.

On the day of the move, he left early for work, kissed her and arranged to meet later at the small hotel they would stay in for the two weeks in the difference between contracts. It would be an adventure crossed with a strange city holiday, as someone else made the bed and cleaned their room while they talked of paint schemes and cushions.

She really had no idea that anything was wrong until she got to the hotel that evening. There was no record of a booking. She rang Pete's mobile but it rang out again and again. There had to be a rational explanation and he would give it as soon as he could. She waited in the claustrophobic bar until it was clear that he was not coming, then spent the night telephoning the police and hospitals checking for him. Clearly something awful had befallen her husband.

Against all odds she fell into an exhausted sleep on a sofa and awoke to the fresh and horrible fear that he was dead. There could be no other reason for this behaviour. The police were polite and understanding but pointed out that he hadn't been gone long enough for them to take the case on, and no body had turned up matching his description. They looked at her with pity and one even went so far as to explain that people go missing all the time and sometimes they want to stay that way. He seemed to move away from the counter as he said this and in her perception the distance between them took on a surreal bend, and the air closed in as time stopped. But something in what he said triggered a notion so awful it felt accurate.

She struggled to press the numbers of his workplace. The receptionist was offhand but helpful while Lucy lied about who she was. Pete had left his job a fortnight earlier and they had no contact details other than the old address and mobile number. Her eardrums shattered in agony at the news, her limbs turned to jelly. Her brain was a miasma of nonsense and noise until she forced herself to clear it and take stock. Pete had left her alone and isolated. She was weak to think of it, shocked and utterly embarrassed, and she knew she would tell no one else what was happening. It was a real situation but she couldn't bring herself to admit that to anyone else, to dignify it with the breath of fact, to admit her stupidity and frailty. Her short-sightedness was a disgrace to women everywhere. She felt guilty.

She found herself back behind the wheel of her car, without hope for the future or a short-term plan. In spite of all, she was a practical woman. From nowhere she remembered a cul-de-sac she had driven into by accident once and went there, as much to think in solitude as a place to hide while she tried to make sense of what could not be made sense of. Had she been too proud before her fall, too pleased with her lot? Fortune was a predator cruelly deciding who should have the good and who the bad. She had brought herself to attention through her unthinking hubris, and now had to deal with the fallout.

It was time to harden against the vagaries of the world. Experience was her guide. She would never trust anyone else again. Humans were too weak to be tested in such a way. They couldn't help themselves for faults and it was unfair to expect too much. But even so, now as her second week of living rough came to an end, it was time to come clean with a select few. Tomorrow would be the start of a new Lucy. She was not looking forward to it.

TEN

Building was in the Richards' blood. Bill's grandfather had been a labourer all his life and was followed into the trade by his son and then by his son in turn. They were all called William. Bill bucked the family trend in two ways: he set up his own business, and named his sons Stephen and Archie. Like all of the Richards men, though, Bill loved to get his hands dirty. He could never give in to the idea that he was management now and not expected to help lay a pipe or mix cement. The Richards were all-rounders and this stood to Bill, investing him with an understanding of all aspects of the trade, but his particular pleasure was joinery. He phoned his site manager Sean Harris and asked if he could be put on manual labour for the day, if the other lads wouldn't mind. He needed to get back to what he loved about his work. He needed the very basics.

It was building that had brought Helen into his life. He had spent years labouring with the Irish on the sites of London. 'Paddy was never afraid of a hard day's work,' they would tell him and he knew it to be true. They were lonely individuals for the most part, driven out of the Old Country by economic necessity. Each week saw an envelope go home to family. Each night saw the tired wrecks nod off on the Tube back to Willesden and Kilburn, faces grey with dust and nails chipped and ingrained with dirt. Then it was a quick shower and a bite to eat and off to the pub to hear news of the old sod or just for a bit of company to stave off their solitude. They built this town and it killed many of them. When it came time to go home after years of hard labour it was impossible for most. They didn't fit into the new order back home and were practically institutionalised, in a Britain that had nowhere for them to go to once their work was done. Helen came looking for one such man, her uncle Felim.

Felim was born in the nineteen thirties, the second of a family of seven. This was just as the Second World War began for the rest of Europe and eventually America and Japan, but Ireland entered into a more whimsical state called The Emergency, a neutral state on the edge of the chaos. His father was a butcher of modest means and there was no money to put Felim through school or into an apprenticeship. When he hit his teenage years, it was decided to send him to an aunt in Hammersmith who put him up till he found his feet, which was a job and digs in North London. The city was being rebuilt after the bombing and work was plentiful. He got a mate who could write to send a weekly letter home with some money for his mother. He returned for a week every year in a new suit, full of extraordinary tales of the streets of London.

But over the decades his visits became less regular and more likely for funerals or a wedding than for his annual holiday. He seemed the worse for wear and there were whispers of a problem with drink. All contact ceased in the seventies after the deaths of both his parents. There was nothing to tie him to home any more; the surviving members of the family had scattered, some of them too young to remember Felim when they were growing up. He dropped off the radar. Helen had heard stories of Felim from her mother, mostly reports of his derring-do as a young man when he was a force within the family. He gained a mythical proportion in her childhood thoughts and that, coupled with her mother's tears while pining for a flesh and blood relative carelessly lost, led to her decision to find him. Her search led her to Bill Richards' door.

The story was a familiar one to Bill. He had met these men, worked with them. He helped out part-time in a hostel that looked after these casualties of society. When their working life was over they found themselves without pension or state benefits and often without a home, the uttermost irony as they had helped build so many. They belonged nowhere, now, lost in a hinterland between the countries they had served and abandoned by an economy that had no further need of them. Together, Bill and Helen searched the company records for a Felim O'Neill but they could not find him. They went further and contacted the various organisations that looked after the dispossessed Irish. Finally, on a cold March day, they stood before a small, unadorned plot in a Harlesden cemetery and paid their respects to Helen's uncle. He had died the year before. They enquired after him at his last lodging, a hostel in Cricklewood for elderly Irish gentlemen. He had been a quiet man who loved the movies and watching soap operas on the television. He had lived a hard life of drinking and gambling, but had quit all that during his last years. His name was down for a trip to Dublin with some of the other residents that March to celebrate St Patrick's Day, but he hadn't made it. He would be missed, they were told. 'He didn't say much, but when he did it was worth listening to.'

And there was a last surprise. The staff had kept his suitcase. 'There won't be much inside,' they warned. 'He was buried in his good suit and shoes.' It was a battered brown leather affair. Inside was a white shirt, a sober tie, a bundle of letters from his mother and an old-fashioned shaving brush and bowl. It also contained a doll, still wrapped and ready to be given to a child on a birthday or at Christmas. They would never know for whom it was intended.

Helen went home to tell the family of Felim's death and her own romance and permanent move to London. Like her uncle before her she chose exile. She quickly found a job as a computer programmer with a financial house although Bill had offered her a place with his company. They were sure of one another and delighted.

Bill looked out at the garden and into the tree at its foot. He had built his boys a house in the branches and it was here that his wife had set up home. She was safe there for now, so he could go to work. And if the rope ladder was down when he returned that evening, it would mean she was open to company. He crossed his fingers in hope and gathered his work clothes. This might yet be one of the better days.

It only took a brief look and a lip curl and he was Ulrika's. They repaired to a private bathroom used by the staff and started to tear at each other's clothing. She pulled at the boy's hardened cock and whispered something about not having a condom. He dropped to his knees and saw to her. Ulrika couldn't believe how alive she felt. Every nerve ending and cell in her body tingled with a vibrancy she had all but forgotten in the months of worrying about her weight. As she bucked onto the student, grunting and whispering urgent instructions, she fought the urge to giggle.

She had been apathetic for so long it was pleasure enough to have put on her stockings that morning. Her own hands had caressed her cool flesh and she had let her curious fingers stray to her bush but only enough to leave her wanting more. She had eschewed panties and, looking at the boy's head working between her legs, she was glad she had. She enjoyed the vision of his dark hair bob by the creamy whiteness of her leg and the laced tops of her hold-ups. She didn't even bid him goodbye as she pulled down her skirt and walked away along the corridor. She simply relished the stickiness on her thighs, the extra moisture a triumph for her new self. By then she couldn't even remember what he looked like, really. Her nipples chafed ecstatically against her bra and her cheeks felt coloured by her exertions. She was sexy and confident, and strung out to her eyeballs.

The office was bright and open-plan. The company had toyed with hot-desking for a few months but the result was mayhem and an all-out war between the Data department and Issues. Now, desks were set in satellite around a central oasis of plants and a water feature. The better ones were by the south-facing window and it was there that Colin was billeted. He was head of his section and could do the work of five in half the time it took the rest of that five to accomplish it. Consequently he had plenty of time for breaks and mischief. He twizzled a spoon in his coffee as he reviewed the office. 'I think I need to take up a hobby,' he said.

'Besides screwing and shopping?' Stella asked, seeking clarification.

'Yes. Botox, maybe. Or kick-boxing.' He threw the spoon from where he stood by the door of the tearoom into the sink.

'Shot,' Stella acknowledged.

'I'm so bored.'

'You're at work, you're meant to be bored.'

'Mmm.'

They both turned to curl their noses up at a brown-clad man called Eddie who was whiffing up the air with a pot noodle.

'Eeyuw,' Colin gasped. 'What is in that? Scrote?'

'You'd love it if there was,' Eddie observed.

He was feisty for such a no-hoper, Colin thought, so he let him be.

'This world is closing in on me, stifling the very life out of me,' he continued. He was going for a histrionic finish but that was a ways off yet.

'You really are worried about this date,' Stella observed.

'I am not!' Colin was perched above indignant now, a place he adored.

'Yes, you are. I haven't seen you this nervous in a long time.'

Stella was getting too good at seeing under his skin. He would have to do something about that. 'Don't be ridiculous.'

'What are you so afraid of?' There, she was at it again, putting her pointy finger on the nub of things.

'I am anything but afraid,' he gushed.

'Are so,' Stella chanted.

'Who's an arsehole?' Eddie wanted to know.

'No one,' came the chorus of two.

Eddie slurped on his noodles, then held them in his mouth as he breathed air quickly in and out to cool them before mastication and a swallow.

'Although it is a pleasure to see you enjoy your food,' Colin said, 'it would be nice not to have to watch its *entire* journey *and* listen to the epic soundtrack.'

'Your problem is that you cannot relax and trust someone,' Eddie told him. 'Just let go once in a while. Not everyone is out to harm you.'

If he had looked behind after his exit he could have conducted a major inspection of both Stella's and Colin's dental work.

'When did he catch the savant genes?'

'He likes you. He's yours forever since you helped him out of the mess with head office over his section's short-fall in February.'

'I only did that to annoy the suits. Besides, I couldn't believe the stink they made about it. All we do here is push notional numbers around on spreadsheets. It's not real. Show me the money is what I say. Show me the fucking money and less of the faffing.'

Stella laughed. 'You're not such a bad sort, really.'

'Keep that under your Philip Treacy hat,' he warned. 'It's not something I want getting out.'

Lucy was tired to the bone. This would be one long day. Danny Brock was in the middle of it now, which was less than ideal. She looked at his face, which was too round and had all of his features too close together in the middle. She couldn't fathom why the others liked him so much. He was so sharp, so quick on the attack. She shirked any contact with him. He was solicitous today, which irked her even more than usual. Obviously the rumour of the pregnancy was totally common knowledge now. She ground her teeth and got on with the job. She wanted to appear as normal as possible to scotch the crazy notion that she was expecting a child. She would remain even-tempered and tackle the smelliest job with gusto. If she could have she would have mainlined red wine and espresso just to prove they had no power to make her ill. As it was, she had drunk so much coffee her head hurt with a caffeine overload and all she wanted to do was lie on a bed and sleep it off.

Her mother phoned several times to witter about the tiniest problems imaginable. Lucy testily pointed out there was nothing she could do about any of these as she was at her other work and perhaps it was time to enlist the help of whichever young male friend was posing as today's pin-up. After declaring that Lucy hadn't always been so unreasonable, Evie said, 'And there's something blue in your voice that I am determined to unearth.' Superb, now they were all on her case, and not one was of any practical use to her.

'Darling, you're not pregnant, by any chance, are you?' her mother asked.

Lucy ground her teeth hard, snarled in the negative and hung up. She sat with her head between her legs for a moment to regain some equilibrium. She was letting the day run away from her and as it was the only little bit of power she had left she decided to chase back control. She popped two aspirin, took a number of calming breaths and re-entered the fray.

The lunch rush was a bad-tempered affair, the population tired of the endless sunshine and cantankerous with heat. But Lucy wore a glued-on smile and patiently attended to all, even talking a few people back into good humour, she liked to think. She drank two litres of water throughout and felt the better for the hydration. She munched defiantly on a cheese and onion baguette, a combination she felt no pregnant woman would touch. Especially with the amount of onion she had heaped onto it. She whistled a happy tune while clearing up. She refused to bow under pressure, was the declaration, and she hoped everyone was paying attention. She took tea with Greta though she remembered little of their chit-chat afterwards. The important thing was to be seen to be hyper normal. Then she left the premises and walked into a local park where she found a secluded bench and sat to cry her eyes out. The lingering taste of chopped onion taunted her.

She needed a change, but a better one than the last that had visited her. At least to be pregnant would have been something to work on, a focus for life. She had nothing. And in the grand scheme of things she was now also nothing. The headache returned. She longed to sleep, exhausted by the interminable misery of the now and a grim future stretching ahead. It looked too long from here and, frankly, not quite worth it in the end. She didn't care about the journey or the destination. She was so lonely it hurt.

She got to her feet and began to walk to the gallery but her limbs were rubbery and she sat on the next seat along, crying again but gently, noiselessly this time. She craved the comfort of an embrace, the physical circle of arms about her and when it came she looked up to find Danny Brock hushing and soothing her.

She laid her head on his shoulder and murmured, 'Who'd have thought it?' Life had one weird sense of humour but somehow it didn't surprise her any more.

ELEVEN

Colin's famous timing was off. He was early for his rendezvous which was so unacceptable he hooked up with a Homo erectus he hated in order to appear in company when his putative date arrived. The other creature, Max, worked in advertising and thought he was God's gift to mankind. Anyone could have told him he'd overdone the dyed hair and should lose a few pounds, but Colin was delighted to be able to rub his nose in the fact that he was meeting someone and merely passing time with Max, if one could believe that was actually his name. Rumour had it he was born plain old brown-haired David Wall on the Isle of Wight and not the perma-tanned, white-blond Maximillian Schrieder he liked to pass himself off as.

Colin and Tony settled busily at a low table by the window in full view of the self-styled advertising guru. Colin looked back at his erstwhile chat mate and declared him 'an alabastard if ever there was one' as he waved back.

'Is he one of your lovers?' Tony asked.

'Funnily enough, no. He's too shallow even for me.'

'You put yourself down a lot.'

Colin sipped a spritzer. 'When it suits me,' he admitted.

Tony let his eyes wander over his companion. Colin was tall and thin, though not scrawny, and expensively clad and shod. Tony had changed out of his overalls but he felt grubby after his day's work in the garden centre and conscious of the mud under his nails which only a good soak would remove. He tucked himself into the floppy armchair as far as he could go to disguise or hide his vulnerabilities. 'You dress beautifully,' he said.

Colin preened visibly at the compliment, knowing it to be true. 'Thanks. I don't have anyone else to spend the money on and it has to be said I do enjoy spoiling myself. I wasn't always rolling in it, of course. I've seen the poorer day too. I prefer having money, if only for financial reasons, as they say. God, this wine is shite. I'm switching to pints. Being a fairy is so fraught with difficult decisions.' He beckoned a lounge boy and ordered, giving the youngster the benefit of a cheesy leer. 'That's sorted the wee lad out,' he declared. He returned to his subject. 'Famke is a godsend too. She owns the house so she charges a very minimal rent just to cover expenses and to make it so that someone is boss.'

'How did you meet?'

'Through a mutual fag. We got on immediately. Me and Famke, that is. So when I dumped the guy so did she and we've been together ever since. Better than any marriage, really.'

It was the elephant in the room so Tony capitulated.

'OK, what do you want to know?'

'Well, you obviously don't live together . . .'

'No. How do you know that?'

'Elementary, my dear. If you did, you couldn't stay out the night without being in shitloads of trouble. Easy-peasy so far. What's she like?'

'Fun, pretty . . . boyish, I guess.' It was clear that Tony had been thinking a lot about this.

'And?'

'This is really difficult for me to discuss.'

'Try,' Colin said.

'I'm an English Catholic so I'm supposed to be a bit repressed, I guess, when it comes to sex. And I find it hard to talk about it.'

Colin looked sympathetic. 'English Catholics are the worst,' he confirmed.

'I suppose what I'm trying to come to terms with is that I don't think I'm gay but, equally, I think it's clear that I'm not altogether straight either.'

'Oh God,' Colin groaned. 'Not another I-want-it-all bisexual. Really! You know I actually prefer the straights, they're much more honest about what they want from a man. Lord knows I've had plenty of them, before and after marriage, sexual tourists.'

'I'm not trying to mess you about. I would hate to do that.' His face was lined with an endearingly gauche sincerity.

Colin put his hand on Tony's arm, looked into his eyes and said, 'I know.'

'I'm sort of floating at the minute. Can you put up with that?'

Colin finished his drink. 'Back to mine, so.' He waggled some fingers at Max. 'Heard he had a tiny dick, actually.'

Tony smiled. 'Not something you have to worry about.'

'No.'

As Danny walked Lucy north to the gallery, his shoulder steamed as her tears vaporised into the London sky. She was grateful for his intervention, despite misgivings about him on a daily level, but had stalled short of telling him the whole truth. She settled for trouble in the marriage exacerbated by the house move. This was a version of the truth. If he suspected a withholding of information he didn't mention it.

He finally asked the question she dreaded and it had nothing to do with Pete. 'Why are you always so nasty to me?' he wanted to know.

'I'm sorry about that, Danny. I find you a bit sharp, a bit too arch.'

'You bring that out in me, I'm afraid.'

'Eh?'

'I don't mean to make it sound like it's your fault,' he qualified. 'It's mine. I react badly to women I find . . . attractive.' There, he'd said it and it was an enormous weight off his damp shoulder.

Lucy halted, mouth wide. 'Now that,' she admitted, 'is the last thing I expected to hear from you.'

She was beginning to think she knew nothing at all about people.

'Obviously it's not a problem with the rest of the staff, particularly Mario and Ivan,' he joked. 'Although as an ex public-school boy there might have been moments, I suppose.' He gave a wry shrug which she found endearing. She had been so wrong about this man. She stole a side-ways look. He wasn't even nearly as horrid in appearance as she'd let herself believe. He was of medium height and solidly put together, with mid-length well-cut hair and a strong profile. He also had a remarkably sensual mouth, which had previously made her feel very uncomfortable. Now it issued forth a level of friendly comfort. This man could be a pal. She needed one of those.

'Come in and tell me what you think of the exhibition,' she said. 'It would be good to see it through fresh eyes. And don't worry if you hate it. That's valid too.'

'You'd have made a good American,' he observed.

'Just gearing up for the art-speak later,' she admitted.

Tony ran a hand down his lover's silky back. Colin turned to him and said, 'You don't have much to worry about in the size department either.' Tony laughed and thanked him for the return compliment. Then he kissed him and began to enjoy himself all over again. Inside, Colin was screaming, 'Don't marry her, don't marry her, be with me,' while outwardly he murmured, 'You'll miss this in a few weeks' time.'

'Or maybe not.'

Something snapped inside. Colin sprang from the bed, stung, but trying not to show it. 'You thirsty?'

Tony was bemused. 'Sure, but there's no rush, come back to bed.'

'No point in getting too used to something that can't last,' Colin said and exited for the kitchen.

Tony wasn't sure what he'd said wrong but knew that he had. Dealing with a man was no easier than dealing with a woman, he recognised. He waited what seemed an eternity, realised he'd been forsaken, swung his legs over the side and wondered what to do next. He didn't want to leave, that much was clear. He couldn't casually shrug into a robe and saunter around as if he was at home or at ease because he was not and because Colin had left in the only robe available. Nor did he want to get dressed. He settled for a T-shirt and jeans, but no socks or underpants, and went to the kitchen also. Colin was ensconced at the table and pretended not to notice that he had not returned as promised with water or any other thirst quencher. He was tucking into a red wine. He indicated the bottle and said, 'Help yourself, as with everything else.'

'I think you may have misunderstood me back there,' Tony began.

'Oh, don't I know it,' Colin sniffed.

Tony held up a hand to quieten him. 'I meant that I don't want to have to miss all of this. It's seems clear to me that I can't get married. After that, it's all a blur and a bit frightening, if you must know. I'm sorry if that's not good enough for you, but it's all I have at the moment. Please don't be mean to me.'

'It just proves that I like you,' Colin said. 'A lot.' He poured a second glass of wine and tempted Tony to his side of the table. He kissed him gently. 'But I'll try to be nice.'

'That'll do fine for now,' Tony agreed. 'Can I ask you something?'

'Do your worst.'

'When you left the room just then, was that a flounce?'

'*Mais oui, mon cher.* If I missed an opportunity like that I'd have my union card taken away from me.'

Danny was having trouble with finding the correct words, but thought 'colourful' and 'too much' said most of what he needed to communicate. 'Not my cup of tea,' he apologised.

'Not mine either,' Lucy admitted.

He slipped easily into helping set out the glasses and wine on the serving table while Evie worried about the last-minute details, checking price lists and the guest book were all in order. When he said it was time to go, Lucy felt a panic and held on to the front door to stop shaking. She wanted protection from the evening ahead, from her life in general. Why was this not getting any easier? She was going to have to toughen up considerably more than she had done to date, but the hopelessness of her plight was leaving her demoralised. She put a course of vitamins on her mental list of things to do.

As Danny faded from view, her mother said, 'Nice boy.' Yes, he is nice, Lucy thought with something approaching relief. One less feud to pursue, one less distraction in a way.

Her mother joined her at the door and put an arm around her shoulder. 'Ready for the hordes?' she asked.

'Not really,' her daughter said, wearily.

'We'll get through it. And tomorrow you can tell me what it is that's making you so blue.'

Lucy's stiff face tried to crack a smile; Evie always thought in colours.

The first of the revellers appeared around a corner and stumbled along the cobbles to the White Rooms. They were well oiled after a late and splendid lunch. Lucy looked at their florid complexions and swore inwardly. Three drunken artists from the get-go were hardly helpful. She shook herself mentally, trying not to be negative. She knew it was sapping her energy. She needed to be a lot more positive. The proper way to deal with the outcome of this lunch was to realise that the triumvirate felt particularly confident so she would not have to spend the first hour bolstering their egos while they whined about attendance and consumerism destroying their muse. This outlook made her feel better already. There now, not so difficult. Her mum smiled over and for a moment Lucy thought she could manage.

Her mood lasted a surprisingly generous length of time. She doled out the grog and sold a few of the less alarming pieces. It was altogether a jollier gathering than she had expected. The sun was less of a drain by now and everyone was content to enjoy its fading rays over some free booze.

It was inevitable that the whiff of cynicism would intrude. A loud gathering wheeled into their orbit. These were the art gurus, mostly the self-appointed arbiters of London taste. Any critics that were to come had been and gone and kindly told Evie that this was not for their paper and they would pass on mentioning it, while pointing out that it needed no help to sell. Everyone was placated and had their dignity intact. This latest cabal would spend the evening looking over companions' shoulders to clock who 'if anyone' was here and torturing the young art students they had in tow. The latter were prepared to listen and nod as long as they too could freeload and gather ammunition for mockery later. Although Lucy might agree with their estimation of the exhibition she was utterly loyal to the family business and damned if they were going to ruin a lovely evening. It was no accident that they had left this soiree until last where they could drink Evie dry and undermine her with faint praise and talk of old comradeship. Some were such clichés as to be totally ridiculous. Lucy tuned in to hear a suspiciously well-preserved specimen get into a complete tither about the red wine.

'It's not so much perspiring as sweating, my dear Evie,' she declared, waving a charm bracelet like a rattlesnake before a strike.

'And that is precisely why I have a tasty little Chablis chilling especially for you. It's just the thing to take the thirst off such a warm evening.'

'Thank goodness,' the woman declared, clutching a bosom that Lucy reckoned was precociously new. 'For a moment there I thought I was going to have to drink the house white.'

Her mother tutted and reassured. 'No, no, we would never let that happen.' She caught Lucy's eye and winked.

Finn Beaker sawed away on a viola while Jez Anderton read some doggerel. Lucy knew nothing about poetry apart from what had been rammed down her throat at school. It seemed pretty crazy to her but she really couldn't tell the good from the bad from the downright trite in this field. It hardly mattered tonight as no one paid them a blind bit of notice. Rita, the painter, was scouring the exhibits for red sale stickers and dashing back to report in a frenzy of excitement and more wine.

Lucy noticed a group of well-heeled businessmen and women huddled by the door gossiping and laughing. There seemed to be at least three languages involved, including a fabulously guttural Russian. They were clearly having a wonderful time. Her heart sank a little to think of returning to the car and the impossibility of laughter there. She put the tray down and drank a quick white, then grabbed a bottle and mingled. People knew where to go if they needed refills and she could kid herself that she was more useful plugging the exhibition and perhaps selling what was destined to be left on the walls otherwise. One of the most handsome of the men broke away from the group as she pretended to check for empty glasses.

'What do you make of it?' he asked, spanning the exhibition with attractive, dark eyes.

Something about him made her want to tell the truth but as that might preclude commerce she fudged and said, 'It's very accessible. A lot of art these days is frighteningly dense and it scares the public, I think. There's really no need for that.' She congratulated herself that she hadn't told a lie yet.

He looked thoughtful. 'My wife, well, ex-wife, bought a lot, and this reminds me of it, I'm sorry to say. I mean, to be honest with you, that one there is psychotic.' He gestured to a work, which Lucy knew was still wet and gathering flies by the new time.

She laughed lightly at the fair cop. 'I can't disagree about that particular one.'

He had a pleasant smile and was immaculately dressed in a linen shirt and trousers. The crumpled fabric suited his air of carelessness. He also smelled good. For a moment she wondered what it was that had ruined his marriage. Was it down to him? Or was his partner to blame? Perhaps they had both seen other ways of living and opted for that. Marriage was not the guarantee of happiness Lucy had once thought. Had she loaded her own with too much as a result? Was that a selfish thing to do?

'Was your wife a customer here?'

'I believe so. Perhaps you'd like to see some of the pieces in question and take them away for resale. I don't know much about all this and I'd do anything to get rid of the stuff.'

'We could arrange a consultation if you like,' Lucy said. She felt stiff in her manners and wished she could loosen up but casual was the last thing she could hope to pull off then. Besides, this was work, in spite of how attractive she found this man.

'No time like the present,' he declared. 'How about tonight?'

She must have shown her surprise because he added quickly, 'I am so sorry. That was entirely presumptuous of me. How dare I think that you might just drop everything to do that. I have lost my manners. Forgive me. I'm not used to getting divorced and all that goes with it so I'm regularly out of character these days.'

'You also haven't told me your name,' she pointed out.

'Ah.' He was pink with embarrassment. He held out a hand. 'Jack Smith.'

'Lucy.' She shook the hand, pausing ever so impercep- tibly. 'White.' She nearly bit her tongue off invoking her old surname. 'I'm Evie's daughter. She owns the gallery.'

She saw his forehead crinkle as an unspoken thought worked through his mind. He looked over at her mother who was laughing with an old friend. 'I see the resem- blance.' He quickly returned to her. 'I mean that in a good way. I know how touchy people can get about compar- isons. I hate to think I'm turning into my dad though I know I am in many ways, barring the being dead bit.'

She liked his self-mockery and easy way. 'You work in the media, don't you?'

He grimaced. 'It's that obvious?'

She nodded and said, ''Fraid so, sorry,' as a smile dallied on her face.

'Yes, I'm a glorified spin doctor. Public relations, publicity, I do it all. Bend the truth and make it palatable, in bite-sized pieces of inanity.'

'That good?' she teased.

'You better believe it.'

Lucy refilled their glasses and they raised them in a silent toast. So much for my businesslike reticence, she thought. I'm flirting with this guy. Jack Smith's voice was musical and soothing, trustworthy-sounding, but given his profession she couldn't help but wonder if it was an affectation. She hoped not.

'So what about looking over the Smith Collection?'

'How would tomorrow evening be? I work till late afternoon so anytime after that is good.'

'Great. Let's say six thirty for a glass of wine and a tour of the house. I'm at six Farewell Square in Vauxhall. Do you know it?'

Lucy was struck dumb. He could have no idea how well she knew it, including his back wall and gate. Her cheeks burned and she thanked the fair weather for offering the excuse of excess sun. She couldn't concentrate on an answer. How could the world be this small? It was intolerable. Just as she thought she was getting to grips with her new life the sands shifted again and she was left flailing for stability or even just a shred of what composure she once had. It was, after all, much too late for dignity.

'If that doesn't suit, we could reschedule,' Jack was saying, a frown spread across his face.

'No, no, that's fine,' she heard her voice say. 'Perfect, in fact. See you then.' She walked away, afraid she might laugh in his face. Perfect was the word for this turn of events. Fate was a punk and deserved a good kicking. She reached for a fresh bottle of white and began another round of the floor.

TWELVE

They were such an ordinary family that she and Bill often laughed to think of them as extraordinary. Normal, run-of-the-mill and, most poignantly, happy were all ways of describing them. They were innocuous, really, just what you'd expect of a family. There was nothing to make them stand out from a million other family units. They were commonplace, until the boys died. Then they became the other extraordinary, though not unique, she was to learn.

It was an ordinary day. March was complaining, with loud wind and rain howling around the house. The children indulged in the usual morning bicker at the breakfast table. She could still smell orange shampoo on Archie's curls from their bath the night before. Stephen thought they probably tasted of orange too as they had guzzled back some juice and spilled as much again on their pyjamas.

'We are orange inside and outside now. If you ate us we would be yummy, Mummy,' he trilled, delighted with his rhyme.

Archie shot him a look and muttered, 'Idiot.' His entire

vocabulary seemed to be made up of insults. He used most of them on his brother but could lash out a selection at others when it suited. To be fair, he was careful to praise his parents, who knew he thought they were slightly retarded, but he sometimes slipped and let his guard fall. Only the day before he had called Helen a 'silly cow'. The trouble with Archie was that he was really funny when he let loose and it was hard not to laugh, and therefore well nigh impossible to check him or stay cross with him for long. He could charm the birds down from the trees.

Stephen was a big soft boy, devoted to his mother. She could do no wrong, whatsoever, and if Helen ever had a bad day all she needed to do was look into his adoring eyes to feel the most wanted person in the world. He was serious and sincere and they sometimes called him the Vicar when he was out of earshot.

Archie, for all his villainy, adored his brother. He had absorbed all of Stephen's knowledge easily, living in the slipstream of his sibling's experience, then forging on alone when it was required. He often asked for his things to be 'like Stephen' and so, for all his machismo, it was obvious who his role model was. They passed the baton of bad behaviour between them, then united defences when needed, and it was a brave adult who tried to breach that battlement. They were tiny and formidable Desperate Dans.

Bill dispensed kisses and admonitions to the boys to be good for the day, pecked his wife's cheek and went to work. Helen looked at her watch and started the long journey of marshalling the children back to their room to dress and the longer trail of getting out of the door, into the car and perhaps making the kindergarten school on time. Archie wanted to walk everywhere now that he was three and BIG. After his umpteenth stop on the stairs Helen felt justified in picking him up and carrying him the rest of the way. He allowed this with a stoic sigh.

'You've been here before, buster,' his mother told him.

He rewarded her with a grin.

In the bedroom Stephen had chosen bright red socks, turquoise trousers and was mulling over a selection of loud shirts. He was a flamboyant dresser, a sideswipe at his otherwise steady nature.

Archie threw a hissy fit as a vest was pulled over his head; he was going through a phase of hating anything to be pushed down on him like this. 'A bit of a control freak,' Bill had commented. Archie had to be twisted into a shirt as he lay heavily on his bed, still busy with the outrage of the undergarment incident. Stephen's shoes were changed to the correct feet and he was ready, while Archie continued to sob, prone on his bunk. Coats were the next hurdle then schoolbags were located and finally Helen led the two out onto the back garden path, her arms full of accoutrements and keeping an iron grip on Archie.

'What is the sky?' Stephen wanted to know, his head tilted as it always was when he was curious or thinking hard on a conundrum.

Archie shook his head at his brother's obvious simplicity. '*Why* is the sky?' he corrected.

167

This one question, twice put, encapsulated their personalities, Helen thought. It always amazed her that each boy was half her and half Bill, made in the same way, yet so utterly different from one another. 'It really is quite mad,' she would tell her husband. 'Mad.'

They struggled to the car and Helen lashed the boys into their special seats. Archie began to shrug out of his coat, complaining that he would be too hot. There was a lot of goading over and back about who was the most stupid and a fully fledged row erupted over a toy that Archie felt was his. Helen tried to intervene but they ignored her, shouting and screaming, and trying to connect kicks from their respective seats. She gave up and put the key into the ignition, then reached for her seatbelt. They were tugging on the piece of yellow felt when she noticed the back gate was still open. She swore lightly so as not to add more naughty words to the boys' growing canon. The door was banging heavily and looked as if it could shake off its hinges. She got out and leaned against the wind to return and close it. Rain pelted and the wind raised her hair and twirled it into knots. In the background she could hear the muffled squeals from within the car. She still did not know why, but she turned just before pulling on the gate handle and saw the car backing out of the cul-de-sac, under its own momentum and gathering speed with each foot.

She began to run but her legs were weighted down and leaden. A scream lay stillborn in her throat, all impulses concentrated on reaching the car. She was an arm's length from the bonnet when the car entered the traffic and the articulated lorry bore down on it, ripping and grinding while the driver frantically pushed his brakes to the floor. She could still see him standing on them, practically upright. Her car was a mangled wreck still travelling under and in front of the lorry so she kept running after it, hell tightening its grip on her. She could not see her children, but she could see their blood spattered on the window. The scream broke free and was whipped away from her by the wind.

Helen lay shivering in the tree house. She pulled Stephen's threadbare comfort blanket close about her and tried to smell her baby. He was gone. But at least he had touched and loved this and so would she. Her Archie talisman was a bear with 'trouble' knitted into his sweater, a forlorn and tattered affair that he had hugged tight, and so would she.

Someone phoned the emergency services and when they arrived they found her struggling with the doors of the wrecked car screaming her boys' names. The truck driver had joined her efforts and was tearing at the metal with poor judgement and inappropriate tools. They were both crying. A small crowd gathered, closely huddled, not knowing what to do or say but unable to leave. They were surrounded by flashing lights and sirens. Firefighters pushed through with cutting equipment and a police officer pulled Helen to one side. She kicked and swore at the woman, wanting to reach her babies and help them. Others in uniform began to tape the area off, moving the onlookers away. Someone began to redirect traffic. They've done this before, Helen thought. They have roles, specific functions. Her only purpose was to save her babies but she was merely flailing and of no practical use. She was frantic with the notion that they would not try as hard as they might if this was partly a routine for them. She screamed as much, or thought she did. The air filled with the smell of burning metal as grinders dug into the car's shell. The layers were peeled back. Even now odd details returned. For instance, Helen was sure she had smelled another metallic odour, blood. Surely it was only her mind trying to collate and make sense of the scene? Surely such fancies were untrustworthy? But even now, she would swear she had also smelled orange but that was probably not the case and didn't take into account the weather. It just seemed so real.

The WPC tried to talk to her, to ascertain a chain of events. She hiccoughed a brief description, unable to concentrate on what she thought was irrelevant. She finally told the woman to fuck off with her questions, that there would be more than enough time for them later. She lunged for the car and was sure she heard the firemen say, 'Dead.' She wailed so loudly she thought her head might burst. The policewoman pulled her back again. She began her mantra, 'My babies, my babies,' hoping this would breathe whatever life was needed into them. She saw these tiny people lifted, limp, from the vehicle and laid on stretchers. Medical staff worked feverishly, moving all the time towards their ambulance. Helen rushed over. 'I have to travel with them,' she shouted at the policewoman. 'I have to. They are my babies.' And again she started her chanting, this time their names. She got close enough to brush Stephen's hair from his face before being thrust aside. 'Please, madam,' the orderly pleaded, 'let us do our job.' Afterwards she realised that they had both died at the scene, but she would not let herself think it on the journey or indeed initially at the hospital.

The lorry driver approached as she was led to a squad car to follow the ambulance. He looked into her eyes, weeping, and said, 'I am so sorry but there was nothing I could do.' He gestured to the car. 'It came out of nowhere.' She noticed police photographers snapping at the debris and someone measuring the ground. A hive of personnel was taking statements from the shocked onlookers. Then the doors closed and they were borne away with sirens blaring. Her hands were covered in the sweet blood that had nourished her children but could not save them in the end.

She answered questions like a robot: Bill's mobile number? Why had the children been in the car alone? Had she left the handbrake off? 'Don't be stupid,' she said, thinking she sounded like Archie. Then her breath came in sharp, staccato gasps as she struggled with the awfulness of that idea. She hadn't released the brake; that was certain. And yet the niggling doubt returned, again and again. She replayed the scene in her mind. The children were bickering, fighting over the toy. She had climbed into the car but had returned to the gate to close it. No, at no time did she even touch the handbrake. She had only had time to put the keys in the ignition before exiting the vehicle again. How could it have moved away without her? It hit her like a thunderbolt and she doubled over with the force of the realisation. The car was in her charge and filled with her precious children and she had failed them. She wailed like a banshee. She had as good as killed the boys herself. The police must have thought so too because they took a blood sample and breathalysed her at the hospital. In her hysteria, she barely registered the procedures. They could have amputated a limb and she wouldn't have missed it, so focused was she on the fight to save her sons' lives and her traitorous role in the unfolding tragedy.

They waited until Bill arrived to confirm the worst, fobbing her off with blandishments, but not lies she later recalled. They simply stalled her. And as a result for the first while after that she associated Bill's presence, unreasonably, with the boys' deaths as if she could erase the deaths if he was not in the picture. She lay thinking of how unbearable it must have been for her husband to drive to the hospital knowing the worst awaited him there, to be confronted by a mad woman and then to hear for sure that the lights of their lives had been taken from them. His shoulders had stooped that day and never fully regained their swagger and breadth.

Helen was beyond reason when he arrived. She clung to him one minute, pulling at his clothes, only to fling herself at the wall the next, wrenching at her hair. 'I did it,' she sobbed. 'I am to blame. I killed our children.' He finally allowed the doctor to administer a mild sedative, just enough to keep her controlled for seeing the bodies, which they both insisted on. 'The boys need us now,' Bill said. 'They need their parents.' They stood together looking at the tiny broken bodies and Helen remembered all of the nights she had watched them sleep the unmoving and untroubled sleep of the purely innocent and contented. Now Stephen seemed to tilt his head trying to figure, 'What's this, then?' while Archie no doubt wondered, 'Why?'

Lucy looked around the gallery, listening to the careless laughter of people on a nice night out. I don't belong here, she thought. She was an outsider now. She had been removed from polite society though not of her own volition. She was also slightly drunk and worried that she might start mouthing off about her problems, a situation which she was too proud to allow. She needed to get out of there and fast. She stashed a bottle of wine in her bag and cleared away the glasses on the serving table, hoping this would also be a hint to the liggers to leave. There would be no more selling tonight. Her mother arrived by her side. 'It's a shame Pete didn't make it,' she said.

Lucy searched for agenda in her voice but there was none. She hated herself for the paranoia. Evie meant well. 'He's really busy,' she told her. And for all she knew that was true.

Her mother sighed. 'I hope this lot clear out now. And at least the exhibition is a moderate success, enough to get those ninnies off my back for a while.' She nodded towards the drunken knot of artists with a mixture of frustration and affection.

Lucy chuckled. Her mother never lost the ability to surprise. 'And there I was thinking they were your very bestest clients.'

Evie grinned. 'You mean you were worried that they were. This really was the most effective way of getting them off my back. We can return to proper business now.' She hugged her daughter. 'Call in to me soon and we'll discuss what you want to do next.'

You have no idea, Lucy thought. 'Actually, Mum, I wonder if we might meet up tomorrow or the day after. I do need to ask a few things.'

'Whatever you need, my chickadee. I'm always here.'

Lucy felt her eyes moisten and turned away. 'Thanks, Mum. I'll phone tomorrow and we'll fix something up.'

'Thank you again for tonight, dearest. I really couldn't manage without you.' She ruffled Lucy's hair as she had since she was a child. 'You are my jewel.'

Lucy practically broke into a trot trying to get away before tears began to pour down her face. I'm just a bit squiffy, she told herself. And about to get a lot worse, she promised. She made her way blearily to the Tube and found herself on the other end at Vauxhall not quite remembering the journey. Good, she thought, oblivion is a nice place to go. The heat had not abated with darkness and she could feel her shirt stick to her back. At least the smokers had stuck to the outdoors and she didn't reek as much as she'd expected. She staggered up the slight incline of the cul-de-sac and took three goes to open the door to her home. She fumbled in the glove compartment and unearthed a corkscrew. Dib, dib, she giggled: ready for all occasions.

She sat on the front seat, half in and half out of the car, idly kicking the kerb and sipping her drink. Evie broke her heart sometimes. She had always done her best for her daughter, probably spending well outside of her resources to send her to the best schools. Lucy could never remember having to do without. That must have been tough on her mother, a single parent running her own business. Tomorrow she would tell her how much she loved her and how grateful she was.

A sudden shiver ran through her. What was that? Someone walking over her grave?

Love. Why was that such a mystery? Some people deserved it and some demanded it, it seemed. Evie was one side of the coin and her husband the other. Why hadn't Pete told her his problems? They couldn't have been closer, or so it had appeared to everyone at the time, including her. Now that was exposed as nonsense. Had she missed the signs? Mind you, chances were she would have exploded if he had shared his troubles. To divide culpability took none of the edge off the cruel turn of events. If only he had run off with some floozie it would have meant a conventional tale of marital woe and she could have told the world. There would be a third person in the equation and with it a chance to apportion blame.

Without this mythical third party they were back to Lucy and Pete, the fallible duo of a sham liaison, as she now saw it.

The fact was he had not chosen to share. And now everything they had was hollow. One lie, even if it was one of omission, had tainted every other aspect of their life together. The whole fabric of the marriage was rancid with it. She couldn't trust the good memories because of the pall cast by his betrayal. She was alienated, on the edges of society, unable to tell anyone what had happened and unwilling to admit her different circumstance. She was a social pariah.

She took a moment to let the melodrama dissipate. This was the wine talking for her. It was clearly ridiculous to maintain this stupid façade but what else could be done? Tomorrow she would go to the gym and to work as usual. She would arrange to see her mother in order to spin more lies to cover her disappointed tracks, to borrow money. For the gloss that would burnish this sheath of pretence and saving face. She laughed. She would even view her neighbour's art collection and recommend a course of action. What she could not do was drum up any helpful advice for herself. She had no master plan and couldn't bear the thought of her life becoming a series of diminishing returns. But she really had no idea what to do next. She marvelled to think that this might all add up to a stiff upper lip of some sort. The thought made her smirk. What a state of affairs, she said to the thick, hot air. She drained the bottle and threw herself back into the car still fully clothed. I'll deal with it all tomorrow. I really should take off my . . .

She was unconscious before the sentence was finished or the thought anchored in her brain.

THIRTEEN

Jack enjoyed an Italian meal in Soho before returning to the square. He was tipsy and amazed that he had chattered out so much information to a stranger at the gallery. She was a pretty little thing, for sure, but that was no reason for a seasoned pro like him to spill any beans. It was the release of saying the unsayable to someone he had just met. He had called the end of his life with Laura and had even begun the process of offloading her artistic legacy. She would go ballistic but as he recalled he had paid for every last diabolical specimen she had dragged through the door. Hadn't she always joked that these were her gifts to him, he just didn't know how to choose them for himself? Well, he would certainly choose the manner of their departure.

He felt slightly out of control and that led him to a place he didn't normally frequent, hence the blabbing to a stranger. He was proper and believed in decorum. He gave a Gallic shrug. Well, the rules had changed when his back was turned and he was doing his best to vamp till ready. This would be some ride. And if he didn't drink at least a litre of water he would have the mother of all hangovers in the morning. He stumbled to the kitchen and forced it down. He could see his reflection in the window glass, a shambolic ghostly presence clad in crumpled linen with wild hair pointing in opposing directions. He laughed at his overactive imagination, casting him as a Heathcliffe. He also had an urge to sing which was not a usual activity. Damn it, why not sing? He was practically a free man now and could do as he pleased. He hummed tunelessly, unable to decide on a song from his vast and to date silent repertoire. It morphed into a caterwauled medley of butchered phrases and musical non sequiturs. Maybe he needed not to get out more. This struck him as hilariously funny and he laughed his way up to bed.

The medical explanations were all given in hushed, technical terms; the translation was that the boys were too small to survive the trauma of such a major collision. They were too soft, too tiny and vulnerable. They had been crushed. It didn't make anything easier; if anything it made it worse. Should they have had a stronger car, or a tank? The fact was, as a doctor tried to point out, Stephen and Archie were just very unlucky indeed. He had meant to help but the remark seemed so trivial once it had left his mouth that Helen said, 'Go away,' and he did, skulking off to examine what it was he had got wrong. His deathside manner needed work, she thought as she floated in an anaesthetised ether above the rest of the planet. In retrospect she could see that whatever he had said would have been wrong so he was damned either way. Still, it had been another lesson in his training, one that she begrudged as it had taken her sons' demise for him to learn it. Demise was a useless word, she decided; it had none of the anguish needed. A pathetic description of cataclysm. She would ditch it from her vocabulary. It was for doctors and undertakers and those who sought to keep things calm and socially acceptable in this most outrageous of situations.

They sat with their darlings all night, none of them stirring. None. Voices echoed with disproportionate loudness throughout the building even when they were the inconsequential whisperings of cleaners getting brooms or cloths. Everything sounded above itself with self-importance and very far away, in another world, probably a better and happier place than this. How could anything matter when their boys lay here lifeless? Now and then Bill would clear his throat, the only indication that he was crying. She didn't know how he could do it so silently, almost neatly into a handkerchief. She was covered in tears and snot and her clothes bore the tracks of the children's blood, which she steadfastly refused to trade for an anonymous hospital gown. Gently, the staff moved them on in the morning and they were ferried home by the police.

They entered the square from the front, naturally. The day was remarkably light and the sun sat happy in the sky. There was not the slightest trace of the bad-tempered wind and rain of the previous day. Blackbirds, blue tits, sparrows were out in force, singing their hearts out in a riot of preening and nesting and preparation for a new season of life. Bill and Helen Richards were returning to their home childless. Helen felt she would snap, or explode into a million pieces. She couldn't remember what happened for the next hour or two and now assumed that she had indeed passed out. Her system simply shut down. When she came to she sat upright for a moment, disorientated and wondering where the children were and why they were so quiet. They had to be up to some mischief as this was the only time they were silent. Her addled mind fought to keep up with unwanted images, each piling on the unbearable realisation of the truth. Then pain sliced through her like a razor. This was the quiet of the morgue.

She rushed from room to room shouting for Stephen and Archie. When Bill got to her she was sobbing in the boys' bedroom, running her hand along the bedlinen as if they were underneath and whispering endearments.

'They're not here,' Bill said, the words choking him.

'Say it's not true,' she pleaded. 'Please, Bill.'

Deep down she hoped that if she willed it with all her might it would be so: if she banished the thought that the children were dead effectively enough they would appear around the door laughing and running to hug her. She looked at this room full of their things. The trinkets, the colourful duvets and pillows, the rows of toys seemed bereft. They had no reason to be here if their owners were not. Helen felt apprehension rise like vomit in her throat. She bent and spewed on the carpet. Bill held her close, soothing her. She could not stop shaking. He lay her on Stephen's bed and he sat on Archie's. They held hands across the small divide.

'We'll get through this,' he said.

'I'm not sure I want to,' she replied.

The most immediate reaction to stun her was that of the other mothers at the kindergarten: they stayed away. All of their voices were noticeably grateful when the answering machine kicked in and they could leave their rehearsed message. The machine worked overtime, collecting offers of condolences and catering. She felt certain they were genuine in their way but to have taken up any of them would have caused major consternation on the other end. She was to be avoided, which was under-standable. After all, she was a woman who killed children and others were fearful that she might take theirs also, even with a look. She was almost mythical in proportion, a legend worthy of a Greek tragedy: the mother who killed her sons. They wondered what it was she had done to deserve this awful retribution, but no smoke and all that. It didn't bear thinking about, so they tried not to. There was a communal oasis spray of flowers on the day of the funerals and that was it. Let's hope there'll be no more about the whole sad, terrible catastrophe, darling. One doesn't want to bring things upon oneself and what goes around comes around, and all of the nonsense spouted when people were too shocked to think a thing through. Helen and Bill were left to cope without the community of local parents.

'They're not deliberately being cruel,' he said. 'They're afraid and they don't know what to do about that.'

Although Helen felt they were merely cowards she didn't mind because ultimately she didn't want the attention or company of her peers. She just wanted to be left alone.

She spent a lot of time in a Valium haze. It took the sharpest edges off the shocking reruns of events in her head. Sometimes the reel was like a continuous film, a narrative of such horror that she screamed to be released. Other times snatches of a scene would sneak up on her, an ambush preview of the heart of her darkness. Bill drank whisky by the bucket but it did nothing to rid him of the demons who had taken up residence in his life. They wandered anaesthetised through the motions. Rituals were set in place for these trials, support from family, visits by neighbours, calls to undertakers. There were decisions to be made. They changed their minds about the funeral arrangements several times a day. At the beginning of that mist-filled week, a day seemed interminable then suddenly the time was gone and they were pushed into making a final choice.

Helen realised how little attention she had paid to her convent education, particularly religious studies. Her grasp of Catholicism was vague. What stuck with her was the sacrifice expected before eternal life was granted. It seemed unfair, too much like a lust for blood and pain. She was at the point where she didn't believe in salvation. Even if it was in the offing it would always be too late for her as of now. Every time she tried to clutch at faith it rewarded her with snippets of inane hymns that rattled round her head and drove her to even further distraction. She couldn't get the face of her old school chaplain out of her mind. He had been a quiet man who smelled of candle wax. His lips were always wet which gave a damp sibilance to his speech, a creepy whistle that reeked of unctuous piety. Looking back from her private hell she realised she envied him his unquestioning faith. She was in free fall but to clutch at any of this ill-remembered background would be nothing more than religion à la carte, a convenient spiritual cherry-picking. There was no comfort to be had in any of it and she worried that it would demean the boys' memory to pretend otherwise. She gave up.

In the meantime, the nightmare continued unabated. Her children were dead and she wanted to join them.

Bill was raised heathen, according to himself. His family relied on a morality based on fair play and socialism. There weren't many of them left and so it was with Helen's family too. She had a brother who lived in Dublin and though they spoke regularly on the phone they often spent long patches without meeting. He had his own life, wife and a daughter. Bill's mother was alive but living in a home, unaware of her surroundings or visitors. His three brothers lived in Australia, Canada and Hull. They rallied as best they could but it was unknown territory for the lot of them. To bury children was a mockery of decent world order. There were no words that could comfort sufficiently, no actions that could properly console.

They decided on burial so that they could visit their boys, although clearly they could just as easily view urns and scatter ashes. Somehow they felt that the boys had endured enough and a further trial by fire was too much for any of them to bear. The vicar at St Olaf's led a simple ceremony. He sent the children on their way with dignity and without sentimental platitudes or claptrap. Again there were no words to sufficiently cover the loss. Helen was devastated not to accompany them on this journey and keenly aware that their final one had been of her doing. She upped her Valium for the day but it didn't erase it, not even the merest scintilla of a detail. It would join the never ending spool in her head.

They were touched by the neighbours' contributions. Famke made her own shrine for the grave of the little boys she had laughed with so often. She liked to joke that they were her mental age and she loved them for their honesty and confusion over what art actually was. '*Exactly*,' she would cry, punching the air. 'The children understand! Everyone else is a fool.' Ulrika made their favourite Scandinavian snack and tucked a little into both coffins to see them on their journey, 'like the ancients', they all decided. And Colin put money in, to pay the ferryman. 'You never know,' he said. Jack and Laura were there, and that was enough. At times of crisis it's amazing how little is required, Helen later reflected.

Life had become pointless. She stayed in bed most of the time and rarely washed. Although family members hung about and neighbours rallied as best they could, this was something so out of the ordinary that people were unable to know what to do to help. They drifted away, hoping that some new routine would take Bill and Helen forward. A week after the funerals her body descended into a rigor, teeth chattering like clackers banging riotously against each other. Her limbs shivered in an ecstasy of suffering, her mind unhinged. She passed into a fever and emerged pale and thin a week later, feeling just as bad as she had seven days before. She had run to standstill.

They went through the actions of living, joylessly. They were referred for bereavement counselling which they took up in a desultory sort of way, supposing they had to do it because the authorities were involved. Helen could not bring herself to speak of the accident and they eventually stopped going. Letters poured in the door with offers of swamis, gurus, self-help groups as well as the post that Bill filtered and destroyed; these were the vindictive missives of the mad and lonely. Some called Helen a murderer, some wrote that she was no better than an abortionist, while others carried dire warnings of further tragedy if their god was not embraced and appeased immediately. There were a lot of chain letters, as if their state of grief made them hostage to all fortune thrust their way. He binned the lot.

Helen made an attempt at alternative therapies. She was burned by hot stones and stabbed with needles. She wore chunks of quartz and semi-precious gems, always wondering why semi and not the full fat precious but too torpid to ask. She breathed in oils, practised yoga and drank

187

her own urine. Sometimes all in tandem. Nothing worked. Nor did she expect it to. She watched Bill struggle to hold their diminished household together and loved him all the more for it. But she found it hard to speak about her feelings. Every time she opened her mouth it ended in a plangent wail and she felt that was doing more harm than good. She began to clam up. This suited her as she came to view words as hollow tools that didn't even approach descriptions of what they were going through.

The police paid many visits as they tried to piece together the events leading up to the tragedy. The tests on both her and the truck driver had come back clean, so alcohol and drugs were ruled out. The vehicles were checked for faults but none was found. Helen told them to keep the car forever if they wanted as neither she nor Bill ever wanted to see it again.

She found she didn't want to leave the house. She lay in bed, willing the mattress and pillows to swallow her whole. She ignored the uppers and tranquillisers left by the doctor. If I am alive, she figured, I should suffer. She did. Bill played nurse and helper. He needed to stay busy. He plied her with food, water, vitamins. He wondered if they should stay, go away, clear out the children's room? Helen took to sleeping in the boys' bedroom after that to prevent him changing it in any way. They passed like shadows along the hallways. He thought it best to let her be, hoping the solitude would pall and she would return to his arms. He needed her. She needed him. But somehow they could not reach out to one another and make the significant contact needed to bind them again. Instead they were locked in parallel, lonely orbits.

Helen began to venture out to the cul-de-sac to watch over the place where the boys were last alive. She spent most waking hours out of doors, hardly noticing the time pass, lost in her misery and the meaninglessness of life without her family. She was like a soldier returned from war: exhausted, shell-shocked and searching for reason. It took only a small adjustment to stay out there on a more permanent basis. She wrote a warning on the nursery door forbidding Bill from shifting an iota. She used the house to wash and change her clothes but neglected to eat unless Bill made her a meal. He began to leave her food on the garden table, needing ever more elaborate arrangements to keep it from the birds and the cats of the neighbourhood. She picked at the food, hardly noticing it. Bodily nourishment meant little to her. She was too taken up with the dark province in her head.

Flowers appeared to mark the place of death on the road. As they withered and were replaced, Helen saw that it was becoming a makeshift memorial. Famke sought her out to assure her that this would not be assimilated into her oeuvre of roadside art. If Helen heard or understood her she didn't bother showing it. When the people grew weary of leaving their floral tributes, Helen tied a plain, green ribbon to the fencing at the mouth of the cul-de-sac in memory of Stephen and Archie. From then on she could sit in safety and see their tribute. She hadn't liked going out to visit the road shrine at all.

One day her despair reached a nadir. There was no catalyst to speak of, it was simply time. She was consumed by an unmistakable urge to hurt herself by way of atonement. She prepared her instruments in the shower room but gazing at her white skin shielding the blue veins carrying her blood through her unasked, she stopped short of cutting her flesh. Disgust flooded her. Her life was worth nothing so what was holding her back? She was too cowardly to do it, to make appeasement. She had all the moral fibre of chicken shit. If she was squeamish about blood why not take the myriad tablets her doctor had lined up in little brown plastic bottles? There were certainly enough to do the job and she wouldn't make a mess. If she seriously wanted to end it all, one large dose of paracetamol would take care of things and produce the painful death she thought she deserved. She had reached a boundary and it horrified her that there were things she wouldn't do, even now. She was doomed to her living hell. She was so gutted with this sentence that she used the razor to hack off all of her hair. It was a pathetically small gesture and she loathed herself even more afterwards. Bill found her later, asleep in the tree house, shorn. He brought bedclothes and made the little cocoon warm and habitable for his wife.

Bill often wondered how far he would let Helen sink before stepping in. There was no definitive answer to this and no help to be offered on the subject. He would have to feel his way around it. He was close to getting professional help after the hair incident but her demeanour was largely unchanged and at least she hadn't hurt herself. He couldn't bear the thought of her leaving altogether, to be cooped up in a sterile institution. Helen needed to be here close to him and to their children's memory. They did talk, sometimes, which gave him hope, even laughed occasionally as they remembered little vagaries their sons had displayed. And sometimes he was allowed to hold her, to comfort and reassure her that it was not her fault. They both cried together and tried to make sense of a world where sense had abandoned them. They were sinking but still horribly alive. A pattern emerged over time: if the rope ladder was slung down from the tree at night he knew she wanted to see him. If not, he left well enough alone. The cul-de-sac beyond was her solitary world and he didn't impinge out there. It was a system and they accepted anything that would get them by, doomed as they were to continue this sorry existence. He watched her from the tree sometimes as she sat or paced and worried for the past, eschewing a future. But it was out there, waiting for them.

The police continued to investigate the evidence. Archie had been found coat-less and loose of his seat-belt, although Helen clearly remembered securing it and Stephen's. They formed the opinion that Archie had somehow loosened the harness and lunged for the toy the brothers had been fighting over. It was found in the front passenger footwell. Somehow on his journey he had disengaged the handbrake, perhaps he snagged his coat, and the car had moved backwards along the incline to the main road. The truck was within its speed limit though traffic was not heavy that morning. It clipped the car just as it hit the road and the resultant spin crashed it into a wall at enough speed to crush it and the occupants. It was a terrible accident. A coroner's inquest would take place to reach the same conclusions. This did nothing to alleviate Helen's sense of blame. She had been in charge. She had been neglectful. She had killed her babies. She deserved to die. And now she knew that she wouldn't be able to bring that about she was yet again at the mercy of fate, a puppet in a malevolent universal scheme. She kissed the blanket and the teddy and asked for her boys' forgiveness.

Colin lay thinking of this new turn of events. He seemed to be dating, if that wasn't too fuddy a word for it. Tony was sweet, funny and presentable. And deliciously rent with problems. He could still smell a damp earthiness from the side he had lain on. As a gardener Tony had a healthy interest in sex and death too, he supposed. Colin had broached the subject with typical style.

'I suppose you have terrible trouble keeping the Wandering Jews from running amok with your Black-Eyed Susans, my own little Capability Brown?'

Tony smiled indulgently. 'Oh, every time I turn my back there's some sort of congress, though not usually between Tradescantia and Thunbergia alata. As to old Lancelot Capability B, he dealt more in greenery, really. The man for pollen and sex was a guy called Thomas Fairchild. He encouraged cousins to marry and invented the carnation, pretty much.'

'So I was correct. It's all sex and filth of the highest regard.'

He fidgeted in his bed now, wondering where this was going, if anywhere. He was unsettled by the stirrings of affection he felt for this new man. They brought fear with them, trailing commitment in their wake. In Colin's book that meant weakness could not be far behind, lurking to ambush. He was trying to get up a good head of emotional speed but the sounds of clattering and then a vacuum cleaner interrupted his reverie. He rose to confront Ulrika who had obviously lost her sense of community if she could tackle housework at this hour of the night.

'Sorry, I just can't sleep. I'm full of energy.'

She was wild-eyed and looked a little crazy. Colin crinkled his brow, wondering, then shook his head. No, Ulrika was way too square to actually be on something. She was high on ordinary shit. 'You've got to stop drinking coffee so late at night,' he told her. 'And if you must continue this purge, please concentrate on wiping down the kitchen and bathroom surfaces. Silently. I need my sleep or I turn into an axe murderer and we didn't enjoy the last time that happened.'

He returned to his room and lay down again but could not settle. He was convinced he could hear the pfft-pfft of sprayed liquid. He reached for his earplugs and drowned out the world. He was still uneasy about the Tony situation. Had he let this go too far too soon? Was this one destined to be the sort of problem he now avoided?

Ulrika thought about what Colin had said. He was right about the caffeine but she knew she had also taken one of her new tablets too close to bedtime. She had been hungry and didn't want to give in to her appetite. She was going to have to regulate the pills better, which wouldn't be a problem. It wasn't for long, after all. This routine was only until she reached her target weight, then she could say goodbye to her little chemical aids. And there was no harm in any of it. It wasn't as if she was some junkie dependent on the stuff. Ulrika did not approve of drugs but she would make proper use of them until she had what she wanted. That was just being smart. She was a prudent, educated woman and in no danger whatsoever. She needed to think this through a little better was all and everything would fall into place, especially her weight. That thought made her smile.

Helen lay in the tree house listening to the night. Heat oozed into her and sweat oozed out. She drank from a large bottle of water. She felt like nothing more or less than a giant puddle. She heard sounds of wood and metal and shifted to see a man leave by the back gate of number 5. He was tall and had a hulking walk but she couldn't distinguish any features. The lights in Famke's studio were ablaze. Burning the midnight oil, her mind said, casting up the cliché.

This reminded her of a therapist she had seen. He was

big into maxims. At the time she found it enraging, but she found pretty much everything like that then. She had been eviscerated by guilt and was raw to the world. She went through the motions of seeking help but none could be forthcoming until she found it in herself. It was still elusive. She sat in monkish silence, waiting for salvation. I have made the blood sacrifice, she thought, now it's payola time. She looked back at that time in therapy with benign fury but was grateful that the man with the letters behind his name had helped pass the time.

He was a furry creature who liked to sit in buddha-like serenity then offer up his gem towards the end of the session. She spent most of the time crying and hardly noticed he was there, perched in his armchair, leather creaking softly as he shifted to avoid sleepy legs. 'Be true to you' was a mind-morsel he had intoned near the beginning of their journey. She could imagine teenagers texting it in the new language of modernism, using numbers and as few vowels as possible. 'You are your own key' was more of the jabber (she having fashioned her own lock), and 'reclaim the inner you'. He threw in a version of 'no man is an island' when he thought she was making progress. It felt like attending a fridge magnet, trite and safe but ultimately useless. Life is cruel and vicious and inexplicable. The magnets don't work. The only day he got any decent reaction from her was when he suggested that 'recovery is not a straight line'. She exploded.

'I don't want to recover,' she raged. 'What would that

achieve? Would it change what's happened? Would it erase the memory of my boys?'

His left eye gave a tic, which she took to be delight at this response. 'Your anger is a valid reaction. Let's explore that.'

'Let's not,' she said, pulling together her things for departure and beating a retreat. Outside the building she stood amongst the furtive smokers and felt ashamed, not of her reaction, but to have let it happen in front of a man she regarded as a charlatan. She retreated again.

She looked up at the sound of another distraction: feet crunching stone and dried dust. She saw Lucy stagger up the little road, struggle with the locks and fall into her car. Someone's been out on the town, she thought. She could hear the young woman mutter and sigh awhile then bang the car door shut.

The heat lay on Helen like another skin. It was heavy as if even the air was tired of being hot now. She lay on her side and turned from side to side as she tried to get comfortable and go to sleep. She realised then that she had been waiting for Lucy to return home, safe. She didn't like that she cared.

FOURTEEN

Helen slept a little later than usual the following day. It was seven thirty before the birds had fully roused her. I've become a disgrace, she chided, allowing herself to enjoy a modicum of dark humour. She climbed out of the tree and made for the kitchen, ravenous for cereal and raspberry yoghurt. She must fill out a shopping list for Bill: they were low on the supplies she most wanted. She scarfed the food then slipped into the spare shower in the washroom at the back of the house. She sloughed off the perspiration of a sound night's dreaming and baking in the freakish temperatures they were experiencing. It was time for the weather to shoot them a break or both mankind and nature would go mad altogether with this endless sunshine. This was what the ancient crones who'd taught her would dub 'too much of a good thing'. She now understood the phrase and hated them for ruining the good thing in this sneaky way.

She caught sight of her hair in the mirror over the handbasin as she reached in to wet her toothbrush. It had grown to an unruly length where combing was a waste of time and the only option was to cover it all up with a hat or pretend not to notice how ridiculous it looked. She was mildly surprised to have given herself a choice. She couldn't give a toss what it looked like. Could she? She was inured to social niceties here on her margin. She grabbed some clean clothes from her laundry pile and dressed quickly. She went to the kitchen, scribbled a note for Bill, filled her water bottle and headed on out.

Beyond the garden gate the red car lay in wait like a tomb. She couldn't bear the sight of it. After the funerals she had cried off any journey in one of those hell cans, sticking to the Tube wherever possible. It suited her to be underground, burrowed and hidden. She liked being ignored by the other passengers. There was no question of talking or even catching another's eye. Silence was the social etiquette on public transport. She was anonymous and no one cared whether she existed as long as she didn't disrupt the journey. She was a nonentity. But how strange that they could not tell she had wrought so much misfortune and was simmering over with grief. I must look quite normal, she imagined. How strange.

She stopped to get a feeling for the day. The solid points of the cul-de-sac had already started to shimmer. It was going to be another hot one. '*Quelle surprise,*' Helen muttered, as she pulled a straw hat down on her head. She could hear the low drone of passing traffic, humming like a nascent threat.

Colin went by at eight thirty and said his usual 'Hello'.

She nodded and could see his obvious surprise, perhaps even delight. Easy to please him, it seemed. He left a stamp of cologne in his wake. It held for an age with no wind to disturb or disperse it. Ulrika sped by fifteen minutes later, hardly pausing to wave. When Helen gestured back she stopped short, almost tripping over in the process.

'Eh, see you later,' she gasped, clearly stunned that Helen had acknowledged her.

She was losing weight too quickly and looked a bit haggard to Helen's eyes. If she continued to shave away the pounds from her body, her head would begin to look too big. Why would any woman aspire to the shape of a lollipop? Still, there was no denying that she also looked happy and that was heartening. She was a lonely soul who deserved better. But life didn't cut up that way, as Helen had found to her cost. Her heart chuntered to a stop, loss ripping through her. She stumbled to the kerb and lowered her aching body to the ground. She knew she would be wrong-footed like this for the rest of her life. It carried with it a perverse satisfaction. I will never forget you, she promised her sons. I will carry you with me, always.

The woman in the car did not stir. Nine o'clock passed and Helen began to get anxious. She was usually up and gone by now. It was none of her business what this Lucy did but she was on Helen's territory and that involved her whether she wanted it or not. Liking this arrangement didn't feature as an option. She threw a few pebbles at the car. They bounced off without making much of an impression. She tried a volley for a rapid-fire rat-tat-tat. Still no result. She edged closer to the car and tried to peer round the edges of the screens. Lucy was still in there. Helen returned to her perch. She would give her another quarter of an hour then formulate a new plan.

The minutes ticked by, punctuated by trickles of moisture rolling down Helen's back. In the distance the church clock tolled the quarter hours. St Olaf's was their mini Big Ben. Helen had no call to tell the time any more but if she wanted she could while it away by comparing the peals from Ollie's and the height of the sun. She also recognised the passing people and traffic. She could distinguish between deliveries that happened each day or once a week. She saw the clockwork toing and froing of nannies and parents and their charges. She knew the dog walkers. They all added to the tempo of inner-city life.

A clear blue sky let the sun beat its fire into the concrete and onto the roof of the car. She must be sweltering in there, Helen thought. She heard the muffled ring of Lucy's mobile deep in the car. There, that would do the trick. She switched off the Lucy problem and cleared her mind to deal with the day.

She sat in a gauzy shroud of unhappiness and wondered about the phases of grief. She supposed she had endured denial at the beginning of the ordeal, not wanting to believe the boys were dead. This was as short-lived as their lives. It was hard to sustain in the face of bodies and the sheer absence of their wonderful energy from the house. They were gone. At times she prayed that she would wake up to find that they had been stolen away, that they were alive somewhere, even if it meant never seeing them again, as anything was better than the truth that they were lying dead in a hole in the ground. Guilt, of course, featured in every day, and it would until she died too. Anger had been a huge presence and it was never far from the surface. Now it had been overtaken by despair. A desperate sadness enveloped her. It would be the base note to the rest of her life. But there was another note sounding and she needed to talk to Bill about it. They had something big to discuss and he had no idea it was coming. She hoped he was ready for another change. Life was moving on with and without them and they had to deal with that accordingly.

She noticed that the church was calling eleven o'clock. That couldn't be right, surely. If so, the woman had been in there too long for comfort. Even if she was sleeping, the heat must be punishing her terribly. None of the windows in the car was open even the tiny amount she normally allowed. Helen began to worry again. She walked up to the car trying to gulp back the revulsion she felt for it. Bile rose then retreated. She searched about for a stick to beat the bodywork with. There was nothing robust enough to make a noise big enough to rouse the sleeping occupant. Finally, she settled on a kick. She booted the passenger door with force but her sandal wasn't designed to protect her foot from this sort of violence and she decided not to repeat the process. She was going to have to touch the thing.

She balled her fist and thumped the door. No reaction from within. She went again. Nothing. She gave a good drubbing but it made no difference. The woman was unconscious. Shit. She was going to have to break a window. Helen's heart battered at her ribcage and she could smell underarm perspiration, which she knew was to do with the act of touching a car rather than complete worry about the occupant. She went in search of a brick.

It's a lot harder to wield a weapon *and* break a window with it than any television programme or film lets on. The weight of the missile dragged Helen's arm out of its socket let alone having to swing the thing for breakage. It took three goes. She reached in the driver's side and unlocked the door. She opened it to release the boiling air within. It reeked of overripe alcohol and processed human vapours. Lucy was out cold or rather she was stewing in the can, unconscious. Central locking meant Helen did not need to reach across the prone woman to undo the passenger door, so she didn't have to spend any extra time actually in the vehicle. She ran around the other side and pulled Lucy out onto the ground. Still there was no perceptible movement. She splashed water on her face and was rewarded with the mildest of squirms but Lucy didn't come round. Helen realised that Lucy was dangerously dehydrated now and held the bottle of water to her lips to try to make her drink. She succeeded only in drenching herself and her supine charge. But bit by bit she dribbled the liquid into the unconscious woman.

St Olaf's had tolled another fifteen minutes before Lucy

opened her eyes. Her hands reached out to stop Helen slapping her any more. Then they reached for her head.

'Oh fuck,' she said. 'I think I'm going to die.' She gagged a few times and added, 'Fuck! The pain. I hope I'm going to die.' She leaned gently to the side again and vomited. 'It's not much but it is my own,' she apologised, pawkily.

Helen tried to move off but Lucy held her hand in a vice grip.

'Please don't go,' she said. 'I don't think I can do this on my own.'

Helen reluctantly stayed put. You won't want me here when you see what I did to your car, she thought.

Lucy rose from the ground in stages. First she rolled onto her tummy and lay panting in agony, eyes clenched shut. Then she made it to her elbows and gave a few dry heaves. She gradually opened one eye then the other and sat up on her knees. She groaned and her stomach rumbled ominously. Her hand went to her mouth but wasn't needed to stop any emissions. She swung her eyes towards Helen but quickly shut them in pain again. She turned her head a second time and said, 'That hurts less, but it still hurts.' She drank some water. 'I cannot remember when I last felt so bad. What possessed me to drink so much wine?' She obviously remembered because she shook her head and whispered, 'Let's not go there.'

They sat, silently wondering what to do next. Both felt awkward. The silence stretched.

'What time is it?' Lucy asked.

'Not sure, eleven thirty or so?'

Lucy gave a low moan. 'I am so late for work.'

'I think they phoned you.'

Lucy struggled back to the car and hunted down her phone. Four missed calls: three from Mario's, one from her mother. When she turned back to Helen she was faced with a blank space but the gate to number 7 was open. She walked gingerly towards it and went inside calling, 'Hello.' All she wanted was to lie down in a bed and pass away. Her legs were weak and shivering, her back ached and her head throbbed energetically. She needed to kill the pain or the vomiting would return. Helen came out of the house.

'Do you live here?' Lucy asked.

'I used to.'

Lucy waited for more but didn't get any: this was a woman of few words. What she did say was in a soft lilt and Lucy wondered if she was Irish.

Helen held out some tablets and a glass of squash. Lucy knocked them back and held her breath in case they decided to repeat. When she felt safe she mouthed her thanks. She sat at the garden table under the umbrella.

'You're Helen, aren't you?'

'How do you know?'

'Famke K told me yesterday.'

Helen felt odd hearing that her neighbour knew this parvenu.

'I'm Lucy.'

'I know.'

'Oh.'

'You introduced yourself to the air the other night and I was still awake, listening.'

'Where? If you don't mind me asking.'

Helen pointed at the tree. 'I stay up there.'

Lucy really didn't know what to say to that. She closed her eyes briefly to let the painkillers kick in. She could smell stale alcohol on her face and from her armpits. It was seeping out of her pores, sweet and sickly, and she began to feel bilious again. Her mobile rang.

'Mario, I am so sorry. I was ill this morning and didn't wake until a short while ago. I hope you weren't overrun.'

Helen watched her little head slowly move from side to side. She could imagine the awful pain torturing her dried-up, fried-up brain. She pushed more liquid in her direction. Lucy sipped it gratefully.

'I'll be in as soon as I can. Are you sure? Well, thanks. If you're sure? Thanks, Mario.' She gave a sigh and a laugh tried to escape. 'I work part-time in a café and the staff think I'm pregnant. This will add fuel to the speculation, a nice bout of morning sickness. It's just as well they're not standing here or they'd be able to smell the booze.'

'You should have a wash. There's a shower to the left of the kitchen. Then, perhaps, a proper sleep. After that we can talk about what you should do next.'

Lucy frowned.

'About your husband and all that mess,' Helen offered.

'Oh. You really were listening.'

'It was . . . interesting.'

* * *

Colin liked his life to be compartmentalised. It was easier that way. He had his home life with Famke and Ulrika, and occasionally the neighbours. He had the office, with his best work friend Stella. His blood relatives were mostly still held captive in Northern Ireland which separated them by hundreds of miles of land and sea and therefore involved air travel or crossing water. And there was his social scene, which also yielded up his sex life. Now he felt as if some areas were spilling over into others. His perfect system might fall apart. Tony was starting to turn up at home and had been mentioned in the office, even if it was just Stella who knew. And his work situation could lead to a return to his family and Northern Ireland. He was going to have to take stock and he hated to have that foisted on him.

The easier problem to start with was his job. He regarded it as money for old rope. He could do it blindfold. He shifted money around on a computer network and goofed off for most of his working day. For this he was well paid and worked in the midst of the City buzz. The position in Belfast would mean prestige and more moolah but honestly it wasn't really a runner. He was not going back, blaze of glory or not. If he did, he would smother in the arms of his extended family and too finite a circle of friends. Belfast was small and although it might be ready for him now he was not prepared for it any more. He would string the company along for some fine lunches with his direct supe-riors then decide to stay and wait till a better position arose here in London or on the continent. Maybe he should brush up on his languages rather than taking up a hobby. He slated that for discussion.

Tony was a more difficult proposition.

Spillage was inevitable between his life categories really and just needed careful handling. Above all it was about control and Colin didn't like to think that he might not be in charge. He wasn't a rabid control freak or anything. Live and let live as long as annoyances stayed out of his orbit was a good rule of thumb. But after being hurt, physically and emotionally, last time out there was no way he could let his guard down again. And the Tony situation was the toppestmost pile of dung waiting to be flung at a fan that he'd seen in many a long day's mince. For all that he was a nice guy, Tony was clearly also a sexual tourist who would stand by his boyish fiancée. Backing out of a wedding so close to the day was unheard of and would take courage beyond Tony's capability, even if he wanted to, which he probably did not. He would be a spicy addition to the volume entitled 'Colin's Inamoratae', maybe even a whole chapter, but there it ended. Colin would enjoy what was offered: gift horse, mouth, et cetera. Then it was, 'So long, have a nice life,' and a gentle shout of, 'Next.'

Sorted. That wasn't so hard.

So why did he feel so down?

'I blew Jonny off,' Stella said as she perched on his desk.

'Ooh, matron!'

'No, you filth bucket, I cancelled the date.'

'Are you insane? He is *hot*.' Colin groaned as if a

realisation too awful for words had presented itself. 'Oh, dear God in heaven above, don't tell me you've turned dyke overnight. You know I detest lesbians.'

'They can look but they can't touch, as yet,' Stella confirmed, stanching a hoot from Colin with, 'It's not the worst idea in the world though, the old Sapphic route.' She was thoughtful. 'It seemed too glib, even for me; Jonny, that is, not the girl-on-girl action. I was only going to date him to tease you and I can think of more enjoyable ways of doing that, with you in tow. No, I guess I'm looking for something more. I'd like to go out with a nice man, a real one. Not a pipsqueak upstart like Jonny. And he is full of himself, you know.'

'When you find this Mr Ideal guy, ask if he's got a brother.'

'Trouble in Camp Paradise?'

'He's getting married in a few weeks' time. It's hopeless. Although that makes the fabulous sex totally hollow, which is a plus.'

'Of course.' Stella wore a sardonic smile. 'You like him.'

'Yes. And I can't really explain why. Which makes it very serious. That's a worst case scenario.'

Stella shrugged. 'Then fight for him.'

Helen was amazed. She had allowed someone *in*. She had spoken more than in months. She had spent time in her own home. And she was engaged in someone else's life. As Lucy slept she pottered around her house, reintroducing herself to its contours and fixtures. She sat at the kitchen table stroking the pine and thinking about how it held secrets, of its own as well as the Richards family. It had hosted many, including her precious boys. Bill usually sat here alone now. She thought of his obvious plight while she was living rough out in the cul-de-sac. She had abandoned her spouse and that put her on an ignominious par with Lucy's husband. Bill deserved better. She had isolated herself and, in that act, had isolated Bill too. When they should have united she had cast off the closest and dearest person to her in a devastating act of selfishness. It was time to come home. It wouldn't be easy. There was a central blank in their lives now but she had to make an effort. She loved him. And he had proved over and over again that he loved her. He must have been so lonely as she trod her solitary path, keeping him at arm's length, using him for material comforts. It was time to stop being so self-centred. He may not thank me for it, she thought, when he gets a load of the inside of my head.

In some ways they had remained true to their marriage vows. A surprisingly regular sex life had continued throughout the grieving process. It veered from the urgent clasping of the other human beloved, on to slow and trembling journeys around the fact that they were still alive and functioning. It was the one thing they could give without having to speak or make the common mistakes of language and action. This was the most basic level at which they communicated and they did so with the respect and love of two people who had travelled together, and needed to stay together too. It cemented the trust they had in each other, even when Helen felt she had destroyed everything they had ever hoped for and had. Especially then? And she had blithely taken it all for granted and tested her husband sorely.

Well, they still had a life and she was going to rejoin it properly as of now.

She heard noises upstairs, her guest moving about. She went to the fridge and began to assemble a snack. She hunted out the last of the paracetamol and filled a jug with water. She had a little mission now and a bigger one later. Helen was coming home.

Lucy took a few moments to get her bearings. She was sunk into a bed, which was luxury beyond all imagining. A window blind stopped the sunlight from blasting the room and lent it a hazy glow. She felt sleepy and safe. Her head thudded, still, and her tummy was mangled but she would live. She felt withered and parched and needed to deal with that but hesitated to get up and confront the rest of the day. It meant acknowledging her homeless status again and all that came with that. The worst aspect of the whole mess was that she had done nothing about it for so long. She had prevaricated to the point of idiocy and the future could be put off no longer.

This hangover was a respite, oddly enough. She allowed herself a short wallow then made her way down the corridor looking for the bathroom. Her chemical make-up had been altered. Her steps were unsteady, her balance off kilter, and her heart pounded to an irregular beat. She opened a door onto a child's bedroom and stood taking in the scene. Actually it was a room shared by two boys, by the look of it. The beds were in the shape of fire engines and little shoes were lined up underneath. Toys were neatly piled into what had once been used as a playpen. It was very neat so the inhabitants had not been in it recently. Lucy closed the door quietly, feeling she had transgressed and should not have gone in there. She had been welcomed into a home and shouldn't pry. Her mind was gluing together the fact that Helen was living in a tree, basically, while her family life was in the house, so there was obviously a story behind these facts. Lucy felt a chill warning that it was not a happy one. They've been taken into care was the persistent solution her brain offered.

She found the bathroom and tried to smarten up. She had expected a puckered face, prune-like from dehydration, but she looked in reasonably good nick. She splashed her face and rinsed her mouth. She needed more painkillers and a gallon or two of fluid. Those and a new life and the job was Oxo. Helen was pottering about downstairs so she went to join her to thank her for her kindness and apologise for the intrusion.

'I've been out to patch up the window of your car,' she was told.

'Oh, did it need it?' Lucy was lagging behind, mentally dried up as yet.

'Well, I had to smash it in to get to you. Sorry.'

'Of course. Right. I've rejoined the human race now.

Bit addled there for a while. Don't worry about the window, it'll be easily enough mended.' Inside, Lucy squirmed. How much was that going to cost? The free wine from the gallery was coming home to roost in a costly way.

'We better get you fixed up too. You need to eat something, drink lots of water and have some more tablets for that head of yours.'

'Agreed. I'm sorry to be such a pest. Just get me tied together with string again and you can send me on my way.'

'I've also been thinking about your problem.'

'Yes?' Lucy could still not recall telling her about that.

'I hear everything that's said in the cul-de-sac from my tree and you went into some detail one night.'

'Ah.'

'We need to follow the money.'

Neither woman remarked on the word 'we' but it resounded.

FIFTEEN

Thursday was Ulrika's least favourite of the week. It had something of the nothing about it; the warm-up man for Friday and therefore the weekend. She also had her most pugnacious class to deal with. They were in mid-argument about fine art versus the popular and/or vulgar, a subject she revelled in and which was always full of length and depth. They were proceeding at a lick through Damien Hirst, advertising, even politics. She might have sat back and let the students dissect one another but they involved her fully, putting her to the pin of her schoolmarm collar to justify opinions and theories. Again this might have been enjoyable but she always got the impression from this particular group that they had no respect for her and were just waiting to trip her up. She was also feeling dizzy and had acid running through her stomach and veins. She should have eaten breakfast but had just popped a tablet and got on with the day. The heat was beastly and the faces of the students began to take on the aspect of trolls. She could see their twisted mouths open and spill forth bile but only heard a garble of connected words that managed to remain meaningless for her. 'Morality, functionalism, spin.' She could identify the concepts but was unable to marshal them.

She stood to clear her head and felt the ground shift ominously beneath her. It seemed to travel in and out of focus. She could feel a damp stain spreading under her arms and along the back of her blouse. She sat and the room eventually stopped spinning. Mercifully, the bell rang for the end of the session and she was spared further attention from the group. She remained long after they had gone, unable to move with confidence, thinking that her legs might fail her or that she might faint if she tried any kind of journey. Her heart pounded at her ribs and she shook all over. It was altogether unpleasant and she was going to have to ask the girl if these were side effects when she bought more of the magic pills. If so, she needed to know how to combat them. She had not yet reached her target weight and was not going to give in halfway there this time.

When her breathing returned to a fairly normal pattern she took her bag and books and tottered in the direction of the staffroom. There she would sink into a sofa and have a lovely cup of tea. Her shoes looked very far away on the ends of her legs and they slid about as she stumbled forward. Could feet lose weight? A little light refreshment and she would be back to normal. She would find the girl later. And she really must ask her name this time.

⁕　⁕　⁕

Famke was puzzled. The cul-de-sac was empty. At this time of the day she would certainly expect Helen to be on duty, but she was not. And the side window of the red car was bashed in. If she hadn't worked so late last night she would have been awake a lot earlier and could have checked out the action. She worried that something had happened to her ladies. At the back of her artist's mind the selfish gene was kicking in and wondering if her project was in jeopardy. I am a slut, she admitted. The art was everything. It'll be here long after we're gone, she thought, if I can make it in the first place. She dressed hurriedly and went to investigate.

She was poking at the broken window when a voice said, 'I did that.' Helen had emerged from number 7. Famke checked her for signs of mental breakdown. Had she simply tried to wreck the car, or taken her venom out on Lucy too?

'Bad, aren't I?' Helen asked and Famke couldn't escape the idea that she was toying with her. Helen let her off the hook. 'Lucy's having a rest upstairs. She got drunk last night and is totally incapacitated today. She'll be fine but she's got a thumping great hangover, as you can imagine.'

This was a gabfest from Helen for which Famke was unprepared. She was slack-jawed with astonishment.

Helen curled her lips ever so slightly and asked, 'Know anyone who'd do a cheap replacement window in a hurry?'

There was a time for allowing the world to toy with you and a time for action, Colin told himself. Stella had a point. If he wanted Tony he would have to make that known. Tony was many wonderful things, potentially at least, but clairvoyant was unlikely to be one. It was a quality Colin would not have appreciated, at any rate, as it always meant the back foot for one of any couple so afflicted. Unless of course two clairvoyants got together, and that must be a nightmare, a kind of binary predictions hell. He was getting sidetracked again and he knew why. He was reluctant to commit. Well, really he was reluctant to hope. It meant leaving himself open to hurt. But were we not put on this earth to suffer? He liked the high drama that smacked of. It almost removed the danger from the exercise.

He picked out the number and listened to the phone ring far away, not knowing what he was going to say. It was unlike him to go off without a small rehearsal in his head. He needn't have worried. A woman answered. He instantly knew this was Tony's fiancée, a hunch but he would have put a tenner on it. Colin took one of his legendary scunners against the voice, which he decided was a squeaky, doll-like confection that couldn't but be manufactured to lure men to their doom.

'Tony's phone, how may I help you?' She even giggled, another nail banged firmly into her coffin.

Colin was caught now as he hadn't withheld his number and was using his own mobile. He asked for Tony and she wanted to know who was calling.

'Colin Parker.' He loathed her now. 'He's helping me with some gardening.'

If you only knew, witch-girl, he's been pumping my water feature but good.

Tony came to the phone, obviously uncomfortable. His tone felt like rejection and Colin was stung. It was his own fault, of course. He had brought this on by getting even marginally involved.

'That's her, isn't it? The lady-boy type you're marrying.' He bit his tongue but it was too late. He cursed himself for the spite and uncalled-for coarseness. He had also betrayed his feelings.

Tony said, 'I'm afraid I haven't got what you're looking for at the moment, Mr Parker. Can I call you back on that?'

Colin hit the red button and presumed that Tony had kept talking as if to finish a short and businesslike conversation. He had blown it. They both had. But what was there to destroy? Truly? Nothing. They had acted on some basic hormonal impulses. That was the sum total of it. Still, Tony's loss. Colin had had a lucky escape. He packed his briefcase, took early leave and headed into Soho. Time for some mindless fun, he decided. To his surprise he found he was crying.

'Any ideas for starters?' Lucy asked, embarking on her first money trail.

'We need his bank account number or a credit card would be good too. I can trace something from those. He's bound to be withdrawing money somewhere, or using the card.'

'You are going to think me very dense but I don't actually know the answers to either of those. He moved the apartment sale money into a new account of his own and the bank wouldn't give me that. And I never knew his credit card number and don't have any old bills I could consult.'

'Mmn, might be a little trickier than I had anticipated so.'

They pondered the problem in silence. Lucy was struck all over again how organised Pete had been. Who was this stranger she had married? Had every laugh and jape covered some sinister, other motive? It would take more than flowers to make this acceptable behaviour. The flowers!

'I know someone who might have his credit card details, although I don't know how I'll get them without tipping her off.'

'Surely the main point is to track him down and get back what's yours? Why would it be a problem asking for the details?'

'Well, I haven't told anyone what's happened. Or where I'm living now. I was just too mortified.'

'Was. Hold on to that.'

'You're right. I'll get the information, whatever it takes.'

'Good. Now while I was thinking this through it struck me that although I can probably do this myself, Colin from next door is definitely more advanced on a computer than I am. I say we call him on board too.'

Helen took in Lucy's expression. 'He's a good sort. He'll be a great help and he has a special gift for lightening most moods.'

Lucy jigged her shoulders. 'Don't suppose my shame can grow any more than it has already. The world and its mother will know soon enough, so yes, why not?' This was not necessarily a case of the more the merrier but she needed to get beyond that sort of pride now. It reminded her to call her own mum. They had to talk. She didn't think it was time to involve her in the entire story yet, but she needed to sort out her accommodation crisis, which meant borrowing money. Especially as her current home was compromised even further as a home by the broken window.

'You need somewhere to stay.'

'I think with the car being the way it is I'd better stay in it for the time being, just till it's fixed up. I don't want it to get vandalised during the night. It's all I have now.'

'There's a bed here if you need it.'

'I'd only be in the way.'

Helen had to admit to herself that Lucy had a good point. She and Bill had matters to deal with that precluded a house guest. There was only so much you could do to help anyone, as she now knew. She had made the offer and was glad Lucy had decided against it.

'If it gets too much for you, we're always here.'

'We?'

'My husband's name is Bill. I think you saw him when

the fire brigade was out back yesterday.' She paused. 'We had two little boys but they're dead now.'

Lucy held her breath.

Helen told her story.

Jack hit the office feeling seedy but up for some excitement. Reviewing his present circumstance he found he was a) getting a lot more sex than usual and b) it was with varied partners, which was a change. He liked the new arrangements. However, he had to sever sexual ties with Clara as it would ruin their working relationship but other opportunities were presenting themselves and he was pleased with that. He had managed to mix some business with pleasure last night and was looking forward to an evening with the lovely Lucy White as a result. He was intrigued as to what she could tell him about the eclectic collection adorning his walls. There were only a few items he liked and he was resolved to shift the rest. It would be pleasant to have a lady visitor to the house too. It would take the last of the Laura taint off it if he began entertaining his friends now, he hoped.

The last thing he wanted or expected was a communiqué from his missing wife but that was what Clara proffered as he clattered past her desk. It was a curt order to put more money in their mutual account as she was running low. 'I'd rather drink battery acid,' he muttered. And please would not have gone amiss. He asked Clara if there was a return number to call. No, there was not. Well, whoops, I wish I could have contacted you to say how tight things are financially and that you'll probably have to get a job or some maintenance from your sugar daddy but I really couldn't get in touch. She had left her mobile, switched off, at the house when she absconded. It was prominently featured on the hall table so that he would find it immediately and know that she had left deliberately and there was no way of talking to her. She had disappeared and chosen to remain that way. Back then he would have pleaded with her to return, given half a chance, but now he was delighted that he hadn't been able to do that and as time passed he didn't want to.

He spent the day putting together a package for a minor politician who wanted to boost his profile and was also desperate to become a novelist. Jack didn't fancy his chances for the latter, not sure that there was even a reasonable memoir stalking this lesser public figure. Then he fielded a few calls about Jodie, who was thinking of joining an international aid convoy to Belarus, according to one rag.

He had an awkward moment as he left when Clara asked about his plans for the evening. He fobbed her off with talk of the visit of a fusty art critic to value some items he no longer wanted. Clara wondered if she should have a look too, another opinion even if it was an uninformed one. She was so blatantly angling for an invite that he felt a complete crud. She was lovely, but she was a colleague, more accurately an employee, and he had let things get out of hand. He skulked away feeling mean and manipulative. Do I like who I'm becoming? he wondered.

He nipped into Selfridges Food Hall to stock up on champagne and nibbles, surprised at how much he was looking forward to seeing the little Lucy sprite again. She would probably turn out to be better in memory than in person and that would be just as well. He had a lot to sort out. While he was there he thought he should just pop upstairs for a brief look-see at the new stock and ended up buying a silk shirt and trousers that were so effortlessly elegant they took his breath away. He had to have them. The price left him gasping too but there was no denying that the outfit was worth every penny. He was leaving the store when he realised he had probably bought them to punish his ex-wife after her demand for money. If it was spent she couldn't have it. And if this was revenge he loved it. He zoomed home with the soft-top down and grinning like a madman.

Lucy was dumbfounded. There was nothing she could say about the story she had just heard. She was mute in the face of such tragedy. Her own problems seemed inconsequential and to mention them would almost have seemed like a weird trading of woes. This was not a competition. And even if it was, Helen's story topped all. Although it was high time she left she didn't want it to look like she was running out on Helen now that she had shared the truth with her. The throbbing in her head was replaced with an aching sadness for her new friend. It was the impetus she needed to change her own situation. And something in the unfairness of Helen and

Bill's tragedy made her angry at the world. She would use this.

She stood. 'I'll get the credit card number for you and we'll try to locate that fucker I'm married to. I've let this go on far too long. Thank you for the offer of help. And if there is anything I can do for you, just anything, you let me know.'

Helen smiled regretfully. 'I hope I haven't frightened you,' she said.

'Absolutely not. I only wish I could wave a wand and make things better or turn back time or something. God, I don't even have the language to talk to you about this. I'm making a fool of myself and probably upsetting you.' Lucy was disgusted with her jibbering.

'It's enough that you're here. And I don't know how but you've roused me out of the trough I was in. That's got to be worth a return favour.'

They walked down the path to the gate and out into the cul-de-sac. Lucy's red car sat, good as new, on the road. Helen saw her bemused expression and said, 'The window fairy came while you were recovering.'

The favour lay between them awkwardly.

'What do I owe you?' Lucy asked, dreading the price, which would certainly plunge her into bankruptcy.

'You can pay me back when you're on your feet again, though I suspect if you were charging me for the therapy today I would owe a fortune even when the cost of the window was deducted.'

'You're joking.'

'I'm not, actually. Will you be OK out here?'

'Oh yes. In fact I have an appointment to keep this evening so it's nearly business as usual again. And I have a plan to get some money and a place to stay. I've let things slide a lot and it's time to get cracking.'

'I know how you feel,' Helen said. 'Good luck.'

Bill fitted out a complete apartment at the site that day. He felt the old satisfaction return.

Sean pointed out that his work was too good for the price they were asking. 'The buyers have the work of a master joiner here and they'll probably never know or appreciate it,' he said.

Bill beamed. Somehow there was hope in the air today. It was a delicate scent and he didn't stand still to locate it, preferring to let it waft around him. He bided his time to relax with it, sure that it would blow away again if he sought it out or worried it unduly. He knew not to expect much any more. Time was when he expected a lot, not as if life owed him but just in the natural scheme of things: when you worked hard and reared a family as best you could, you wanted the best for them and enough for you. The humbling lesson had been unnecessarily harsh but he had paid attention.

When the klaxon for down tools sounded he was gratified to be asked out for a pint by the other lads but decided to head home. He had the buzz of a good day's work firing inside of him.

He wheeled by the supermarket and picked up Helen's

requests. On a whim he bought her some freesias, her favourite. This sort of gift hadn't been appropriate before now but it seemed right tonight. Again he couldn't explain why. He smelled the cheerful scent of the flowers and smiled. There were still simple delights out there, tiny moments that kept us going, in spite of all that the cosmos hurled at us.

The house felt different and it took him a moment to pinpoint the reason. He stood stock still in the hallway and listened. Someone was moving around in the kitchen. His heart was frantic. This hadn't happened in so long. He crept along the hallway to the door, not wanting to startle her into a bolt. He gave a casual 'Hello' and walked in to see Helen standing in wait for him. He handed her the flowers and said, 'Welcome home.' He leaned in to kiss her cheek, smelling again the flighty scent of hope.

'Bill, we have to talk.' Her tone was calm and her expression still.

His heart juddered to a stop.

SIXTEEN

Lucy felt almost foolish walking around to the front of the square. I live here, for goodness' sake, she giggled. Nicholas Farewell stood on his pedestal, hand on granite heart, watching her approach. His dates were etched as 1780–1815 and he was declared a Friend to the Needy. His face was kindly in outlook and she thanked him for his patronage as she passed by. She had changed into a summer frock, surprisingly uncreased from its sojourn in the boot of her car. It was white with pretty pink flowers and she wore her favourite suede pumps with it. She was sophisticatedly cool, she convinced herself, in a casual yet feminine way. Why did it matter so much to her that she make an impression? She was a married woman and damaged goods. This was business, not a date. The butterflies in her tummy were working overtime.

Jack answered the door in a shirt and trousers that must have cost most people's monthly wages. Silk, obviously, and beautiful upholstery to a well-kept body. He even smelled expensive. Lucy gulped. How would she concentrate on the evening? He ushered her into a cool marble-floored hall with white walls and a modern chandelier hanging gracefully from the ceiling. Incredibly elegant also. Where was all the bad taste he'd said his ex-wife had visited on the place?

'A glass of champagne?' her host asked.

Although Lucy had vowed never, ever, ever to drink alcohol again, she couldn't think of any other way for her to break the ice she had made here and which only she was prey to at that moment.

'Lovely,' she answered, shrinking at the sound of her whiny voice. She feigned a cough to clear her throat. 'Pollen,' she murmured. Was it her imagination or did he crack too wide a smile?

She's just as nervous as I am, Jack thought, leading her through to the conservatory.

'This is a beautiful house,' Lucy said, wondering how any woman could give it up.

'Thank you. I've had it quite a while now. I'd love to tell you it was a complete dump when I got it, but no. An architect had his tremendously tasteful way with it before me. I did manage to snag it before any of the frightening booms though. I don't think I'd be able to afford it now, to be honest with you.'

He handed her a glass of pink fizz. The cool bubbles hit exactly the spot that needed massaging and her hangover was finally banished.

'How long have you been divorced?' She stepped back in alarm. Did she just ask this most personal of questions?

She wanted to scream at her faux pas. 'I can't believe I asked you that,' she admitted.

To her relief he laughed. 'Probably as well you did. We're separated at the moment. But it'll end in divorce.' His tone hardened for the last nugget.

'I'm sorry to pry.'

'You're not. Well, perhaps you are but you're up front about it. I can't stand to catch people gossiping about it, particularly people who profess to be friends with those sickly sincere moon faces.' He was thoughtful for a moment, then puzzled. 'Don't know why that surprises me. In my line of business I'm guaranteed a bit of truth bending.'

'It's always sad when something special dies,' Lucy remarked, not as lightly as she would have liked. Then to clarify she added, 'I mean like a marriage.'

He grinned. 'As opposed to the truth.'

She giggled too. 'Something like that.' She liked the way he put her at ease, but couldn't deny that she was still skittish with nerves.

'What about our private view of the collection?' he asked, giving the question a healthy dose of mockery.

'Lead on,' she said, surprised that she didn't want to break the tenuous momentum they were building.

He held his arm out to usher her on their tour but they still managed to set off at the same time and collide. An electric jolt ran through them and they stepped away more gingerly. This promised to be more of an obstacle course than either had anticipated.

Some of the pieces were fine, including small works by established artists from their early years. These were often figurative and very pleasing on the eye. The more abstract items were problematic, some brashly coloured, looking slapdash. They had to have been introduced by the vendors as 'sound investments'. Jack declared most of them hideous and marked for the saleroom.

'Crikey, that's an abomination,' Lucy squealed, pointing at a lurid specimen.

'Madly expensive,' Jack confirmed with a grim nod. He brandished the bottle for refills. 'You'd need a drink to get past some of these monsters. No wonder the artists were willing to part with them. This house is like one giant orphanage for unfortunate pieces of drudge.'

'They're not all bad,' Lucy cautioned. 'I think some of them are probably quite valuable.' She caught his cynical eye. 'Though certainly hideous. There's a lot of contemporary art here so I'm surprised you don't own any Famke K. Particularly as she's a neighbour, I believe.'

She sensed a hesitation in him. 'I don't mean that her work is ugly or overpriced. Far from it.'

'I could never afford a Road Shrine,' he offered.

'She's painting now, a series about living here in London.'

'Yes. I've actually seen some of that.' He was clearly stalling. 'It's very powerful.' And now he was covering madly.

She gave him a quizzical smile. 'Do I sense a history?'
He reddened.

'Oh my word,' Lucy said. She began to backtrack, aware

of her trespass. 'Of course, it's absolutely none of my business. I apologise.'

Jack held his hands up. 'I think it may have been a . . . a mercy shag. Women seem to want to, I don't know, help out since my wife left. It doesn't mean anything.' He felt his liver curl to hear his dismissal of Clara and her attentions. Famke, he was sure, was a sexual gadfly. Listening to his last statement he wasn't much more. 'I don't think our eminent artist intends to repeat the exercise. And I have to point out that I was never unfaithful to my wife during our marriage, or at least not until after she did her runner.' He sounded to his own ears like a man telling lies or making convenient excuses. 'I'm a slut,' he admitted.

'I think that's OK as long as you're a gentleman slut and treat these ladies well.'

Lucy found it reassuring that he even bothered to explain. She couldn't blame the women or fault their taste. This man was gorgeous. In a way his admission helped ease the voltage between them a tad. They continued to walk, which stretched the breathing time.

Their trail led them to his office and here Lucy clucked delightedly over a small Beryl Cook.

'One of mine,' Jack beamed.

'I love it. In fact I love anything she paints. It's fun and approachable and wonderful.'

'You'll hear no arguments from me on that score.'

'Good, because I was running out of superlatives.'

'But this is my favourite.' He led her to an oil above

his desk. It was a painting of a baby and it took her breath away. She sank into his swivel chair and stared. The tiny mite was curled asleep in a pink gingham rug, fists balled and touching her face. The observer immediately loved this baby as the artist clearly did. Brushstrokes seemed to caress the baby's face. The colours were warm and pulsating with the wonder of gazing on a new life.

'I can't believe I'm seeing this, that I'm actually in front of this painting,' Lucy said.

'I bought it years ago at a retrospective exhibition of the artist. Wish I'd got a lot more. He's dead now and I really like his work.'

'Me too.' Her voice had a melancholic catch. 'His name is David Mason and he was my father.' She turned to him with tears in her eyes. 'That's me. I am the baby.'

'I know. I guessed it when I met you at the gallery.'

'I haven't seen this one before. It's beautiful.'

Jack hunkered to her level. 'So are you, now even more than then.'

She began to cry softly, leaning her head to one side and revealing a smooth white neck. Jack couldn't help himself. He leaned in and pressed his lips to the soft flesh. He heard her moan. He cupped her face and kissed her wet cheeks, tasting salt tears at first, then moving to her mouth and tongue.

'What's happening here?' she gasped.

'I don't know but it's wonderful.'

The man was rough-hewn from granite. His muscles were taut and huge, bound into boulders that served as limbs. His shaved head topped a shallow forehead and dark, malicious eyes. His skin was coloured by tattoos. He was the classic 'heavy' from central casting. You'll do, Colin thought. I've been looking for you all night. He checked his phone: five missed calls so far, all from Tony. He barged his way across the bar floor, bumping into several tables along the way and slurring apologies.

'Got any more tatts under there?' he asked the giant, waving a hand over his torso. 'You seem to have them everywhere else.'

'What's it to you if I do?'

'Just wondering.' He coquetted a smile. 'If I'm gonna fuck a guy I like to know what to expect.'

'Surely that takes away all the surprise?'

Colin batted his eyes. 'How right you are. Let me find out for myself. Shall we?' He gestured to the back door.

The hulk followed him out into the alleyway behind the bar. Colin pulled at the man's flies and released an enormous erection. 'My, oh my,' he said and fell to his knees. He took the penis in his mouth and realised he was too drunk to fellate without barfing. Oops, miscalculation, an inner voice sang. To his relief, he was dragged up almost immediately.

'Turn around and bend over,' he was told.

He did, and as the man pounded into him he thought, 'This is more like it. No love, no hurt.'

❈   ❈   ❈

Famke was enjoying the setting sun from the roof of her studio. Orange and pink streaks flared across the sky, cloud and smog co-mingled on a fading cornflower-blue canvas. The human swarms were returning to their hives in planes, trains and automobiles. She had finished some of the smaller pieces today and was pleased with the efforts. The paint was so layered and dense in places they would take an age to dry. It was all she could do to resist pushing her face into them like a cream cake.

The status quo was changing in the cul-de-sac and that was exciting too. She wondered about asking the women to pose formally for her. She wasn't sure why or if this would help the work along but it was always time well spent to study the human body, to recap the techniques at the very least. She sipped on a cold Sancerre and sighed contentedly.

She was turning to climb down when she spotted Ulrika returning from work. She was about to wave when a young woman approached her housemate and they had what looked like a fraught but brief conversation. Something exchanged hands and Ulrika hurried to the gate. The girl watched from the roadway. Was she smiling? There was a creepy feel to the scene that Famke didn't like but she couldn't pinpoint exactly why. She went to join Ulrika to find out.

The girl had left Ulrika speechless with fury, and unnerved. She had searched for her all over the campus earlier without success and because she didn't have a name she couldn't ask for her or look her up in students' records. She needed a new supply and dreaded falling behind with her regime. As she approached the back of Farewell Square a familiar figure approached her with a smile. Ulrika was pulled up short.

'What do you think you're doing coming to my home?' she asked, fury gilding her voice. The scenario darkened even as she spoke. 'And how do you know where I live?'

'I told you I'd find you when you needed me,' the girl said, ignoring Ulrika's tone. 'Here I am.'

'I tried to find you earlier,' Ulrika stated. 'If I had known your name it would have been easier.'

'My name isn't important.'

'It is to me.'

'Look, miss, the less you know the better. What we're up to here is not exactly legal so the less you're involved the better, OK?'

She had a point. It would be the end of Ulrika's career if she was discovered buying drugs from a student.

'As you please,' she said, trying to sound as if it was her decision not to pursue this point any further. 'What have you got for me?'

'I'm a bit short at the moment which means I have to charge a little more and I have to ration, but that's just until my supply improves. I'll have more soon, then we'll be back to normal.'

Ulrika handed over the money and took the small bag of pills. 'This will not become normal. This is only for a short while,' she promised the girl.

'Sure,' she replied, giving a toothy grin. She might as well have added, 'That's what they all say.'

Ulrika felt no better than a junkie. She didn't like where this was leading but at least no one else knew about it.

The girl gave her a critical once-over. 'Have you been eating sensibly?'

'Lectures are my business,' Ulrika told her, curtly.

'It's no good to ignore these things,' the girl warned.

Yeah, yeah, like you care, Ulrika thought. She waved the girl off dismissively. She would be glad to see the back of her when this was all over, which would be soon, she reasoned. She would allow herself a light meal when she got in.

Jack and Lucy stood in his study, panting and bewildered by their experience.

'Will you stay the night?' he asked. 'I really want you to. I understand that this is sudden, but it feels so right.'

He could not believe the charge he felt when he kissed Lucy. How could it be so strong when he had only just met this woman?

Lucy was now further down the road of her problems. She should tell him that she was married. She should go home. She should explain where home was. She also wanted to stay. She wanted to feel this man's arms around her, to feel his nakedness pressed against her own. She wanted to feel him inside her and to watch his face as he made love to her. She didn't care whether it was in a bed or not, and until then she would have listed a bed as the number one requirement of staying the night anywhere. It had paled as a demand in the last fifteen minutes.

'I want to but there are a lot of things you should know about me first.'

'There'll be plenty of time for that,' Jack said and he believed it. It was as if he saw the truth about romance for the first time. He didn't care how overwrought that sounded; it fitted the moment.

'I'm not entirely free to do this,' Lucy explained, haltingly.

'Neither am I,' Jack pointed out.

'You should know that I'm married,' Lucy said, grinding out the words and feeling every one of them rip her lips as it passed by. 'My husband has left me.' In the lurch, she wanted to add, but that came with so many shameful details that she couldn't bring herself to admit them.

'I understand that,' Jack said.

She knew that he did.

She smiled then. 'If you throw in another glass of champagne you might have a deal.'

'Done.'

He bent to kiss her again and they forgot the drinks for more than an hour. They eventually finished the bottle naked and propped up in Jack's bed. They feasted on antipasti and got breadcrumbs on the sheets. They pondered another bottle of champagne but decided against it as it meant moving off the bed. Lucy was afraid to concentrate too hard on what was happening in case one pinch would make it disappear. When they began to make love again, it was slowly and with infinite care. Lucy felt she would dissolve into this man in rapture. She didn't dare think further to what happiness that would be. Jack, in turn, marvelled at the ecstasy he felt and the melting glory of this woman's body, given wholly to him. This was what it was all about.

Colin went to the pub loo to clean up and make himself presentable for the journey home. His boxers were slightly bloody and smelled of condom. He felt defiled and debasement brought satisfaction. He could begin again. His face looked haunted in the mirror. I'm drunk, that's all. I need to eat. I need to go home. He gathered his bag and jacket and walked out into the busy city street. No one paid him a second glance. He was an anonymous piece of human trash. In his pocket his phone vibrated as another call went unanswered.

He lowered himself gingerly into the Tube seat, aware of how sore he was after the bar encounter. He saw his cadaverous face reflected in the dark glass as the train sped from station to station, hurtling him forward. He closed his eyes and listened to the thundering engine fill the tunnel. It sounded like the inside of his head. He longed to curl up in bed, to forget the week so far. He felt tears well again but refused them purchase. They had no place here. There was nothing to mourn. He was young, free and single; wasn't this the pinnacle of his London summer?

He tried to sneak into the house but Famke was on guard and caught him in the act.

'You look awful,' she told him

'Many thanks,' he breezed. 'I will admit I'm fucked.' He hated the sly truth of the admission.

'And pissed,' Famke remarked.

'It is so.' He manufactured a credible yawn. 'And now I must bid you nighty-night, oh most precious muse. I must get my beauty sleep.'

'Tony called for you, wants you to phone him back.'

Colin waved a hand dismissively. 'Not my problem. I'm not a social worker.'

'There's a note under your bedroom door, too, that you have to do something about.'

'Sure,' he said, as he passed round the return on the stairs and disappeared from her view.

What the hell was going on? First, Ulrika had stomped off to her room like an unruly teenager, and now Colin had arrived home in rag order. Famke felt like the mother of a dysfunctional family. She swore aloud in colourful Portuguese. Neither had noticed the paella she'd made to share with the entire household. She chided herself for her chintzy image of the modern family eating a meal together. The last thing she needed was to go all soft on the world. She ate her portion alone and disappointed. This is not what I signed up for, she sighed.

In his room, Colin tried to make the words on the note stand still long enough to read them. It seemed to be from Helen asking for some sort of technical help but that couldn't be. He put it aside and climbed onto his bed, burying his face in the pillow and pouring his soul into it in tears and sobs. Success was bitter, he reflected, but he had had his way. There was only him to blame for the evening. And if he had it all to do again he wouldn't change a detail. Or would he?

'I have been so negligent,' Helen said. 'I don't know how to make it up to you.'

'You're here with me now, that's all that counts.'

Bill was afraid to smile in case his mouth took off with happiness. His wife was back in residence. Or so he hoped. There were good signs. She had put the freesias in water and taken a long satisfied smell before placing them in the middle of the table. The room immediately looked brighter and lived-in. She began to arrange dishes for an evening meal. He didn't dare ask what it was they had to discuss. He wanted nothing to disturb this delicacy. He wanted to welcome back whatever normality they could salvage and he would take anything that was offered without over-analysing it.

'I'm not sure how this will work out so it's still one day at a time stuff,' Helen said.

'That's fine.'

They sat. It was like starting over. There was a strange novelty to asking for a glass of water, passing the salt. He talked about work and she told him about Lucy. It seemed this other woman was the catalyst for Helen's return. And still there was no mention of the topic they needed to 'talk about'. Just when he thought it had been forgotten, it was back on the agenda. Helen refused coffee.

'I don't feel like it.'

A bell went off in his mind, trying to remind him of a detail stored away. What? It was so close. He knew the answer but didn't have time to tease it out.

'There are a few things I won't be having from now on.' Helen's eyes were downcast and he couldn't read her expression.

'Yes?' He was developing a nervous tic and his voice sounded breathless, both in a bad way. His legs jiggled independently.

Helen breathed deeply, holding for a moment while she galvanised her words.

'I'm pregnant, Bill. We're going to have another baby.'

He rushed to her side and they held each other tight as they both subsided into tears. This was their miracle, a chance to begin again.

'We are the luckiest people in the world,' Bill sobbed.

'Yes, love, we are.'

SEVENTEEN

Number 5 Farewell Square was a casualty zone the following morning. Colin rushed to the bathroom. He bypassed the mirror, unable to face his reflection, and retched his guts up into the loo. He could not stand up, the only straight activity he ever had any truck with. Ulrika knocked on the door and asked if he was OK.

'No, I'm not. This is my last day on this sorry earth, so start planning my funeral.'

She wanted to shower but decided to leave him be for another fifteen minutes as he did sound *in extremis*. Besides, she was weak with hunger, the sort that sent hot, molten lead coursing through her and made her feel nauseous. That, accompanied by the soundtrack of Colin being ill, was almost too much for her system. She went in search of food, mindful that she had missed her previous evening meal because of Famke's prying and her own storm off to her room. When she calculated, she found it meant she hadn't eaten in about twenty-four hours, barring one digestive biscuit with afternoon tea in the staffroom. She deserved breakfast.

'Will he make it?' Famke asked when she appeared.

'Jury's still out. I must admit he does seem very, very sick.'

'That's not like Colin. He has the constitution of a horse, normally. I'll go play Florence Nightingale.'

When Colin heard her voice he spluttered, 'Death be not proud,' through vomit-encrusted lips. 'It's all over, Famke.'

She heard another tremendous bile-filled bawk. 'I'm ringing you in sick.'

He didn't argue.

'Will I see you again tonight?'

'Would you like to?'

Jack and Lucy had that awkward second-date atmosphere hanging over them, in spite of the fact that they would have recognised the other from many different and adventurous angles by then.

'Sheesh, how needy does that sound?' Lucy gasped, disgusted.

'It's OK,' Jack assured her. 'I'm not sure what to say or do either.'

Lucy lightened her tone. 'You know, now that we've got the sex bit out of the way, as it were, you really should know some things about me.' She was dreading the exposé but once it was introduced she reckoned she would have to follow it up. She took a breath and let it all out. 'I've been living in my car for the last fortnight.' His mouth opened. 'It's in the cul-de-sac, your cul-de-sac, out back there.'

'You live in the red Micra?'

She nodded sadly. He began to laugh, then choke, thumping his chest and wiping his eyes to clear the tears. 'That is just remarkable,' he cried, laughter bubbling up again. 'I don't know what to say. That really caps it all, Lucy. Bloody priceless.' He regained his self-control. 'You can't stay out there. You must move in here.'

'Isn't it a bit early for that?'

'You can have your own room. If we share a bed on a night, all the better, but I really cannot have you going back to that tin can whenever we're not together.' He raised a hand to quell her arguments. 'It's not up for discussion. You're moving in.'

Lucy tried to sound forceful. 'As long as we're clear that this is a temporary measure.'

Jack's phone rang and effectively ended the conversation. He glanced at the number. 'A client, born with a silver spoon in her nose; charming and kooky, and pays very well.' He shrugged. 'What can I tell you? I'm a whore.' He winked, then pressed the answer button. 'Jodie, good morning. What can I do for you?'

Lucy looked around at her new lodgings. She stretched her arms wide. 'Room to swing a cat,' she murmured happily. She twirled once and went out to transfer her possessions from car to house.

Ulrika stood before the mirror and cried. She finally fitted into a dress she had bought as an aspiration three months ago. It was still a touch tight but in a way that made her

245

body look voluptuous rather than fat. And all this after two slices of thick white bread toasted and smothered in butter. Whatever was in those pills worked quicker than anything else she'd tried. Another half a stone and she would only have to worry about weight maintenance. She ran to the kitchen to show Famke her success. Colin was sitting with his head slumped on the table, groaning as if nursing a fatal wound.

'Have you phoned the undertakers?' he muttered.

'Shut up,' Famke ordered. 'You'll live.'

'I'm glad you're so sure. Believe me, from here it's Armageddon all the way. I am on the brink of annihilation, facing into the vortex. The last of my kind.'

'You can still talk, that's a positive sign,' Famke said, drily.

Famke was spot on, as Colin knew. As long as he could articulate, and be funny, he could keep things trivial and therefore manageable. His suffering from the hangover was so severe that he didn't need to confront the emotional vacuum inside of him. He could put everything down to chemical imbalance. File this one under 'later' and then ignore it when the time comes. QED.

Ulrika cleared her throat and waited for their approval.

Famke brightened. 'You look great,' she told her. 'That dress is a vast improvement on the Spartan look you've been cultivating recently.'

Colin raised his head a notch and squinted through bloodshot eyes. 'Fab. Well done, you.' He quickly reached past the table and screeched, 'Famke, bucket!' She placed it under him and he gagged into it.

'No reflection on you,' Famke said to Ulrika. 'Too much to drink last night and who knows what else.' She turned to Colin. 'By the way, Stella was so worried when I rang your office she's coming over this evening after work.'

Ulrika grinned. 'Great. We've not met her yet.'

'No. It will be an event,' Famke promised.

'My lives have merged,' came the wail. Colin stretched out his arms. 'Slash them now,' he begged.

Ulrika extricated herself, delighted to have ducked out of any explanation for last evening's visit from the student. Colin was the perfect smokescreen and would remain that for the day.

Although Bill was an early riser, Helen was still up and gone before him. It wasn't too much of a jolt initially to wake and find her side of the bed empty, then the absence hit him as something worse and he was down the stairs and into the kitchen, fast. She was coming in the door.

'Force of habit,' she said. 'I had to check that everything is all right out there. It is. Breakfast?'

They tucked into juice and cereal. Bill drank coffee. Helen a peppermint tea.

'The tummy is a bit dodgy,' she admitted.

'Your punk hairdo is coming along.' He was treading dicey ground here mentioning a previous, bad time. He waited on his tenterhook.

'Yes.' She ran a hand through the mop. 'It has a certain charm.' Fine, they had negotiated a hurdle.

'Bill, you know when I lived outside?' Here came another.

'Yes.' Easy does it.

'It wasn't because I didn't trust you or anything. It was something I had to do.' They were getting back in touch. 'It's not because I thought my grief was greater or more important than yours.'

'I know that. Anytime you want to talk about it is fine by me and if you don't, that's fine too.'

'Thanks.'

The kitchen air itself seemed to breathe a sigh. Relief and hope were still on the agenda.

'What will you do today?' he asked.

'I'm not going to be able to break my routine immediately, so I'll sit outside for a while. But this afternoon I'll start the hunt for Lucy's husband on the computer.'

'Is there anything you need, anything I can do?'

'Just be Bill.' She paused. 'This isn't a disease so we mustn't let it get out of proportion. We're having a baby. We've been granted a new lease and I know you're as worried about that as I am, but we can do this, and the worst thing we could do is to make it into something it's not. This baby deserves its own time, not to be foisted with making up for other lives. I hope that makes sense.'

'Perfect.'

'Good. Now get out of my sight, you're late for work. If you get fired then we're shanghaied.'

'The boss's wife loves me, so we should be fine.'

*　　*　　*

Lucy stood in the guestroom giving herself a hard time about what a pushover she was. Even after all I've been through, here I am flinging myself at a man who shows me just a soupçon of kindness. This is such a temporary situation the word temporary doesn't cover it adequately, she promised. Anyhow, it seemed entirely based on sex, and as enjoyable as that was, in fact very darned enjoyable, it was no basis for a proper relationship. Whatever that was any more.

It hadn't taken long to move in her three bags. She sat on the bed to read the note she'd found under her windscreen wiper. Helen suggested they hook up late afternoon to start the search for Pete, which meant she had to get his credit card number before then. Fine. The paper smelled faintly of cat spray and therefore of her car. If she caught the little fur bag that was doing it, he was in for a sound telling off. From what she knew of cats, which was not a lot, this would have next to no result. Cats had insouciance that humans like her could learn a lot from. She needed that sort of inscrutability. She was firmly of the opinion that she was the easiest read woman on the planet. Although that was a problem right now what she needed most to continue with the day was a shower and to phone her mum to beg some money to rent a flat. At today's prices she might be better setting her sights on a shed.

She showered and sat down again to tackle her mother. She was going to have to share some truths. She took a deep breath, let it out and dialled. She told Evie that she and Pete were having difficulties and she needed to rent a pad but their money was tied up. It was causing a lot of friction, she explained. Her mother was not in the least surprised.

'Darling, I could tell something was up. You're not your usual sunny self.' She chuckled. 'You smacked those artists from pillar to post the other night. They didn't expect to have to actually put hammer to nail and there you were cracking your whip. It quite suited you, I thought. So, you want money to rent a place. Are you sure you don't want to move in here?'

'No, Mum. Thank you, but I want us to remain friends.'

Again the tinkle of Evie's laugh came down the line. 'You are so wise.'

Lucy was aware that her mother was probably using 'you' as in the plural for her and Pete, whereas Lucy meant her solo self, but that was for another day. She remembered a detail for Evie.

'Mum, you'll never guess what. I've discovered one of Dad's old paintings and it's of me.'

Evie's breath caught. 'Is it a little oil of you in a pink blanket?'

'Yes, how did you know?'

'I didn't. I hoped it was. That was my favourite. Has it found a good home?'

'Yes. A nice man loves it.'

'Good. Perhaps he'd let me see it one day. Must go now, sweetheart,' she said, and Lucy could tell she was crying.

'I love you, Mum.'

'I love you too, Lucy.'

❋   ❋   ❋

Famke rehydrated her ailing housemate and ordered him back to bed.

'Could you carry me?' he wheedled.

She laughed, as he knew she would, and refused.

'There was a time when landladies did all sorts for their tenants,' he moaned as he struggled to the stairs. 'If I should die before I wake, et cetera,' he said, 'the music for my funeral is listed in the pad on my bedside locker. Burn everything else, though some of my past lovairs and pets will want mementoes. You may dispense my Armani jocks, but only the very good ones. And don't let my family bring me back to Norn Iron. Christ only knows what class of cack-handed send-off they'd give me. I'd end up in some hetero limbo for all eternity while Satan and God fight over my tight little faggot ass. Oh, and that goes for if I have a stroke too,' he added with a shudder. 'No Belfast. Am I making myself clear? Kill me rather than let that happen.'

'Consider it done,' Famke said. 'The pleasure will be all mine.'

He wound his tortured way to his room and sat on the bed to check his telephone for the umpteenth time. It insisted that he had seven missed calls from Tony, and one voice message. He dialled in and heard, 'I'm sorry about earlier. We have to talk. I have something important to say.'

'You're mixing me up with someone who gives a shit,' Colin said as he switched the mobile to mute. He flung his body back onto the pillows and watched a feather rise and fall. I am a modern Icarus, he thought. I flew too high and now I am in descent, wings singed. Well, I'm damned if I'll crash and burn. He kissed the feather and tucked it under a pillow. Then he lay on his side and willed sleep to come and take him away, to heal. When he was thus restored he would emerge a new and better version of Colin. As he drifted off he realised that he lived his life one day at a time like a recovering alcoholic, so perhaps the hangover was an appropriate sign.

Lucy felt like a movie star as Jack's sports car whizzed her into town. She wanted to wave at everyone they passed. She wished she had a scarf to billow out in the wind they created with their speed.

'Note how it's the men of a certain age who stop and stare at the motor,' Jack said. 'They are all as sad as I am, clinging to their disappearing youth and trying to stop the march of time with expensive toys.'

'Thank goodness it's not the woman who's being ogled,' she remarked.

Jack hit his hand against his head and went, 'Duh.' He looked across at her sheepishly. 'Sorry about that. I really didn't intend an insult. Of course they're eyeing up the talent too. How could they not?'

'Stop digging, you're only making it worse.'

But it was true that men in their forties were admiring the car.

Lucy laughed at his earlier self-deprecation. 'You don't seem so desperate to me,' she said.

'Oh no?' Jack replied, unconvinced.

She would have liked the staff at Mario's to see her arrive in such style but it would have provoked too many questions. In their eyes she was, after all, an apparently happy, pregnant, married woman and it would have been exhausting to explain otherwise. She was tired of being tired and decided to keep her circumstances to herself. But first she had to indulge in a little sleuthing, which she realised meant lots of lying.

Martha was slumped uncomfortably on a stool by the cash register as usual. Wasn't she supposed to be learning the trade? The air conditioning felt silky against her skin and Lucy thought the shop smelled coolly green.

'Busy?' she sang, unable to resist a tiny jibe in the face of the girl's obvious stagnation.

'Yes,' was the surprising reply. 'We've done the morning's orders and are just about to unload the deliveries and sort them.'

'Oh,' Lucy muttered, stymied.

'We start at six thirty most days,' Martha explained. 'We take in the fresh flowers, do up the bouquets and displays and usually have a little rest about now.'

Fi popped up from behind an exotic hedge. She waved a carnation and pointed to an elaborate arrangement ready by the door. 'That's Martha's latest and I must say she has outdone herself this time.'

It was exquisite: a study in relentless grace and form, with muted colours and taste screaming from within the cellophane.

'Wow, Martha, you are talented,' Lucy congratulated.

Martha shrugged. 'Keeps me off the drugs.' She held Lucy's eyes till they both laughed.

How much more wrong could she have been about this young woman?

'The coffees are on me,' Lucy announced. 'Actually I do need a favour. Pete's gone and lost his credit card and what with the move and all we can't find his last bill so we don't have the number. I know you don't need all that to cancel it but it might help to have it and to check what's turning up in the transactions. Hopefully he'll know which are his and which are not.' She threw in an eye roll to illustrate that he was a ditz when it came to his card. 'Would you mind awfully looking it up from his order the other day?'

They didn't bat an eyelid, just found the information and passed it on. Well, why would they worry? I am his wife. He is my husband and I'm not asking how much he spent on me, just helping out in his crisis. Also, I don't seem the sort of sneaky bitch who would use the information wrongly. They trust me. That was the sticky moment when she realised that all lies, no matter how well meaning, had their immorality. Oh, how wrong can anyone be about someone else? she again thought. She left Fifi's Flowers with the number burning a hole in her pocket. But she couldn't feel that bad about it. I may be on the slippery slope, she admitted.

Well, so be it.

*　　*　　*

Famke watched Helen make her slow journey to the main road. She paused at the green ribbon, pressed her lips to her hand and put the hand to the fabric. She stayed still and silent for an aeon and from the back of her head Famke could only surmise the unwelcome memories that Helen was dealing with. Then, as if each foot were made of densest lead, Helen stepped ever closer to the edge of her world. She stopped and looked back at her cement sanctuary, as if about to flee back beyond it to the safety of her garden again. With what must have been superhuman effort she turned towards her goal. She stepped from foot to foot on the spot, limbering up. Then suddenly she hurtled forward until she was standing on the public pavement beyond the cul-de-sac. Famke could almost hear her yelp, a mixture of fright and triumph. Then she turned left and went on in the direction of her continued healing and Mr Patel's deli-cum-newsagent.

'Bon voyage,' Famke whispered. 'And safe home when that time comes.'

Now she had to figure out how to transfer this drama onto a canvas.

EIGHTEEN

Colin rose and showered without disintegrating. This was a pleasant sensation, though not to be trusted. He found that paranoia was the term best describing his mood now. If he were to apply logic, which he loved to use regularly at work, he would have admitted that his system was still under the malign influence of his hangover. But it suited him better to view it as a malaise which threatened his whole way of life and which he needed to vanquish immediately. That, at least, had a little excitement to it and he needed to keep boredom at bay. Boredom was when unwanted things happened, like dialling the wrong phone number and looking like he cared. He noted no further calls from Tony, which meant the flake didn't even have persistence in his paltry make-up and so was better consigned to life's rubbish heap.

He thought briefly about the man because it seemed *un peu* unfair to dismiss him so out of hand. Well, no actually, it wasn't. This was about survival and Tony was dragging him under. He had to get back into the old Colin mode as soon as possible. To critics who opined that he had a fear of intimacy, Colin would point out that his past record spoke for itself. 'I have no fear of intimacy. I relish it, as long as it is often and temporary.' There now, that was better already. And that was enough thinking about it too. Like Scarlett O'Hara, Colin felt he'd go mad if he thought about it today. He would think about it tomorrow.

Maybe.

However, a further problem existed. Stella had texted to say, 'over 2 c u 18r. dyin 2 meet roomies + c crib.' If he hadn't been so out of it earlier he could have nipped that in the proverbial. Shite on a stick, she was crossing the line and there was naff all he could do about it. The girls knew she was on her way to visit. And if he stopped her they would all realise he had been deliberately keeping them apart. He cursed himself. Arse and piddle. What he needed now, after liquids, aspirin and carbs, was a distraction. He revisited Helen's note. Promising, he decided, and a definite point of departure.

The weather was beating the living daylights out of the city for yet another day so he threw on his most casual linen trousers with the tie waist and a painfully white T-shirt. It was a gesture of defiance to his rotten head and necessitated the immediate addition of sunglasses. Now the world had a more peaceful glow, the pale brown lustre courtesy of the Gucci corporation. God bless the Label. He slowly drank a litre of water to dilute the toxicity in his beleagured tubes and organs. He wondered at the joy of water. How could it be so good for the body when there was nothing in it? No drugs, no vitamins, no roughage. He introduced solids to his stomach without disaster. So far, so good. Time to visit his neighbour.

And here was the curiosity. Helen was not sitting at her station. He thought nothing of it initially as she might be gone for water in her ex-kitchen or a snack, or she might be having a siesta in the tree house. But when she had not surfaced within twenty minutes he felt the stirrings of worry. He knocked on the gate of number 7 and shouted her name. Then he dialled her home number from his mobile but the answering machine kicked in. He left a short message asking her to call him immediately in what he hoped was a light-hearted tone and which was anything but what he felt then. He began to sweat and it brought with it the odour of excess alcohol leaving his system by all routes available. He particularly disliked the rivulet heading south along his back, knowing full well where it would end up and how uncomfortably moist that would be. His body began to protest again at its recent rough treatment. Before he could get to thinking that through he ran back into the garden calling for Famke, wanting to share and halve this problem of their missing neighbour.

'You know, you are always so cute when you're worried,' she said.

'Famke, *liebling*, this is no time to come on to a gay friend, much as I appreciate and understand your admiration. You're lovely too, but not my type, dear. OK? This is serious. Helen is gone. What are we going to do?'

'Wait for her to come back.'

He couldn't believe her hard-heartedness. Even for a selfish artist this was going too far. He began to berate her.

'Relax the colliewobbles. Helen has left to do a little shopping. She's started to go out again. She even spoke to me yesterday. It was quite a day, I can tell you. In fact I would have told you if you hadn't been so blathered last night when you got home, or so diseased today until now.'

Colin sank into the studio settee. 'I am getting way too old to care about humanity any more. It's too exhausting and the results are usually catastrophic. I've had it with people.'

'Sure you have,' Famke said, unconvinced.

'I have. I renounce them. They're nothing but trouble.'

'And what of your great talent which is handling said people and entertaining them?'

'Speaking of talent, I can't believe I cried off work today.'

'I know, it's not like you to risk the boredom of a day at home. You must have been suffering greatly to have to do that. Or perhaps you've finally rebelled against the Man? Or you've hit rock bottom? Whichever is the case, I expect a full show of self-laceration.'

'Well, a little flagellation would not go amiss, I suppose. It's always worthwhile.'

'And now are you really going to tell me what's wrong with you or shall I guess?'

'Perhaps a wee guess would be in order, just to start the bidding?'

'Tony.'

The transparency of his life began to sicken Colin. He wondered where all the effort he made to distract people went? Did it count for nothing? Did anyone appreciate how much energy it took to be this outrageous and devil-may-care all the time? He slumped further into the velvet sofa.

Famke didn't feel qualified to dispense useful advice. 'My love life is scattergun at best,' she pointed out. 'I'm too selfish to be with someone and too much of a libertine to be tied down.' (Colin made a feeble attempt at a fnar fnar double entendre but he really was whacked.) 'That's my excuse anyhow and it suits me. For what it's worth I don't think there's much you can do about Tony. He's got a lot to sort through, a lot that doesn't involve you directly. He's put himself in an unenviable position and you may have to sit this one out.' She shrugged. 'But what do I know?'

'I've decided not to care because I agree with you that there's fuck all I can do about it. Which is also why I went out and got soundly rogered in a squalid alleyway by a thug I met in Soho last night. There is no low I cannot sink to and I felt I had to prove that to myself.'

Famke clicked her tongue a little in exasperation. 'You should be nicer to you, Colin. You deserve more.'

'Tell me about it, sister.' He brooded a little. 'Why has this one got to me? That's what I don't understand.'

'I think that deep down you're looking for someone permanent, even though you can't admit it to yourself.

You want to be half of a happy couple. I could strangle that carpenter or whatever he was for ruining that for you.'

'Oh God, the ignominy of it. I'm nothing more than a boring old looking-for-love bloke. I'm so traditional it's pathetic.' He wallowed in self-pity and disgust. A spare piece of medulla threw up another question that was bothering him. 'Why is Tony sticking around?'

'He's obviously confused and this is a great refuge.'

'Plus I'm a great ride.'

'As you never tire of telling me.'

'I can organise some written statements to back me up, if you wish, my Thomascene doubter. And no, I don't know if that's a word. The point is, my reviews are excellent. I'm too good, actually. That's why he's back for more.'

'Could be.'

Colin groaned and held his head in his hands. The dual panics of his hangover and errant life were taking their toll. Mess piled upon mess into a smelly compost heap of reconstituting gunk. He didn't like the horticultural reference he had summoned up, it smacked of Tony the Gardener.

'And what the fuck am I going to do about this promotion back to the Olde Country? It's nothing short of deportation.'

'You may be in destructive mode right now but I have to draw a line there.'

'Keep reminding me of that. I'm feeling a bit vulnerable now and I don't want to bolt into the easiest escape route, especially if that means going home to my family. I love them, but that's precisely because they're miles away.'

Helen found it hard not to shake. She was not frightened of this outside world, per se, but was nervous of its re-introduction. She had forgotten the most basic rituals, like opening a purse and choosing money to pay for a service or item. A comestible? What was that when it was at home, eh? And had she been searching for the word commodity? She'd have to look those up. She should regard things as having freshness to them as opposed to exhausted repetition of age-old practices and products. That was the way to proceed. This was starting over.

Her social isolation also rendered chit-chat a foreign territory. A question like 'How are you?' was rhetorical usually and didn't want as lengthy an explanation as Helen had to offer. She didn't have a lot to say as it happened and would have found a lengthy conversation beyond her after so long a silence. It was odd to hear her voice pass off the pleasantries of daily commercial life, though. 'Please' and 'thank you' just like she'd taught the boys to say. They were foreign on her tongue. She even bought a newspaper, a 'commodity' she'd managed without very well during her exile. She was playing catch-up and tried to look forward to the new perspective her absence allowed her.

The traffic unnerved her, but she had to trust the pavement to walk on and the road for the cars to travel on. Similarly the pedestrian crossing had to be used to get to the other side of the road, while passing vehicles slowed or came to a stop. Those were the rules and one had to hope, believe, that everyone would observe them. Anyone who came to grief because of a breach of this trust was unfortunate and ultimately undeserving of the tragedy. Trust was the nub of the thing, with attendant rub, and a world of hope and fear attached.

She saw one of the kindergarten mums in the distance. Cilla, she thought. Mother of Tristram, a brat as far as Helen could remember, given to biting and lies. Or was that Andrea's kid? The other woman stalled when she saw her, wondering if she was seeing correctly. Then she raised a hand and waved hesitantly before disappearing round the next convenient corner. It was tempting to follow her to see how she got herself back onto her preferred route and perhaps even to jump out of a hedge going 'Woo'. She would probably pass away with fright. It was not surprising that Cilla didn't want to speak to her. It would be hard to have a chat without mentioning that rather awful tragedy Helen had precipitated. She would come around. Hell, I nearly have myself, Helen thought.

She had to stop and clutch a bollard when a mother and family passed and the eldest ran too close to the traffic. The old fear surfaced. Images of destruction whirled and loss punched her in the face and gut again. She must expect this to happen. And whereas this might have been a situation guaranteed to result in panic, there would be times when she wouldn't be able to predict when a memory would assault her, or her life would grind to a halt for a painful reflection. She needed to give herself the leeway to embrace what was hurled her way, experience it and move on, one step at a time. She followed this plan, one foot in front of the other, all the way back home.

Colin was waiting in the cul-de-sac.

'Is that not my space you're occupying?' she asked.

'Well, someone had to stand guard if you were going to feck off without telling anyone,' he sniffed.

She flung the paper at him. 'Find me the stories that matter. I haven't got time to be wasting on faff any more.'

'Why thank you, a cup of coffee would be lovely.'

'I like the shades.'

'They aren't even an affectation today. You really do not want to see the bunny-pink eyes under here.'

'I seem to be making a habit of helping locals with hangovers these days. There must be some sort of tag team in operation.' She tutted. 'I think it's disgusting the way young people have no respect for themselves any more.'

'Yes,' Colin agreed. 'But so much more fun than macramé.'

'Come in and tell me everything. I'm a bit behind on details.'

Vida was perky. She gave Lucy another smile, which congealed her blood as effectively as the last one had managed to do. If she hadn't been such an ogre Lucy would not have singled out hers beyond all the other smiles on display that day. Put simply, Vida was not one of life's laughers so any scrunching of her face into a rictus of happiness was enough to curdle cement. She was in her usual widow's weeds, which added to the witchery. Lucy tried to ignore her as she shucked into her work uniform but it was clear that Vida had her directly in her beady sights. She appeared to be mixing a potion and Lucy's radar warned that this concoction could only be on course for her. She leapt on an opening to chat to Mario when he remarked that she looked a lot more chipper today.

'Yes, I do feel much better, thanks.'

'You like my lingo?'

'Oh, chipper, yes, very good.'

'Soon you will be even more. Vida is making her special recipe. Very good thing. When Maria has been pregnant it is all she can have. No tea, no coffee, just what Vida makes.'

Vida took time out to curl her lips again. She only lacked a pointy hat.

'I'm not sure I have room for anything because I had a huge breakfast,' Lucy stuttered. Her stomach gave a loud rumble to announce the lie. She had room, all right, and there was no stopping the Slovenian Sorcerer.

'She's been talking about this since she got in,' Danny offered with a sympathetic grimace. Manfully he tried to distract Lucy's attention from the crone and her hubble-bubble. 'How did the viewing go at the gallery?'

'Great,' she answered distractedly. 'What's in it?' she asked, nodding towards the mug of steaming threat.

'Secret,' Vida growled. 'But very, very good for the woman.'

'Great. You can join me in a cup,' Lucy said.

'Not me, you.' Vida's finger was like a spear and probably as dangerous. She grabbed the mug and thrust it at Lucy. 'Drink.' This was not a suggestion.

It was a grey-green liquid with black specks. Lucy sniffed at the gloop to prepare her taste buds. Bad idea. It smelled like creosote. When she had her first sip she realised it tasted like creosote too, with hints of ear wax, tarmacadam and mud.

'Good, huh?' Vida snarled.

'Mmn.' Lucy was actually unable to speak. She swallowed quickly and expected to welcome the vile potion back to the world immediately. Weirdly, her body hung on to it. Vida loomed over her, blocking escape. She couldn't face doing this slowly so she blew hard on the mixture a few times, took a deep breath and knocked the lot back in one go.

'Well done,' Danny said. Vida whipped round and nailed him with a glare. 'Vida. Well done, Vida. A tonic is just what she needs.' He fled back to the front counter.

Lucy sat, waiting for the inevitable hurl. It never came. Instead, she began to feel fantastic. She tried not to show this but Vida stabbed at her chest saying, 'Vida know. Vida know.'

Lucy couldn't let this go on. 'I'm not pregnant,' she insisted.

'Vida know that.' She pointed at Lucy's head. 'In here it is not good. And in there.' Now she pointed to her heart. 'But you take Vida cure and you will be good again.' She

267

sized her up. 'Something different today. A man? But not your husband.'

Lucy gasped.

'Vida know.'

She bloody well does, Lucy thought. Vida knows.

The atmosphere at Jack's office was strained. Clara had taken a dim view of being left out of his plans for the previous evening. The grin on her boss's chops advertised a successful social encounter with someone else, a female: she knew him well enough by now to read the signs clearly. She had competition. She also had the ammunition to wipe the smile off and despatch it to the far side of the moon. So she did.

'Laura phoned and this time she left a number.'

On cue, the smile faded. Jack was aware of the gauntlet he was running today and decided to tackle the easier problem first. He listened to his wife's voicemail message. 'Phone me. We need to talk.' She was usually a woman of many words so his blood chilled a little to hear such brevity. The fewer the words, the greater the anger, the bigger the bill and so on until infinity. He felt his testicles shrink and waited for them to return to normality. They didn't, which he took as a weather dial for the day, so he set to and dialled the number his wife had so kindly furnished. He expected a rough ride, but at least it would be at a remove down a phone line.

The brooding presence of Clara at her desk was tangible and terrifying, even though she was strictly speaking in the next room. He would have liked to close the adjoining door but didn't dare approach her. It was madness that he didn't think twice about tackling bloodhound journalists who made money from ripping people into shreds but he quaked before these women. They knew him too well and where his faults were and he had lots of those. Cowardice was nudging into the Top Ten now. Perhaps it was time to swear off women altogether.

Jack steeled himself for the onslaught. Laura without endless dosh was a woman scorned nonpareil and he expected her to come out fighting and vicious. He had to remember that she was more desperate than he was at this stage.

'What the fuck do you think you're playing at?' she spat.

'I'm fine, thanks for asking. And you?'

'Jack, don't play your little mind games with me. I am not one of the mentally challenged twits you pen-push for. Where's the fucking money from the bank account gone?'

'How nice of you to worry about our finances,' he cooed. 'It's been a tough season as you know and I'm afraid I'm not the moneybags I was. Of course, that won't worry you unduly as I'm sure you are being well looked after by your new beau.'

He stanched a chuckle. Bet the poor sod had finally put a price on fucking Laura and realised he needed to be the controller general of the BBC to afford her.

She tried a new tack. 'Jack, please don't be like this. I have issues to work through and it will benefit us both when I've sorted them. Until then I need your support. Isn't that what marriage is all about?'

He was rendered speechless. The gall of the woman. The manipulation. It was breathtaking.

'I'll need a contact address for you, to forward whatever comes to the house for you, dear.'

She named a place in Hampstead. 'And what about my running-around money?' she asked.

Running-away money, more like. 'It really has been a shit month, so I can make no promises.'

'Do your best,' she oiled. 'That's always been good enough for me.'

She might as well have stabbed him with a blade and got it over with. He felt gutted by her manipulation and lies. He actively hated her at that moment, which shocked him. But it was her calculated betrayal that heightened this feeling and that was what hurt most of all.

'I'll see what I can do.'

He hung up, shaking and damp. Normally Clara would have been on hand with coffee or sympathy but she kept her head down and worked on, very deliberately oblivious to his plight. Bet I'll be looking for a new PA soon too, he thought. He picked up the phone a second time and called his solicitors. He asked them to begin divorce proceedings. He was not going to take this lying down any more. With that in mind he phoned the bank. He neglected to transfer any more funds to the Smith joint account. Instead he instructed that his personal account be debited for all bills relating to his private life from now on, the business being entirely separate. He thanked the stars that he had never made Laura a trustee of the firm or put her on his board of directors even though she had constantly angled for both. 'No,' he replied, when asked if he and Mrs Smith would be closing the joint account. 'It will remain open. And no, I do not wish to transfer any monies to it at this time.'

That was the simple bit of the day out of the way. He had yet to placate his PA. Even though he should have felt like an invincible after his action-man dealings with Laura, he was scared approaching Clara's desk. His buttocks clenched now, in perfect unison with his shrivelled balls.

'I think I may have been an ass,' he began.

NINETEEN

'The less you know about how I'm going to do this the better,' Colin warned. When he was sure he had their attention he continued. 'I used to shag a computer nerd who loved to show off his hacking skills and I picked up a thing or two, including crabs so we won't go there. At least not right now. Men!' He rolled his eyes. 'But I don't need to tell you that,' he said directly to Lucy. 'As we're using Helen's system she'll go to jail and not me.'

Helen threw him a withering look. 'I really don't think the police want to come bothering me ever again.'

They let that settle.

'While Colin is trawling cyberspace I'll compile a few more details,' Helen said. 'What did Pete tell you about his immediate family? Perhaps that's another way in.'

'His dad died when he was a kid and he was an only child, which was something we had in common. His mother remarried but it ended unhappily and I think he said she lives in a retirement village on the south coast, somewhere outside Hastings. I'm ashamed to say I never showed much interest in that side of his life. And he was always very reluctant to talk about it.'

Colin honked. 'I'll bet he was.'

Lucy felt like a traitor painting this picture of Pete. It also branded her an utter fool. 'I don't mean to suggest he's a complete villain,' she protested, but that sounded so pathetic she shut up again.

Colin wouldn't let it go. 'Of course not. After all, he's only gone and done a bunk with your entire life in cash in his pocket. He's a regular saint, is this Pete.'

Helen jumped in. 'Knock it off, Colin. This isn't easy for Lucy. I'm sure no one is more disappointed in the way things have turned out.'

'I'm sorry,' Lucy said. 'I know I'm not making much sense explaining it, partly because I can't believe it's happening and partly because the situation is too absurd. I feel an utter idiot.'

'Don't mind me,' Colin said. 'I'm hungover and anti-man, both of which I'll survive.'

Lucy blinked back tears. Suddenly she didn't want to know where Pete was. It should have been exciting to embark on the chase but instead she felt frightened and low. She wanted to start over with a clean sheet and ignore the nastiness of the past. But now the process had begun and she could not turn back.

Colin tapped away at the keyboard, muttering computer jargon and swearing. Then he gave a triumphant hoot. He turned to his rapt audience. 'I think we might be in business.'

Lucy's temperature plummeted and goosebumps rose on her arms. She wasn't ready for any of the revelations that lay within the machine's complex universe. It was difficult enough to deal with day-to-day life without the full disclosure of that truth.

Helen noted her panic and came to the rescue. 'Look it over and reduce it to laywomen's language, then we'll see what we've got.' This would give Lucy the breather she needed to compose herself.

It's only money, Lucy wanted to scream. Let him have it. She couldn't do that, of course. She would never regain her pride if she let it go so easily. She would lose the respect of everyone who knew her. She had to face up to reality. There was no other option, unfortunately.

She looked up from her thoughts to see Helen in the garden taking some time out. She arched her eyebrows at Colin.

He kept his voice low. 'I think she gets overwhelmed all the time about the boys. It's to be expected. She knows we're here if she needs us.'

Helen waved from the garden. 'Carry on. I'll be back in, in a moment.' She stood caressing the bark of the tree and collecting herself.

I have got to pull myself together, Lucy thought. My behaviour is plain ridiculous compared with what that woman has endured.

Colin was humming and hawing. 'How much of a creature of habit would you say Pete is?' he asked.

'Hard to say,' Lucy admitted ruefully. 'I base that on

the fact that he has a huge habit, gambling, and I never knew anything about that.'

'I hear you. But, say, shopping or having a choccie biccie at a certain time every day, that sort of thing?'

'Nothing that I can think of. Why?'

'Well, I've got into his credit card account, which is beginner's stuff really. The new bank account will take longer to locate but I'm owed a few favours. Anyhow, it seems your Peter may be doing a weekly shop in a Sainsbury's in Ramsgate. To me that means he's holing up somewhere vaguely remote and coming into town on a Saturday to stock up. Last two weekends he's used his card in the same supermarket. In Ramsgate.'

Helen returned and stood looking over Colin's shoulder at the screen. 'Interesting,' she murmured.

Lucy's head was in a whirl and she couldn't think straight. How should they proceed?

'Tomorrow's Saturday. If it happens again, we can assume it's a pattern,' Helen said.

'Yes. If he appears on our radar tomorrow, we'll know where to go looking for him next week.' Colin stretched. 'I'd love a trip to the seaside. London is beginning to wear, frankly, what with this endless heat and all of the shit hitting my fan. I need a break complete with fish'n'chips, ice cream and slot machines.' He grinned at Lucy. 'So, shall we?'

Lucy had gone a pucey shade of grey. She thought she might hoy.

'Well, I must say there's no need to show such disappointment. I may not be your ideal date, dear, but I am wonderful so you should thank your guardian angel that I'm willing to be seen in public with you, let alone engage my tremendous intellect in your life.'

'It's not that, Colin. You are great.'

He smiled and nodded in acceptance.

'I just realised that if Pete has all of the apartment sale money he may be gambling that away. Supposing he paid off whatever dodgy debts he had, he'd surely still have something left and maybe he'd try to pad it back out by trying his luck again.'

'And he's not a very successful gambler by all accounts,' Helen said.

'I'll consult my little black book and get someone to find his new bank account. My computer skills are only borderline nerd compared with some of the geeks I've encountered. We'll see if we can block the account somehow and stall him frittering the money away.'

'It's probably time to get a lawyer, Lucy.'

Colin was right. Helen was right. She could leave this alone no longer. But the details were getting bigger and almost impossible to take on board.

'I'll probably need a kiss-me-quick hat for our trip to Ramsgate next week,' Colin mused.

The vision of accosting her husband with Colin at her side in such a hat was too much for Lucy. She became hysterical.

'I get the feeling I don't have much choice in this,' she managed between heaves of laughter and eye wiping.

'None. I'm off to locate a cyber-punk and start packing.

Planning is everything.' A new thought struck him. 'You can't go on living in that car.'

'Actually, one of your neighbours, Jack Smith, has kindly offered to rent me his spare room.'

Colin held up the index fingers of both hands. 'Whoa there,' he commanded. 'Rewind,' he said, pointing them now like twin guns. 'Jack Smith and you?'

Even Helen perked to that news.

'It's just a temporary measure until I get back on my feet and can rent a flat.'

'Sure, sugar. And I'm Pope Benedict the Sixteenth.'

'It's not what you think.'

'Honey, it's always what I think.' Colin breezed out, cackling with pleasure at being the purveyor of the toppest gossip available that day. He made a note to skive off work more often, at least a day every month if these were the sort of nuggets he could expect to unearth. It certainly served as a distraction from his own annoyances. Stella would be upon him soon so he needed to phone a friend on the bank account problem, freshen up and get his brightest face ready. He was determined to chivvy his way out of his personal quagmire and return better than ever before. There was never any choice between sink and swim.

'Does he really have a little black book?' Lucy asked.

'Oh yes.'

Famke was pleased with what she saw. She had laid out the series as if she had entered the cul-de-sac from the road and so it had a narrative of its own. Some images were repetitive, underlining nature's attempt to reclaim its space, others showed sections of the women's impact on the area. This portion was finished for the moment, she felt. She needed to feature the women as themselves now. She had plenty of studies of Helen to be working with, but needed to capture Lucy. She decided to ask her to pose. With that in mind she found her way over to number 7 where her subjects were having a glass of lemonade and sitting in companionable silence.

Helen looked drained and Famke said so.

'It's tiring to be back in the thick of things. I'm unaccustomed to all this activity. I might take a nap.'

'I should be going,' Lucy said, taking her cue.

She walked Famke out through the garden gate. As they left she saw that Helen was climbing the rope ladder. She must commune with her kids up there, she decided. She could not even begin to imagine the woman's inner torture. It made everything else seem so silly. But not every hurt was as great and even though her jilting by Pete was of far less consequence, it hurt too and to get over it she had to make him atone for his actions. He also owed her a lot of money and as horrible as it would be to pursue him for it, and to confront him again, it had to be done. She could never move on if she had no self-respect and she wouldn't have any if she let this go. She copper-fastened her resolve.

'I wondered if you'd be free to model for me tomorrow?' Famke asked, interrupting her thoughts.

Lucy ran the unexpected words through her head. Had she heard the request properly? She could not formulate an answer that made sense and heard her voice utter a sound like 'parn?' which Famke took to be bemusement.

She repeated herself. 'Would you pose for me tomorrow?'

'Oh yes, fine. Great, actually. The café where I work is closed at the weekend so I'm free. What time would be good for you?' Now she had verbal diarrhoea. She was mortified. I used to be able to talk to people with a modicum of sense and confidence, she thought.

'Perhaps mid-morning? Another thing is that you should take our box room. It was ridiculous of me not to have offered it before.' Her inner bitch teased her. You're just saying that now because you don't need to have her live in the car any more, you can work on what you have and what you'll get from the new sessions.

'Actually, I'm fixed up on that front,' Lucy explained, reddening. 'As I told Colin, Jack Smith is renting me his spare room.'

'Jack as knight in shining armour,' Famke crowed. 'How very philanthropic of him. I trust the payment is in cash rather than kind?'

Lucy's mouth made shapes but this time no sound emerged.

'You don't have to answer that,' Famke said. 'I couldn't resist a tease. And I am also unbearably snoopy.'

Lucy remembered Jack's confession of a dalliance with the artist and wanted the ground to swallow her. She was useless at negotiating the minefield of other people's relationships. She couldn't even manage her own.

'Relax and enjoy yourself, Lucy,' Famke advised, seeing her discomfort. 'You'll live longer and it'll be far more fun, which I reckon you deserve at the moment. Come in and have a glass of wine and we'll interview Colin's workmate Stella when she arrives. He's been hiding her for ages.'

Laura's first affair had dealt Jack a devastating blow. They had been married just short of two years when he found out she'd been sleeping with a guitarist. At the time he had taken on far too much professionally but found it difficult to turn down the work and resultant money. He was buzzing with success and heedless of his wife, according to her. In the end she was the one who spelled it out for him. He had been crippled by the hurt. They went through the full and awful disclosure of her infidelity and Jack thought he might never recover from the pain. She spared him none of the details. He was tortured by vivid imaginings of their intercourse and there, too, Laura managed to supply details, even when he begged her not to. Honesty was her policy, she said. She was deliberately cruel but he was too in love to see that. It took him months to recognise that the other man was a prig and not worthy of second thoughts and that Laura got off on taunting him. He assumed the matter was all his fault, that his neglect had been the primary cause of the aberration, and Laura did nothing to assuage his sense of responsibility.

Second time out he realised that when she told him about her extramarital activities it was to rid herself of the other man and to involve him in the fallout, sharing the blame and causing maximum domestic drama. The second chosen was an interior designer who had revamped two rooms in the house. They had to be redone immediately after Laura's revelations and so this time the money involved doubled. He dealt better with the second affair than the first, outwardly. But it hurt him more. He genuinely thought he'd never have to go through this again. They had saved their marriage early on and nothing could chink their armour again. They had emerged stronger, better, more in love, or so he had believed.

He acquired a palpable two-tiered ache measured in his wife's name: Lau-ra, Lau-ra. This became the in and out of every breath. It astonished him that he could hurt so much. This time he made scenes of their rows and forsook the gentle understanding he had previously shown. Laura didn't enjoy that. She didn't believe in allotting blame, she said. It was a waste of time and as good as crying over spilt milk. Jack could see plenty of reasons why a person might cry over that sort of waste. Shit happened, she said, and they had to deal with it. Together. This time he wasn't so easily pushed into believing it was his fault and he wanted her to know how hurt he was. Most devastating of all was that he never found her more beautiful than the times when he nearly lost her, or thought he would.

Slyly she suggested that he have an affair too, just to even up the stakes. It would be a holistic approach, she felt. He was agog at the notion. Nothing could have been further from his mind. In fact, he felt obliged to mention that he'd really have preferred it if she had never strayed. Then they wouldn't have to sit through such rubbish. Although he didn't settle back into the role of the passive understanding husband this time, he managed to find forgiveness for her again. He was grateful she hadn't abandoned him. His ego was nothing compared with the need to succeed at his marriage. He wanted it to work. She lashed him regularly with this during arguments.

'Jack,' she would begin, investing his name with scorn. 'Your idea of old-fashioned decency is nothing but sentimentalism. You just don't want to deal with life: proper, dirty, awful, inconvenient life.'

She made him feel so small. Now he knew it was because she had no respect for him, but at the time he was too blinded by panic and affection to see it. He couldn't understand why he was not enough for her. Still somewhere in the dynamic he was lacking. He needed to find out how and why and to remedy this. When she finally left, it was obvious that he had not.

Third strike and you're out, was his rule and he had to obey it now. He needed to run this divorce like one of his public relations campaigns, with thorough ruthlessness and charm. But when he had spoken to Laura earlier, her voice in his ear, imagining her breath on his face, to his embarrassment and shame he had stiffened with desire.

*　　*　　*

The relaunch of Brand Colin took place in the back garden.
A table was laid with wine and snacks and the main man
sat surrounded by what he referred to as 'his bitches'. He
introduced 'Stella for Star'.

'That's from a Tennessee Williams play, isn't it?' Lucy
checked.

'Well done, yes. It's *A Streetcar Named Desire*. One of
my favourites.'

'You love the theatre, then?'

'Who doesn't, *ma chérie*?'

'I wish I got to more shows but I've been very lax,' Lucy
admitted. 'What have you seen recently?'

Stella began to laugh.

'Nothing.'

'But I thought . . .'

Stella leapt in to explain. 'The thing is, Colin loves the
theatre but he's so afraid of seeing something that will put
him off that he's stopped going altogether.'

'Who could blame me? The last thing I tried was in a
wee room above a local pub because it was called *Willie's
Paradise*. I thought it would either be about Shakespeare
or pornography but, to my considerable chagrin, it was
neither. Just some experimental shite where everyone kept
their clothes on. Very dispiriting. And although the place
was minging I didn't catch anything either. I felt like asking
for my fiver back.'

'You got in on a discount?' Famke asked.

'Disability,' he grinned, impishly. 'They didn't ask what
'cos they were too embarrassed, but if they had I was going

to tout my gayness, it being unnatural and a sickness according to the Reverends back home.'

'Apropos of which, I was worried about you today,' Stella admonished.

'Darling, I was worried about myself,' Colin reported. 'I have rarely known pain like it, which for me is something to report. How and ever I am returned good as new, and intend to begin again with a tabula rasa.'

They raised their glasses in a toast to the same.

'Ah, the Good Samaritan returns,' Colin announced as Jack put his head around the gate to check on the noise.

'Why do I feel like I'm going to regret having just done that?' he said to the company.

He took in the gathering. The newest recruit was a handsome black woman in a sharp suit and sparkling blouse. This was Stella, he was told as a glass of wine was thrust into his hand and he was thrust into a beanbag at Colin's feet.

His would-be tormentor purred. 'At last I have you just where I want you. Well, not *exactly* where I'd like you but the evening is young and I am reborn.'

'Lucky old me,' Jack muttered drily.

'You think I'm bad? You should meet some of the carpet munchers that are always hitting on Stella. They are so aggressive. They really cannot take no for an answer.'

'Colin has a morbid fear of lesbians,' Stella explained.

'Who wouldn't?' he squealed, horror writ large on his face.

Jack was a little shocked by Ulrika. She looked haggard.

He asked gently if she was feeling all right, saying she seemed pale and quiet. She blamed a hellish week at school and everyone grunted their understanding.

The exchange was inoffensive in itself but it made Ulrika nervous. She thought everyone had dismissed her as a crackpot. But then she always opted for that. She wanted to exude the confidence of Colin's friend Stella. He was giving her potted history to the assembled milieu. According to him, Stella had been born on the wrong side of the tracks in Brixton, an area which was traditionally the wrong side anyway. He said her family was related to most of the bad asses shooting people, or shooting up, or shooting straight off on Her Majesty's pleasure. Their family unit fled southward to Tooting where she got a good education at Graveney, smartened up with further training in IT and now lived as far away from the Brothers as she could manage, in this case Stoke Newington. That was the sort of reinvention Ulrika found inspiring. She also felt a little queasy wondering what Colin would say if asked to describe her to strangers.

Stella was also a big girl. She had the lush curves and high bottom of all the women in her family, she said, and she seemed proud of that. Pity that look didn't suit Ulrika. Her Nordic genes demanded thinness. She felt terrible but kept that to herself, putting it down to too much wine on an empty stomach. It meant that she contributed little to the conversation and this highlighted her worthlessness, in forensic detail, to her own mind. She thought, I am not interesting. I am that horrible combination of dull and dieting. She felt weak, on all fronts. She nibbled on some hummus and pitta bread and sank further into her back seat. She was hovering around the event, rather than participating in any meaningful way. She wasn't even enjoying it. Normally she loved their house fun, and was content to watch from the sidelines. This was odd, unsettling, unpleasant, but tomorrow was Saturday and a chance to recover. She only needed to find her comfort zone, then she would be renewed.

Lucy on the other hand was lost in happiness. She looked around in wonder at what had happened to her. She had been welcomed by these strangers. They were caring for her. They expected nothing in return. She was overwhelmed with gratitude. Please don't let this turn out to be false, she prayed. I want this to be real and lasting. I might have new friends here and a chance to begin again.

Behind their fence Bill and Helen sat listening to the laughter and chat. It was enjoyable and without effort. There was no need to join the fray and they were content to be in their own little world, separate but in touch. Then there was a collective intake of breath from the other garden and a man's voice said, 'I've called off the wedding. Could I please have a very large glass of strong alcohol?'

TWENTY

They've all met now, Colin reflected. The only missing element of total flux within the categories was his family and he still planned to keep them out of the equation, until his funeral, at which time he would make them listen to his favourite tunes and they would be powerless to advise him on same or do anything about it. Ah well, it had been an interesting experiment while it lasted and probably of anthropological interest, if only that was his field.

He had to hand it to Tony, he really didn't think he'd have the courage to cancel the wedding. He hadn't talked in terms of postponement, it was off. Strangely, Colin didn't hope for anything beyond that. He had mulled over his talk with Famke and realised that Tony stood for something in his life. He was a lovely man and Colin enjoyed his company and presence but there was a lot in the notion that he, Colin, was searching for someone to share his life with. Tony was in the spotlight, but he might not be the one. This had been the reason he banished him to the box room last night. Falling out of one bed and into another was no way to solve a major life problem, he announced loudly at the end of the drunken salon he had hosted. That applied to more than one couple in the room at the time. Lucy and Jack had things to work through too and they looked suitably affected by his decree. He was pleased with his mature take on the situation and glad that he was drunk enough not to care who, if anyone, was in his bed that night.

He was also thrilled that he didn't have the Premiership level hangover he had experienced the day before. Famke had made everyone drink two pints of water before retiring and she was now officially the patron saint of Vauxhall. There was a weariness to his edges and he'd have liked more sleep but when it was clear it would not be forthcoming he hopped out of bed and began the day. The nerd he'd contacted to locate Pete Kingston's bank account had texted to say the details were in the postbox of number 5. He'd probably put them there in the dead of night. This was the sort of subterfuge those geeks loved, Colin mused. He went to collect the data and sat reading it over a weak coffee.

Pete hadn't yet touched the money, which said to Colin that he was hiding out on the thugs he owed. This was dangerous practice. He needed to clear his debts or he'd end up maimed or dead. Colin's friendly computer gnome had put a stop on the account which would last a few days if it was noticed at all, and it might not be if Pete was lying low. Colin checked the time. It was 7.10 a.m., so way too early for their quarry's shopping trip. He rose to go shower and met Tony on his way out.

'Off to work?' Colin asked.

'Yes. I think I'd better maintain some sort of ordinary activity. And earn a living.'

'That's the spirit. It's good to keep busy.'

'Yes. Though it does make me a handy target for my fiancée and her family. I'm expecting cruel and unusual punishments.'

'Only to be expected from mere human beings. I know I'd be spitting with rage and vengeance.'

They both grimaced at their own mental images of spitting and revenge.

'Thanks to you all for being so understanding last night.'

'No problem, that's what we're here for.'

'So, we can still be friends?'

'We are friends. Let's keep things platonic until you've sorted yourself out.'

'Which could take forever.'

'Granted. Or until her family snuff you out. But it will be worth it in the end. You can't stagger wildly from one crisis to another. You'd never figure anything out that way.' He stopped short of adding, 'Ooh, get me, the Sage!'

They hugged and Colin watched Tony's back disappear through the gate. He gave a small whoop that he had been so strong and wise. I'll never last at this lark, he thought, it's way too grown-up.

Lucy examined Jack's hands. 'Do you have regular manicures?' she asked.

'Yes, actually I do.'

'Pedicures?'

'Yep.' He lifted a foot to show off the work.

'I like that in a man,' Lucy commented. 'It's just gay enough.'

'That's me, all right. You should see some of my shirts.'

'I used to go in for all that too: the manicures, leg waxes, hair highlights. Then I became homeless and poor and I had to restructure things a bit. The resources weren't there for general spoiling of the body.'

'You look in good nick to me,' Jack said, truthfully.

'Many thanks, kind sir. It's good to be indoors again and to think of such vanities. Even vacuum cleaning seems possible again.'

'Though hardly desirable.'

They lay lounging on the bed of the spare room. They had returned from Famke's and said their goodnights, Colin's words still resounding for both of them. They had lasted twenty minutes apart and met on the landing, each going to the other's room. They opted for Lucy's because there was still a lot of Laura in the master bedroom.

'I guess we're both adulterers,' Lucy mused.

'Yes, though under the best possible circumstances for that particular activity, don't you think?'

'Yes. If it has to happen this is probably the only acceptable version of it.

'I'll be looking for a place of my own from Monday,' Lucy told Jack.

'Fine. You don't have to, you have an open invitation to stay here, but fine, I understand.'

'Thank you for taking me in.'

'The pleasure is all mine.'

Lucy climbed on top of him. 'Not quite all.'

Bill hosed down the garden before the sun got too hot and scorching. He could almost hear the ground slurp the water in gratefully. Helen sat in the tree house looking down the cul-de-sac onto the road. 'You missed a bit,' she'd call down every so often. He felt like bursting with happiness that they were reunited. And the news of a new life was so fabulously unbelievable that he sometimes pinched himself to make sure he wasn't dreaming. He pottered for an hour then made tea and they sat to savour the silence and their new order. Bill's eye fell on the trug he had taken from the shed. Small tools stuck out at angles, a roll of twine and some packets of seeds. He knew one of them held sunflower seeds. He had planned to grow them with the boys. His throat constricted as he remembered his darlings. Sorrow would walk beside them every day of their lives. He reached out and held Helen's hand.

She squeezed it gently. 'It doesn't get easier, does it? It simply changes.'

She watched some dandelion seeds floating in the air. She remembered a windy day at the end of April when the cherry trees from the front square surrendered their blossoms and they fell from the heavens onto the cul-de-sac like pink snowflakes. Helen had found it utterly beautiful, and pointless. She thought that beauty had no place any more and no function in her life. She would never again know it. But here and now with a stirring life inside her she felt a tiny inkling that it might again mean something.

Lucy headed over to Famke's studio. She was looking forward to sitting for the artist, flattered to be asked. She wore a simple cotton dress and flip-flops. She had buffed her body with a little extra care today. There was the joy of having a bathroom to oneself to do this, so she had shaved off the excess underarm hair, trimmed nails and painted them, sloughed off dried ankle flakes and exfoliated the pallid sluggishness of leg and upper arms. At the back of her mind she also wondered if she would be asked to pose nude. The answer was no.

'Although that would be very lovely I don't think it would suit the series. But can I hold it as an option?'

'Sure.' Lucy was in fact relieved but glad that she had offered. It occurred to her that her body might bear the telltale marks of a fulfilled sex life and it was desirable to save those details for the two people involved in that activity. She settled into the seat Famke had arranged for her.

'Get comfy, close your eyes, whatever. Don't worry if you have to shift about. I don't expect rigidity.'

At first she worried that she would never get comfortable. Her butt ached, then her leg went to sleep and reawakened with pins and needles. She shifted and squirmed. She didn't know where to look and eventually did close her eyes. The studio's roof windows were open and she could hear birds singing and the distant sound of a lawnmower. She was surprised by how relaxed she became. Her mind wandered, flitting from subject to subject. She pictured details from work like Danny being solicitous and Vida mixing her potion. It made her smile. She had a vision of her mum painting the walls of the gallery many years ago, her face covered in white freckles of emulsion. She thought of making love to a new man. She remembered the pleasure he gave her with his hands, his tongue darting in and out of and on her and her reciprocation: she was no slouch in returning the sexual favours. She heard his whispers and urgings, willing them both on. She stretched again, picturing the night-time and morning scenes, all merging now before her closed eyes. What she could not see was Famke's delight at the many different expressions she was making with her face. As she thought about Jack, leaning back with a smile of satisfied languor across her features, Famke deftly captured the attitude like a thief stealing a couple's most private moment.

Ulrika lay on her bed willing her heart to stop pounding. It seemed to be racing out of control in her chest. Surely it was beating too fast? Even drinking too much caffeine didn't give her this strong a reaction. It felt like a coronary, or what she imagined that might be like. She didn't like this feeling that her heart was out of control. Her chest palpitated wildly. She held up a hand and it shook. She tried the other. Same deal. Her blood whooshed through her veins like a flood in maddened flow. It echoed in her ears and thumped behind her eyes. She could see the little veins in her eyeballs in relief against the light. They throbbed dark and bright to the powerful rhythm. She would need to drink a bath of camomile tea to achieve calm. It was obvious that alcohol was having a negative effect on her body. It stripped it of vitamins and as she got thinner she needed more ballast in that line. She would increase her dose of multivitamins.

She decided to have a shower and a light breakfast then sequester in a comfy deckchair to read a book. She could work on relaxing: that's what weekends were invented for, after all. She would only need to endure these strangenesses for a short time more. When she was slim everything would slot into place effortlessly and she would feel just great. She didn't like how she felt right now but it was nothing compared with the self-loathing she experienced when she looked in the mirror. She hated her lumps and bumps.

She showered and dressed, ate some fruit with low-fat yoghurt and had a herbal tea. She still felt hungry so she popped a magic diet pill. She was due one anyhow. All of her limbs were now experiencing a version of St Vitus's dance. This would pass once she was settled. She placed a chair in some shade and sat sweating gently into the foam cushion. She felt a little afraid. At least the chair hadn't groaned when she sat into it, as it usually did. What was a little palsied discomfort compared with the figure she'd always dreamed of? She craved intimacy, tenderness. She wished she had a boyfriend.

◦　◦　◦

Lucy walked off any stiffness during a break. She wandered around the studio, admiring the pieces drying, some finished, some waiting to be completed. She was not allowed to look at any of the pictures Famke was making of her in case it made either of them self-conscious. Tucked behind a drape she found a tiny oil, very abstract and in a naif style. She picked it up and looked at it from a few angles.

'Not mine,' Famke admitted. 'I'd love to hang it on the wall but it reminds me of the artist, who is dead, and also it's so effortlessly good it makes me feel inadequate, which is unhelpful when grappling with a new series. I'll put it back up soon.'

'Only a child or a genius could handle orange like that,' Lucy offered. 'Who did it? I must admit I don't recognise the artist.'

'That was painted by a lovely little boy, called Stephen; Helen's elder son. I'm not sure whether she or Bill know it exists, or remember that it does after all that's happened to them.'

'I don't think I'd be able to survive that sort of tragedy.'

'That's the cruel thing about life: people do. Helen tried her best to fade away but this world would not let her go. There were days out there when I felt like taking a shotgun to her to help her on her way. You could practically taste her pain. Then you came along.'

'What did I do?' Lucy was genuinely taken aback.

'I don't know, exactly. It's like you annoyed her back into human congress.'

'I suppose it's a good quid pro quo, seeing as I'm getting

such help from everyone now. Helen was the one who suggested going after Pete. I wouldn't have known where to start.'

'She's fundamentally a very sensible person with a great sense of fair play. She and Bill are perfectly matched like that. Which is why you'd wonder why the cosmic scheme of things was so pissed off with them. They are good people, yet they were chosen.'

'Perhaps only the best are tested like that.'

'And I have come up trumps, my creatures, because I am the Best.' Colin stood in the doorway wearing his best Cheshire Cat. 'We are off to Ramsgate next Saturday. We have a husband to catch.'

'He went to the supermarket again?'

'Yes. It's almost boring now to be able to predict the movements of this stranger I know so well.'

Lucy sat to digest the news. She felt dread rather than the elated expectation she should have experienced at the prospect of retribution. They were closing in on the man who had left her in no uncertain lurch, but she didn't want to confront that or him. She had to find focus somewhere, grit to gird her shaky spine.

'Should I get a kiss-me-quick hat for the provinces?' Colin was wondering afresh.

'You've never needed one before,' Famke said.

Colin conceded the point. 'True. Superfluous detail. I'm fab as is and those pork pie thingies are shite anyway. I do want to blend though, as we'll be undercover. And I won't necessarily be on the pull.'

Lucy didn't feel comfortable with her future being discussed like this. Her marriage was about to implode, entirely, with a showdown in a car park, and Colin was worried about a fucking hat. She took a deep breath. She needed to maintain a sense of humour along with her perspective and Colin was going out of his way to help so she should be grateful. It was not his fault that she was running scared. If anything, he was diffusing the crap attached to this whole dung heap. None of these new people had made any judgement of her based on the fact that she had let this happen. None attached her any blame. There was no shame here and no reason to let her pride sour the help they were giving. Things were improving. She could snatch back some face, and a modicum of victory, and get on with her life. But what was that going to involve? What did the grand plan that was her life now amount to? She was a single woman again, grappling with all of the usual struggles, no better off than when she had started on her adult path. That was the hole in the doughnut. Time to look at the outer rim: perhaps things were just no worse.

Colin admired the paintings. 'Who are they for? What gallery are you going to?'

Famke smiled enigmatically. 'I'm quite glad you asked that.'

Colin's eyes narrowed suspiciously. Had he turned feed unknowingly? Was he being manipulated?

She turned to Lucy. 'I had thought that the White Rooms would be perfect, if Evie and Lucy would have me.'

Lucy's lower lip hit the deck. The idea was too outrageous, too magnificent to be true. She tried to speak but uttered only a squeak. Her legs buckled. She felt perspiration grow along her upper lip and more flow along her back. A smell a lot like fear emanated from her armpits.

'You know, I've never actually seen a person go that particular shade of puce before,' Colin remarked as he began to fan her with a magazine.

Lucy was aware that she looked like a yellow guppy fish taking air.

'I'm so sorry,' she croaked. 'That's probably the last suggestion I expected today, or any other day for that matter. Are you sure you mean it?'

'Yes.' Famke smiled at Lucy's perplexity.

'This is just so . . . big for us.' She tried to add it up in her brain but looked even more lost. 'We'd bite your hand off for this exhibition.'

'No need to go that far,' Colin observed, squeezing his face into doubt at the efficacy of the whole hand-biting plan.

'Colin's right,' Famke pointed out.

'We would be honoured,' Lucy said, tears in her eyes. Then she began to bawl.

'Now look what you've done,' Colin said to Famke, shaking his head.

She shrugged. 'Shit happens.'

Ulrika was raving now but enjoying it. Her brain had shrunk within her skull and occasionally darted out to touch the bone with its pounding fleshy mass. It was having a party to its own Garage beat, or House, or Jungle. She was levitating, even though she could feel the edge of the chair pinch the back of her thighs. She watched herself from a distance as she laughed at that last image of cephalic gyrations. Her soul had escaped her body. The corporeal Ulrika was feverish beneath a large ceanothus, its fuzzy blue flowers set against deep glossy leaves which shone like her skin. Her breath was a rasp, dry and parched. She tried to rouse her unconscious self to drink some water but that Ulrika was dreaming of sashaying along college corridors naked and proud of her new form. I was the fat chrysalis, now I am the beautiful butterfly. She was all of the drawings displayed on the wall, so objectionable to the cleaner, so pleasing to Ulrika. I am the nude, I am the model body; I have fashioned myself into art. Her happiness sparked merrily in her brain, synapses sending out electric lights to celebrate her achievement, like fireworks illuminating the sky. And then there was nothing. The display had ended. The sky was black.

She was out.

Gone.

TWENTY-ONE

At first no one noticed that Ulrika was unconscious. They thought she was sleeping off her vile week, taking advantage of the day and its manifold pleasures, bathed as it was yet again in bright sunshine. Famke, on her way to the kitchen, remarked that she would burn up if she didn't drink some water. Ulrika looked flushed, a film of sweat glistening on her pale, blotched skin. Famke tugged on her arm to rouse her and realised that something was wrong. She and Colin dabbed her face and neck with ice cubes, then threw a litre over her but to no perceivable change. They called an ambulance and Ulrika was taken away for treatment. Colin travelled with her while Famke searched her room, certain now that her housemate's condition was no accident but a result of stupidity and desperation. She found the baggy with one tablet remaining under the mattress. She rang the hospital to describe it for the doctor and then went over there with it. Everything happened in a haze of disbelief and slow motion, like watching a film at a slightly skewed speed.

'Amphetamines?' Colin choked, unable to compute the idea. 'Ulrika on speed? But she's the squarest person alive.'

'She's also a person who'd do anything to be skinny.'

'Well, she's succeeded. There's hardly anything of her left.'

It was not a matter of pumping her stomach, the doctor explained. She hadn't exactly overdosed; it was more that her system, battered by dieting and the drug, had simply cut out. She was horribly undernourished, which was a major concern, and dehydrated from her spell in the sun, but that was more easily remedied. He spouted the buzz words of her condition: low self-esteem, bulimia, substance abuse, dependence. Now she needed nutrition, rehabilitation and on and on. Ulrika was reduced to a statistic and a type but at least medically there was hope that she was going to survive.

'We have been so lax,' Famke said.

Colin was having none of that. He was livid. 'The silly bitch. She's a grown-up and we are not her keepers. She knew what she was about and we are not to blame.'

'We should have helped her more.'

'By doing what? Dieting for her? Or, as we now know, scoring speed? I don't think so. And we have tried all along to make her feel better about herself but she refuses to listen. There's fuck all you can do in the face of that.'

Neither of them was totally convinced by his argument. Both were stinging with guilt. One of their tiny family unit was lying in peril close by and there was nothing they could do to help 'except not tell her parents', as Colin realised and voiced.

Famke pictured the girl who had first moved in, a hippy chick she'd met after a talk she felt obliged to give to the foundation year art students at Ulrika's college. It was her version of 'giving something back', and perhaps to show the despairing that there was an artistic life after tuition had ended or ceased to matter. Afterwards, the relevant teachers had led her to an airless, communal staffroom for warm white wine and sweaty cheese on crackers. The bright spark was Ulrika, new to her job and still marking papers after hours. She needed a room, Famke had space for a tenant and so it came to pass. There were other adventures they shared, including a brief, but ultimately ill-judged, affair. Neither was gay, both enjoyed the dalliance but Famke was a spirit unable to settle, afraid of losing total control over all aspects of her life. This stopped her from any romantic commitment to anybody, so 'nothing personal' as she liked to say. Ulrika accepted this and in truth had been experimenting even more than Famke, who had taken women to her bed before and would again. The relationship realigned to a genuine friendship between ex lovers, and was a happy state for both. Colin's arrival skewed the house politics and after a period of volatility, when everyone wondered if they even liked the others they shared with, they settled again into a louder and giddier routine than before. When had they lost sight of Ulrika? At what point might they have stepped in and prevented her from trying to erase her body, and therefore presence, from the life of the house? Why had they not told her more that her self-styled spongy bits were truly beautiful and to be celebrated? The dieting had started so ordinarily that they missed the insidious routine of starvation that emerged. But was that any excuse? Oops, I never noticed?

Suddenly Colin hopped to his feet.

'Where do you think you're going?'

'Thought I might ask that doctor a few more questions.'

'Colin, you are not to hit on Ulrika's physician.'

'I'm not. Well, not unless it's very clearly going that way.'

'We're here to support our friend, not to hinder her recovery by messing with the medics.'

Colin was exasperated. 'It's my way of dealing with this crisis. And really, Famke, you know better than to tell me what to do. I react very badly to that sort of thing.'

'The last medical type you brought back was a complete disaster; the nurse with the Oedipal complex.'

'He didn't look so good in that nightie, did he?'

'It belonged to Ulrika's dead grandmother. I'm not sure she ever got over the shock.'

Colin sat, semi-defeated. He sighed. 'It would be nice to have someone with a little medical experience about the place,' he commented. 'None of us is getting any younger.'

'You are,' Famke retorted. 'Mentally.'

Colin fidgeted, flicked through old copies of *Take A Break*, fidgeted some more.

'Oh, go on then, but lay off if he's not interested. Not everyone can be a conquest.'

He scampered down the corridor whistling, which Famke hoped wasn't bad luck in a hospital.

Lucy thought the news of the exhibition too important to impart on the phone so she hightailed it to the gallery. And her tail was up with sheer joy. It was time to shut up shop for the day and Lucy intended to bring Evie to a trendy wine bar. Her mother was subdued so she didn't plunge straight in. Instead she asked what the matter was.

'Bartok's left with Phillipa Douglas.'

'God,' Lucy exclaimed. 'She's . . .' She struggled for adequate words to describe the frightful creature that was Phillipa Douglas.

'Extremely rich,' Evie supplied.

'And extremely stingy,' Lucy remembered.

Evie issued a wan smile. 'It's the one thing keeping me going. He has no idea how tight she is.'

'I know you don't want to hear this now but I didn't think he was your best specimen to date.'

'No, but he made me feel less ancient. You know how I hate getting old.'

'Mum, you look fantastic.'

They both hated that the phrase 'for your age' haunted those words.

'Have you any idea how exhausting it is? All those creams and treatments, not to mention the positive attitude. And all the while nature is whittling away, adding a new line to the neck and lowering your breasts exponentially with the years, or by the month as it is the older you get. I'm knackered, Lucy. The young fellows make me feel like I just might keep time at bay for a millisecond longer. I hate what I see in the mirror, and I confine that to the facial area. I dread to think what's going on at the back of things.'

'You are beautiful, Evie White, and the best mother a girl could have, and I am about to make you the happiest gallery owner in London.'

'Bruce Willis is finally coming for me?'

'No. We've got the new Famke K exhibition.'

Evie peered into her daughter's face with sympathy. 'As much as I would love for that to be true it could never happen, Lucy. You haven't been yourself this last while, dear. Perhaps you need to take a break.'

'Mum, I'm serious. She lives on the same road as I do and we've struck up a relationship. Believe me, I was as surprised as you are. Shocked, really. But it's true. She's ours.' She shook her mother gently to drive home the point. 'We have the new Famke K.'

Evie staggered a little. 'Champagne,' she croaked. 'And fuck Bartok.'

Lucy giggled. 'It's more than Phillipa Douglas will get to do.'

Ulrika loved the meadow. The grasses all had floral tips and swayed in a gentle breeze, singing the happiness of nature and all that is good. Her body rocked with the gentle flow. She felt cherished. The air was like a kiss upon her skin and when she looked she saw that she was plump again but beautiful. Children laughed in the distance and she walked in the direction of the noise. Somewhere behind she heard her name called through a long echoing corridor but she ignored it. She needed to talk to the children. Stephen and Archie looked surprised to see her as if she was early for a party and they were not quite ready yet.

'Hi there, guys,' she said. 'Long time no see.'

They both laughed and continued their chasing. She joined the rally. When they stopped to rest on a grassy bank she closed her eyes and smelled the floral scent pervading this heaven. The thought that this might be heaven checked her slightly.

'You look pretty,' Archie said, curtly honest as ever. Best of all she believed him. Archie never lied.

'You shouldn't be here,' Stephen said. 'It's not your turn.'

'No,' Archie added. 'Not time,' he further explained.

'But I wanted to see you both,' Ulrika protested.

'So do Mum and Dad and they're not let,' the elder boy said.

'You have to go back,' Archie said. 'And say hello to Mummy and Daddy. Tell them we're having fun.'

The words were garbled now because she seemed to be fading from them or they from her. 'Ask them what?' she shouted at the retreating figures. 'I didn't catch that.' The distance between them was increasing, speeding by and suddenly she was looking into an impossibly bright light and thinking I'm dead: this is the light they all talk about. But then it came to her that the only people who ever talked about it were those who didn't actually die. She sniffed the disinfectant and air fresheners and blinked her eyes. She was lying on a hospital bed but the face of an angel looked down on her.

Jack hooked up with Jodie Taylor Jones for a cocktail at tea time. She plumped for Brown's on St Martin's Lane. 'Not the chi-chi-est venue at the moment but it does the best Bloody Mary in W2 and I need a vat of that to see off this latest hangover.'

The place was filled with a pre-theatre end of Saturday shopping buzz and Jack couldn't help but smile. Fun and possibility burnished the air. He loved that he was here, in one of the greatest cities in the world, and it felt like a village; his village.

'You look good today,' Jodie told him.

'I feel it,' he admitted. He didn't go into details because his life was inconsequential to a client. Jodie was aware of it however.

'I met your wife at a party recently,' she said.

Jack's buzz ground to nothing. Suddenly the village was a trifle small. 'Oh yes?'

'Yes.' Jodie smiled wickedly. 'I think it had been thrown by that man she's living with.'

Now he was feeling like the village idiot.

'He's a dreadfully pompous bore, just right for her, I thought. Didn't like her, as you'll have gathered, especially after the way she's treated you.'

Jack thought he might cry at Jodie's loyalty.

'She is beautiful, in an awful sort of way. I think she expects everyone to fawn over that detail. But you know, the soul doesn't match the trimmings, there. If you ask me, and I realise you haven't but I want you to know anyhow, she was bored off her tits and very, very drunk. Now, if I noticed that, and I am usually the drunkest woman in London, you can imagine just how drunk she was. She knew who I was and made some half-arsed comment, which suited her state, and I told her I had never known you so happy or fulfilled. I'm sure she didn't want to hear that.' A thought struck her. 'I do hope I haven't ensured her return. There is nothing like the report of an ex's happiness to send a wanderer rushing home to spoil things.'

Jack laughed. 'Don't worry about it, Jodie. She was probably too far gone to remember.' But he hoped she hadn't sparked the idea of rapprochement in Laura's head. He wasn't entirely sure he was over his wife or her supernatural powers to bamboozle him. He silently prayed for strength from whatever god was listening and ordered more BMs.

Famke and Colin confined their remarks to pleasantries about recovery with Ulrika. She lay wasted and feeble against impossibly large pillows. She babbled about children. There was no point in berating her with the prospects of career ruin and near death. Surely she knew that. And yet, her denial of anything more serious than not eating enough was worrying in the extreme. The young doctor treating her said she was disorientated and when she was up to it they would introduce rehab and therapy. He'd seen it all before, it seemed.

'But he's a toddler,' Famke wailed outside in the car park.

'A heterosexual toddler,' Colin moaned.

'What can he possibly know at his age? He's barely out of nappies.'

'Home, hag, and don't spare the Sauvignon.'

Lucy found them both at their kitchen table later. It was still hard for her to believe that she had been welcomed into their company or that one of her artistic heroines had chosen her for so much. She proffered two bottles of champagne.

'It's the least I can do after all the help you've given me, and the promise of the exhibition is so generous I'm speechless. I can't tell you how thrilled Mum is.'

Famke shrugged. 'She deserves it and I hope it makes her some money. She probably doesn't remember but she once wrote me a letter after a savaging by a critic and it really lifted me. I was starting out and it meant a lot to me that someone like Evie would take the time to contact me and to be so positive. Her generosity is legendary in artistic circles, and not just advice and kind words: she's bankrolled so many young artists it's hard to keep track.'

Lucy's eyes welled up. 'I think it may be because my dad never earned enough to get by and it led to him working himself to death, really.'

'The painter, Mason, wasn't it?'

'Yes. David Mason.'

'Are you the baby in Jack's painting?'

'Yes. Imagine that. What a world.'

'It's a beautiful study. Jack lets me look at it when I need inspiration. I'm hoping to get that sort of passion and honesty into what I'm doing.'

'Eh, forgetting Colin, are we?' asked their queenly company.

'No, Colin, we are not. You're just not our number one priority right now.'

'It's at times like these I'm glad I'm queer. Women are impossible.'

Jack met Lucy on her way out again. She was carrying a small holdall.

'Was it something I said?' he asked, cocking an eyebrow and trying to look suave.

'I left a note on the table explaining.' She was stumped by how awkward the situation felt. 'I know that sounds formal but I don't have your mobile number.'

They both laughed and the tension dissipated.

'What kind of guy have I turned into? No, don't answer that, I will. I'm in danger of becoming a cad?'

'And a bounder,' Lucy added.

'At least you know where I live. So where are you off to? Not that it's really any of my concern, I know.' He held his hands up in a placatory gesture, designed to make her smile. It did.

'I'm going to stay with Evie tonight. She's been chucked

by her chap. It's a bit of a theme in our family this season. Thought she might like some girly company.'

'Men are not the brightest creatures,' Jack concluded. 'I don't mean that as an excuse. Why don't you bring her over for lunch tomorrow? We can have a relaxing day over the papers.' He crinkled his face. 'I predict the weather will hold so we can sit in the garden and be wonderful.'

'Done.' She stood on tiptoes and kissed his cheek, which led to a more intense kiss and then on. An hour later Lucy made another run at leaving and this time she did, hair wet from a shower and the pulse of lovemaking still racing in her veins. She hailed a cab and chortled at the idea that she had a reason to actually drive her car tonight but was over the limit and could not.

It sat quietly in the cul-de-sac awaiting her return. A drunk staggered in on his way home from the local pub. He pissed against the fence and wondered what the green ribbon was for. A minibus, full of elderly bingo players, used the cul-de-sac to turn round and change direction. Sounds of an argument drifted by on the air. A jet roared overhead taking holidaymakers to Tenerife, each wondering why they were travelling all that way when London had the best weather in the world just then. The ginger cat arrived and sprayed the abandoned car once again, cocked it a snook and left.

TWENTY-TWO

'It's interesting that God should have made such a mistake during the Creation,' Colin said, fanning himself with the Style section of the *Sunday Times*.

Famke paused, coffee mug in mid-air. 'I'm hanging on your every,' she told him.

'Well, I mean to say, Mondays, you know?'

She was getting the gist but remained silent.

'Why not make more Sundays when they're so good?'

'You've got me there.'

He flicked through the glossy, admiring some Patrick Cox shoes and gasping with horror at the latest trend in eye shadows. 'There are a lot of skeletons on the scene, to judge by the magazines, so heroin chic is probably the look Ulrika is going for.'

'Was. It ends now. She's straight into therapy faster than you can say calorie.'

He threw the paper aside. Famke offered a news section. 'Oh no, I don't need the world, thanking you. There's more than enough drama in Farewell Square, mercy boocoo. It's been quite a ride around here since April.'

'And who's to say it's over yet?'

'I really don't have the energy for an iota's more excitement or horror. And to what end?' he asked, grandly. 'What does it all mean? What does it all add up to or prove?'

'Maybe it's time you got religion,' Famke suggested, burying her head in the mountain of newsprint.

'I would make a lovely nun,' he confirmed. His face took on a dreamy quality then he muttered, 'I feel a moment coming on,' before leaving the room at speed.

Too late Famke realised her massive error. She had set loose his campest genie. As the album of *The Sound of Music* began to play she wondered if it was too early to have a drink. She stuck it bravely until Colin was sixteen going on seventeen, then baled out of the house. Typical, she thought, Colin is the one belting out the decibels and I'm the one who has to conduct the apology tour.

Helen let her in to number 7. 'It's fine,' she said before Famke began. 'I just wish he could sing.'

'I've been threatening to record him to illustrate how tone deaf he is and that time may have come.'

'Oh, leave him be. The world is harsh on dreamers and he's doing no harm.' They allowed the screeching to invade the conversation. 'Well, not much harm.' Christopher Plummer strummed his guitar, strangely unperturbed by the disharmonied duet now raging through 'Edelweiss'.

Colin sounded like he was choking and in dire agony. 'It is a truly ugly sound, isn't it?'

'If only it hurt him too.'

In spite of the cacophanous impromptu concert two doors away, the silence in the house was undeniable. Where once two small boys would have thundered through the rooms and corridors, now adults crept by, unable to crack the void left behind. The cheeky faces grinned from photographs on the walls and sideboards but Archie and Stephen were missed. This old house had seen some action and Famke hoped it would know happiness again soon.

'How was your trip out?'

'Noisy and confusing; a bit like Colin. But I managed it. I may go for a bigger thrill next time and tackle the supermarket.'

Famke gave a low whistle.

Colin thought about his job. It was handy, do-able, unexciting and profitable. None of these attributes was so heinous of itself, or in tandem with the others, as to make him want to jump ship. He liked the security afforded by his monthly pay cheque, which was almost adequate for a single man of his tastes. He enjoyed the statement that he worked 'in the City' and the vagueness of the throwaway 'something in finance'. All of these things were fine. But the months preceding had dealt such mind-blowing lessons to those around him that he really did have to consider that there was more to living than a dull, well-paid job in a predictable existence.

What were the alternatives? What were his strengths? He was good with people. He would make a superb agony aunt, adept as he was at seeing through to the heart of problems. He had also dated practically every type of person on this earth and need only change gender as dictated by the query. He would probably make a fantastic actor, as he was the ultimate showman and liar, and what else was it but lying for a living, pretending to be someone else for a few hours every day? He spent every day role-playing, with his best being the camp, vain queen of the sarky remark, with the demon sense of dress and the heart of gold. Actually that was him, but he did tweak it up or down as necessary, and detail of tone was everything so that was also a plus for acting as a profession. How hard could it be? A trained monkey could do as much, given the right costume and instructions. He might make an even better puppeteer, which led him to the notion of becoming an agent. That was as camp as three rows of tents back to back. Bitching, sniping, haggling over fees and gushing endearments to wrap up, all were grist to his everyday mill already. It would just mean buying an Armani suit (which was on his things-to-do list anyhow) and he was away. His memoirs would make excellent reading, if a little spicy for some. He could talk the talk so all he needed there was to type the talk and a publishing contract for six figures was his for the taking. The endless possibilities began to confuse him. He did enjoy the daydream, though.

Where did he see himself in five years' time? He

didn't like contemplating that at all. When he pictured it he wanted desperately to see someone alongside him, sharing his experiences, loving him. There was no one. And it made a mockery of his dreams but also of his life. What was so wrong with having a good job and salary, even if it was a bit ordinary? And why did this mad seeking of a.n. other have to be so cussed and dispiriting? It was no wonder he tried to inure himself to it. He didn't like feeling that his life was essentially meaningless and of no worth. He naturally veered towards the happy of a day and he was not going to let this mood get in on him. He would make his life into something, with or without someone else to validate it. He just needed a pointer.

Tony appeared, tired but cheery. At that moment Colin knew he should tell him to turn around and go away. There was something in his eyes that sparkled like zeal. It was bright and shiny and new. It held out hope.

Colin employed his best thwarting tactic. 'You don't look like any of the bullets landed,' he said. 'Her family must be very poor shots. Now, if you lived in Northern Ireland . . .' He never got to finish.

'I've always wanted to work for an aid organisation,' Tony said. 'How would you like to join me?'

'Ah, now, here,' Colin grumbled. 'I've heard of a deus ex machina but this is going too far. There is such a thing as scale, you know.' He walked to the workbench and flicked on the kettle. 'But tell me more.'

❖   ❖   ❖

There are certain rules in life that cannot be ignored or argued over. One is that any book described as 'a meditation' is dull, nine times out of ten, no matter the subject. Another is that a patient will fall in love with his doctor. This can be a little, as in a crush, and nothing much of a concern to either the attendant or attendee (unless the problem being treated involves the reproductive area which throws up its own awkwardness) or it may be a lot, in which case the area being treated is inconsequential as the patient's adoration, misplaced or otherwise, gets in the way of recovery and any of the doctor's attempts at aiding such an event. Ulrika had fallen for young Dr Theo Berger. His was the face she had seen bathed in angelic light when she came to in the hospital. She had smiled back then leaned over the bed and vomited onto the floor. It ranked as one of the most memorable moments in her life.

Dr Theo set about distancing himself. In spite of how attractive his patient was he could not get involved. His expertise was growing but so also was his recognition of sticky situations. He signed the case over to the gnarled and hirsute Mr Wall and returned to his rounds. Ulrika was whirled off on the merry-go-round of her rehabilitation and she didn't see her angel again for another three months, by which time everything had moved on for all involved and the risk of embarrassment had passed.

Jack served up crispy duck à l'orange, al dente green vegetables and some sloppy mash as 'a respite from chewing'. He and the White ladies gossiped over wine and lunch.

They dissected the papers before moving around the house to inspect the walls and objects, scoffing at some of his wife's worst excesses in the modern art market, while admitting that most were still worth lots and therefore sniggering was redundant, if enjoyable. They stood in respectful silence before the portrait of the baby Lucy.

'I can still remember how you smelled that day,' she said to her daughter.

'Milky?' Lucy chanced, gently.

'You were a very placid baby. Probably knew what you were in for in life and conserving your energies.'

'No, Mum. I was happy. I still am.'

She and Jack slipped away to give Evie some private moments with her reminiscences.

They had been careful to be no more than friends in front of Evie, but now, alone together, they found a moment to kiss. It felt dangerous, risky. Lucy began to think about how unlikely the whole scenario was. They were separated spouses with unfinished business. All this suggested they were doomed as an item. That was the sensible summation. But there was no room for that in the heat of their fire. They were new and invincible. No one and nothing could find them out. They played the part of consultant and client well, they felt, and there was no way that Evie would suspect anything more than chance having thrown them together for commerce.

When Evie arrived back to the conservatory, she refilled her glass and sat facing them.

'Thank you for the opportunity to see that painting again,

Jack.' She sipped her wine. 'But now to other matters. I am not a stupid woman, or blind. Above all, I'm a mother which means my radar is acute. I think you two have some explaining to do,' she said. She pierced her daughter with knowing eyes. 'Particularly you, miss.'

It was time to try to put words to what had happened. Lucy was nailed to the spot and didn't know where to start, so she opened her mouth and let it all out.

Bill and Helen had returned to a point in life where they were making plans. It was a foreign country, forgotten in all the other travels. Practicality had to be included in the loop. They were not the only ones involved.

'You must see a doctor,' Bill said, stroking his wife's stomach.

'I know. I've been putting it off because when I do it won't be only our secret any more. I want it to be ours for as long as possible: ours alone. Famke was here earlier and I desperately wanted her to know so that people would stop worrying as much about us as they have been. But I couldn't. It's ours, this baby is ours, and I want to enjoy that feeling a little longer.'

'I'm surprised she didn't notice the bump,' Bill remarked. 'I suppose she was too caught up with Ulrika.'

'She feels she's failed her as a friend.'

'We can only do our best and hope it passes muster.'

'I'm not up to going to a hospital to visit so I said we'd probably wait till she got home before thrusting our faces into hers.'

'Good thinking. Now, what does Madam crave today?

'Her husband and a cool glass of lemonade.'

'Coming up.'

Helen went through the garden door to the cul-de-sac on one of her regular checks. It was still and smelled ripe and dusty. As she passed the car she identified the cat's spray. Grit gathered and crunched between her teeth. The green ribbon was intact, an empty can of export lager lying close by. She picked it up to bring to the waste bin on the main road. As it plonked to the bottom a motorbike sped past with two young women chattering and laughing. They wore helmets but their bare legs looked so vulnerable Helen had to turn away. She imagined the bike skidding, spilling its passengers onto the rough ground, their knees and flesh dragged and ripped to red along the tarmac. She sped back to the garden, lungs burning and heart ready to explode. She tried to relax into the recliner by pinning her back hard into the padding. She shook with the vivid image of frailty fresh in her mind. There would be more of this from now on as she rejoined the city. This day had the feeling of the last of an era. Bizarrely, it also felt like the last day of some warped freedom. Tomorrow would begin a new phase in their lives and she was nervous of all it brought with it. She breathed deeply and sipped on the drink Bill had served. She remembered his words: we can only do our best and hope it passes muster. This carried fleeting comfort but it would do. For now, it would do. She closed her eyes and let the boys come. She remembered Stephen's first smile without wind. It made her laugh.

✻   ✻   ✻

Colin put Tony to work. 'Cooking is your gig,' he said pushing him towards the larder. 'Amaze us.'

'Do you promise to think about what I said?'

'Yes, though it's only fair to tell you that I am always more use in an office juggling figures. That's what I'm good at. Travelling to the poorest areas of the earth might tune the soul but I would be of no practical use in that situation. I'm purely decorative. However, there are many ways of saving the universe and I'll apply myself to thinking about those. That do?'

'Yes.' Tony grinned. 'You're a lot more practical than you like to let on.'

'Of course I am. How do you think I've survived this long? I like the coping to be effortless-looking, if not invisible. A big corporation pays me loadsamoney to look after its fortune, because I am entirely capable. But keep that schtum. I don't like to be too obviously fabulous all the time as it eclipses the rest of the human race, which tends to create an atmosphere.'

'Got it.'

'Good. Now, do you think you could rustle up a cake? Only Famke is having Lucy and her mum over for a cup of tea and there's nothing in.'

Tony poked around the cupboards and fridge. 'I could try.'

'That is all we ask.'

'Lemon drizzle,' he mused.

'Mmn, tart.'

'I have my moments.'

✿   ✿   ✿

Jack felt like a schoolboy caught robbing an orchard. He had found himself explaining and defending his recent movements to Evie also. His and Lucy's stories combined to make a sorry mess and it was galling to think that between them they had seventy years of experience but no sense. He planned to grasp all bulls by their horns the following day, having never knowingly passed up on acting out a cliché. In the meantime, the Whites were with Famke and he was chugging back a bracing glass of wine. It didn't help his vision, actually or metaphorically, but it tasted nice and he needed gratification.

Famke promised to deliver the work in twelve weeks' time. When Evie questioned the sagacity of this undertaking the artist said she'd just expand to fill any extra time available otherwise. A deadline was what she needed now, not a guideline. They all enjoyed Tony's cake. He furnished a soup and salad also, rustled out of nothing, then excused himself. Sunday night was for organising his work overalls for the following week, he explained. He was mindful that he couldn't assume he'd be invited to stay and realised that perhaps it really was best not to. They neglected to tell Evie about his failed engagement and bolting out of a wedding so close to the celebration. She'd heard enough of human irregularity that day.

Famke had some stipulations. One was that Evie wait to see the whole body of work, finished. 'Lucy has seen some of it, and is some of it, so I hope you will trust her judgement.'

'I do, implicitly,' Evie confirmed.

Famke laughed. 'I love the way I've assumed she's given the work a good report.' Before the Whites had a chance to begin their protestations she said, 'I also want the exhibition to be seen by as many people as possible, so I'd like to try for a national tour. I want this to be populist, even in the realms of what snobs might call "low" art, especially there, I suppose. I want it to have access to the majority and vice versa. Anyone who buys a piece must allow it out to the public for the duration of the tour.'

'I think we can all live with that,' Evie said.

Lucy voiced the obvious. 'We're both on the rebound, Jack, so it's a bad idea to be getting so involved again. We need to be careful of ourselves. We're both fragile and vulnerable.' And horny, she thought. 'And it's not exactly casual, is it?'

Jack gave in. 'Well, no. I still don't see why we should have to be spiteful to ourselves just because we were dumped by two shits.'

'No. But, to reiterate, we have to be careful.'

'I agree. Can I just mention that I have initiated divorce proceedings? I'm not in denial about my marriage, or its failure.'

'And I would get a divorce too, if I could just find my husband.'

'Right, well, that's good to have out in the open. Now let's go to bed.'

'Why do I feel that is not the way this scene would have ended in the textbook.'

'It is the way it ends in the textbook, to illustrate the wrong thing to do.'

'Bed it is, then.'

Helen and Bill made loose plans for the following day, mindful not to rush or to expect too much from a capricious world. Helen thought of the new baby. It was the size of an orange inside her now. This called to mind her boys, though they were never far away, of course. She told Bill. He smiled. 'I wouldn't mind if it was the only fruit,' he said.

Ulrika drifted in and out of the bright light of the hospital ward. She was conscious for brief moments of each hour but had no desire to wake up fully. That'll be for tomorrow, she thought. This was not a promise but inevitability. She could not hold it back, try as she might like to. She continued to let her consciousness slip into the light, out to the dark, and in and out, to the nth degree. The content was dreamily real.

She lost any sense of time and was glad of that. She knew it was out there, waiting to catch up with her, but she hoped she could dodge it long enough to get stronger physically. Even that thought seemed remote and unable to touch her in this haze. She drifted off again to a place behind her eyelids where she was moving on a journey with no beginning, no end. To and fro, to and fro, and in this way Sunday became Monday, and it was time to start over.

TWENTY-THREE

When Helen was exiled in the cul-de-sac, she had a purpose to her day. Now that she had returned to an empty house she needed to find things to do. With her role as mother on hold again she was at a loss. She found herself on that Monday morning kissing her husband goodbye as he left for the building site and no idea what to do with her time for the eight or so hours until he returned. She didn't let this rattle her, she had been through considerably worse, but it was a concern. She decided that her boast of a trip to the supermarket might be the place to start. Then she would clean about the house and visit the cul-de-sac to continue her intermittent vigil. She would have liked to do all this in reverse order but wanted to break a touch with her old ways, in the spirit of this new beginning.

She had a shape for the day.

She was so exhausted by the planning she had a snooze in the children's room and dreamed of giant fruits. As she surfaced later, clothes sweat-stuck to her skin, she thought that, all in all, it could have been a worse start to the day.

She reviewed the plan she'd fashioned earlier and decided to go with most elements of it but with a new one thrown in. She would walk to where Lucy worked and see how she was managing on her first day of this potentially momentous week. She chuckled drily at that. 'Every week is potentially momentous,' she said aloud.

Lucy found Danny unloading boxes of exotic blooms from tall metal trolleys outside Fifi's Flowers and decanting them into the florist's shop. The ladies tried to help but he was having none of it. They stared misty-eyed at the old-fashioned chivalry and chittered excitedly at his every quip.

'It's nice to see the world return to Victorian norms,' Lucy supplied, leaning against a wall to observe the shenanigans.

'Feel free to help and ruin the symmetry of the scene,' Fiona said.

'Vida's brewing up in there, you'd better hurry,' Danny told Lucy.

'Killing me with kindness,' she remarked. 'Who'd've put Vida's name down for that, eh?'

Martha followed her in to get coffees, excitedly singing Danny's plus points. Amazingly, he didn't have any other kind, according to the paean. Lucy laughed. Only a week ago she'd thought him a creep, now he was Superman. Vida pushed the creosote-based goo at her, glaring. Lucy downed it obediently and waited for the buzz, which kicked in with the rush she remembered from Friday. 'This is good shit,' she said.

'Very good shit,' the Slovenian attested, holding Lucy's eyes and daring her to comment on some or all of what had just come to pass.

'Thank you,' was all she got. She grunted and walked off, leaving Lucy to wonder what had actually happened and where they were going with this new vaudeville routine.

Jack tried to head Clara off at the pass. 'Before you brandish that letter in your hand, let me offer you a better job title and a substantial pay rise.'

'How substantial?' she wanted to know. 'If I am to be the ultimate corporate whore, I'll expect a suitable bribe to go with it.'

He told her, she agreed that it was in the suitable-to-generous league but would require further haggling before a contract could be drawn up. 'You're still a shit,' she said.

'I am,' he conceded.

'As I have not yet resigned,' Clara said, stressing the yet, 'I can tell you that your wife is on her way in here. She is not happy. In fact, she is what my old nan used to call hopping mad.'

'On a scale of one to ten?'

'Apoplectic.'

'Shit. I need to disappear. Woman the phones and the fort and good luck,' he cried, running for the stairs. If Laura was en route she would use the elevator. She didn't like to perspire on couture garments or to risk breaking a designer kitten heel. That sort of kitten was about as cuddly as she got. He was entering the lobby when he saw her emerge from a black cab. He ducked behind a huge potted plant and thanked the fashion for outsized everything in his venal world.

Her beauty punched a hole right through him. She dripped elegance from within a dangerous dress. Cold accessories chinked against her tanned skin. Her black hair was held in a simple ribbon, so plain it was threatening. She clacked across the marble and pressed the call button with a painted, grape-red nail. As the doors of the lift pinged closed she lifted her sunglasses from her eyes, their olivine clarity piercing from beneath curled, sensuous lashes. Jack gasped as he staggered from behind the greenery into the vapour trail of her perfume. Fuck, that woman is a loaded gun. She's also gorgeous. He was taken aback to realise her power over him still. I am in real trouble here, he thought. Time to escape. He limped to the door, nursing an erection and crippling fear.

Colin sat opposite the exquisitely named Aubrey Love. Not even the surname Darling could challenge that, he thought. They were on the top floor of the building, surrounded by light and the best views of the city that money could buy (and it had). This was but one of the perks of being boss. Aubrey was a furry little man with a genial aspect and a fondness for corduroy. He actively pursued his hackneyed image to excellence, as with the rest of his endeavours. He had a withering eye, should it be required, and was a millionaire many times over. He had started on an East End stall selling vegetables and the standard joke was that he really did know his onions.

'I cannot accept this promotion to the Northern Ireland office,' Colin began, simply and to the point. 'I am flattered by it, and I'm tempted by the salary increase . . .'

'But,' Aubrey predicted, neither delighted to call where this was going nor daunted.

'But,' Colin picked up, 'I'd like to wait for an opportunity elsewhere in the organisation. There may be a better opening in another European country soon and I'd like to hold out for that.'

'You surprise me, Colin,' Aubrey admitted.

He left it there, forcing Colin to ask, 'Why?'

'I had thought that if you were to refuse you'd string us along, stick us for a few splendid lunches, then tell us to go jump.'

'I intended to, but I thought I might weaken in a drunken moment and accept the job so it's best to put an end to it right now.'

Aubrey nodded, pleased with the honesty of the answer. 'I applaud your strength, your fibre, and while I am disappointed you aren't going to Belfast for us I do think a very drunken meal is in order. I hate the way we have all become so abstemious at lunchtimes.'

Colin smiled. Aubrey was a recovering alcoholic and had been dry for twenty years. 'Get your people to call my people and we'll do that.'

Colin returned to his desk buoyed by his moral stand and the fact that he was not going 'home'. He spotted

Stella laughing with the brown-clad Eddie. She looked so genuinely happy that he let the scene play out before he presented himself.

'What was all the mirth as I arrived?' Colin enquired.

'Eddie was telling me about a speed dating night he went on.'

'Pah, old hat,' Colin scoffed. 'Gays invented that centuries ago.'

'Oh yeah?'

'Eh, yeah. Think of how many men I can go through in a single evening. QED.' He held her eyes and waited for her to break and tell him her news. Which she did.

'You're the master,' she said in admiration. 'We're going for a drink after work.'

'See what you can do about his clothage. Brown is so . . .'

'Brown?'

'Exactly. It's sapped the energy right out of me even uttering the description of it. Brooooown.' He feigned a nod asleep. 'Your mission should you choose to accept it, et cetera.' He waved her away.

'Sir!' Stella saluted smartly and disappeared.

Colin spent the rest of the morning looking up aid agencies on the web.

Famke faced her future and wondered, 'Is it good enough?' To be sure, it was incomplete, as all futures are when observed from any sort of present. She believed in Art's power to change a person but in no major way, and, if

pushed, was reluctant to give even the capital A to Art.
To have meaning, for just one other being, was enough.
Even that was a narrow remit, too, as she would be satisfied with the viewer being moved, whether they could
explain that or not. It didn't amount to saving humanity,
nor was that intended. She just wanted to open a new set
of eyes, to entertain, in all of the widest sense of that word.
Did it make her a better person? Perhaps. Probably not.
She didn't care as long as the work engaged. Right now,
looking at what she had so far, she was stir crazy. She
wanted out. She wanted anywhere but here in front of
work that was just that: work. Gone were the glorious early
days of inspiration tripping up technique and ability. Now
it was down to putting the ideas and images on canvas,
making the fucking things. And that was often dull and
seemingly unfulfilling. Plus, if she was honest, she now
thought it was shit and a waste of everyone's time. Oh yes,
there were sections that worked well and were worthy of
comment. And there were others that could not have been
worse if they tried. How could brilliant passages exist right
next to turds? She picked up a brush, daubed it in a vibrant
magenta and rushed at the canvas that was annoying her
most. It felt good. It had its own momentum and reward.
Any more would be overkill.

Time to calm down and settle into the drudgery of creation.

Ulrika was facing awkward questions. She answered them
like a person dealing with a very small foreign child who
didn't speak the language. No, she didn't have a drug

problem. She had merely sought some immediate help with shifting the stodgiest of her weight. She had made an error of judgement, that was all, a mistake. It was simple and brief and done and over with. She was walking away from it. No. Big. Deal.

She encountered a brick wall as if she'd spoken in Latin or Serbo-Croat. Her throat was dry with nerves and every time she swallowed, it felt like her oesophagus was filled with crushed glass. God, this hospital reduced everything to the medical; terms and jargon like voodoo in her mouth and brain. Oesophagus indeed.

Yes, she'd like a different shape. Who wouldn't?

She was hungry, fractious, and feeling a bit of a tit if truth be told. She knew she'd fucked up and no amount of bravado could erase that.

And then, tough questions. About life. About who she was. Who she'd like to be.

Anyone else. Or just someone. Someone interesting. Someone who contributes.

You are a teacher, surely that contributes?

To nonsense. Media studies? What's that when it's at home? I want to be someone who matters.

'Don't you think you matter to the people who love you?'

'Yes,' she replied. 'But who are they?'

'Now, Ulrika, now I believe we are getting somewhere. This is progress.'

Who was this old bozo, with his wisdom and his purple nose? 'You don't look to me like you are in any fit state to advise anyone else. On anything.'

He smiled patiently.

She wanted to punch his lights out. Today will be brought to you by the word 'wank', she thought.

The air was fresh with possibility that morning and Lucy found she didn't want it. She moved about with a vigour that her head couldn't share. It was filled with toxin: dread seeping from one neuron to the next, poisoning the week just as it began. Sometimes she jumped involuntarily, like jerking from sleep at the moment of passing over. Saturday was when she would confront Pete, her husband; her one true love, she had thought. This certainty was tainting everything she encountered.

Her heart lightened to see Helen arrive. It was a while before she thought on the oddity of the other woman's presence. She introduced her new friend to her old friends and served her a fennel tea.

Helen saw the curiosity in Lucy's eyes. 'I needed a new journey and thought I'd try yours,' she said.

You're welcome to it, Lucy thought, but kept it to herself, commenting only that it was a nice walk. The sentiment was hollow through no fault of the city, just her situation.

Helen sat at the window and read some papers and Lucy tried to fling herself back into work but it was useless. She eventually plonked down and asked, 'What am I to do?'

'You're going to Ramsgate and you're going to have it out with him. You don't have a choice any more, not while

Colin is looking forward to a trip, and I see that you have breath in your body.'

I may have breath, she wanted to scream, but I've misplaced my backbone, and my pride was stolen from me by the same man who has all my money.

'He's bit of a terrier, Colin?'

'Don't even bother to test his mettle,' Helen advised. 'Once he's made his mind up, that's it. Roll over and enjoy.'

Lucy sat shaking, an anomaly in the rays of brilliant sunshine illuminating the café. Helen reached out to hold her hand.

'Don't worry,' she said. 'I'm here to help.'

'Thank you,' Lucy said, tears rising in her eyes. 'I don't really trust myself any more.'

'I don't trust me either. But I have a feeling that's where we both have to go before we can return to ourselves.'

She got him when he returned to his office building six hours later. He was waiting for the elevator when she pinned him to the nearby wall and pressed herself tight against him.

'You have no idea how horny it makes me when you play tough,' she said. She let her hand drop to his tightening crotch. 'My, my, we are glad to see me, aren't we, big boy?'

He was enveloped in her scent, his pulse quickening, blood roaring through his head, then south to his groin. He heard himself groan. His cock was hard in her hand now and she crushed her lips to his. He felt her nipples stiffen and knew that she was liquid gold between her legs. Her tongue caressed his and suddenly he was lifting her off the ground and over to the stairwell where he banged her against a wall and thrust into her with an abandon that was animal. 'Come on, Jackie,' she urged as he slicked in and out of her. 'Harder.' Her hair came loose and fell over their faces like a sheet of black satin. He lost all sense of self to lust and as he abandoned himself to release he felt something visceral rip away from within him. The self-loathing was instant.

Laura pulled her dress over her naked ass and grinned into his face. 'That's all I wanted to know,' she said and left.

He sat on the steps, panting and disgusted. He had let her use him once more. He had been manipulated by her calculation and his own weakness. You just made your biggest mistake, he whispered, to both of them. He walked up the three flights to his office, steeling his resolve with each step.

Clara sniffed the air. 'She got you, then?' she remarked, recognising the perfume he was bathed in.

'Oh, she got me all right. But it ends here.'

Jack stood simmering, his eyes unfocused, reliving a private torture. Clara donned a receptive look but his thoughts were clearly not ready for scrutiny. Taking in the creases etched on his features she was sure she didn't want to dig too hard. The air popped in his ears with fury. When he walked away he left an outline of cold rage behind.

He went to his desk and sat, trying to review his past

to this point with a view to changing it for the better. Are you totally out of control? he asked himself. Or a pitiable slave to the snake in your pants? You have had sex with four different women in the last week. These are the actions of someone with a thinking disorder. What the fuck are you up to? He was stumped for an answer.

He let the silence reproach him. Then he made some phone calls to expedite his separation from his wife. Never again will I sink so low, he promised. But nothing could change the fact that he had been unfaithful to Lucy with the bitch he was married to. He was a shit. His mutability sickened him.

Lucy's eyes travelled over the 'rooms to let' ads without paying enough attention to see what they were offering. She began again. Same difference. It reminded her of trying to read *Ulysses* once. She would go fifty pages and realise that she hadn't seen a single word. Moving on scared her. Farewell Square had become her rock and she now could not imagine life without it. In fact, she couldn't think past Saturday, what she had to do to get her life back onto its proper axis. It wasn't even something she could plan for. She had no idea if they would find Pete or how he would react, or how exactly she thought she would get him to give her the satisfaction she needed to move on.

All around her the population sped by. She saw Vida chat to Greta in the porch of the café. They were laughing which sat oddly on Vida's face. Or did it? Was she so blind to the world she imagined wrongs and anger where there was none? Danny served Martha coffees and they were laughing too. The sun smiled, the city sparkled. Why did she feel so mean-spirited? She didn't, she realised. Yet again, she was simply afraid, for the past and the future, stuck here in the present where she felt useless and unworthy. Yet she was willing to stay here. Because to move on meant that Saturday was coming and she could not get her head around that at all.

Jack was distant and a little drunk that night. Lucy hadn't seen him drink whisky before, but then she hadn't known him long. It made her grin to think of them practically shacked up after only a few days. The liquor didn't seem to be doing anything to either inebriate him further or lift his mood. He tried to be upbeat during a meal of lasagne decanted from a Marks and Spencer carton by Lucy's own hand and accompanied by a salad also à la the St Michael chain.

'Bad day at work?'

'Yes. Sorry. I don't mean to bring it home with me but it's hard to shake.'

'Don't worry, we all have those.' She flashed a smile that lit her whole face, wrinkling her freckled nose and bunching up the edges of her eyes with such charm he felt even more of a shit than before, a level he had previously thought impossible to reach. He couldn't forgive himself for what he'd done but he couldn't tell Lucy either.

He put down the crystal tumbler and took her into his arms. She felt to him like a saviour and his heart stuttered. I have feelings for this woman. I cannot fuck this up. He kissed the top of her head. 'I don't deserve you,' he told her.

He retreated again and after Lucy went to bed she heard him put on one mournful jazz album after another, usually instrumental and all depressing. Much later he fell up the stairs, paused at her door, then continued to his own room. Lucy appreciated this. After her speech about the Rebound he had recognised that they were two rogue elements careering forward without a plan or focus. Obviously they needed perspective and a goal, and a hint of separation, while this was achieved.

She missed him in her bed.

Bill and Helen lay talking. It was chit-chat, anecdotes, and reminiscences. The ceiling was so familiar and so far from where she had been for so long that Helen took time to study it. When she was done, she said, 'I've made an appointment to see a doctor about the pregnancy.'

Bill hugged her closer to show his approval. She felt the calluses on his large-knuckled hands graze gently across her arms.

'And I think I might finally be ready for some proper bereavement counselling. I couldn't be doing with any of it while I blamed myself so much for what happened. I still do, but it has moved on now, I think. I suppose I was always afraid that it might be some sort of cure, some unwanted miracle, and that we might forget our children.'

'That can never happen, Helen. We will never forget them. And we'll never get over the grief, but we will figure out how to get around it.'

TWENTY-FOUR

Colin marshalled his troops. 'I have booked us into a quaint and genial hotel called the Royal Harbour in Ramsgate for tomorrow, Friday, night. It is little more than a stone's throw from our stakeout. I want us on duty at the supermarket from early Saturday morning. We know, from the lack of activity on any of Pete's cards, that he has gone to ground again for the week.' He paused for a stagey sigh, then let them have, 'As per my brilliant deductionary powers. So he's probably a little peckish by now and will need to stock up on goodies.'

He surveyed the faces and saw terror in Lucy's and slight glazing over in Famke's.

'Eh, am I getting through here?'

They both nodded.

'I can't believe the week has flown and that we're actually going to Kent,' Lucy said, testing the words as she uttered them to see if she was dreaming or living this unwelcome turn.

'Ignore me, I'm always bad tempered when I'm on

the home run for a body of work,' Famke contributed.

'Great. This should make for a right barrel of laughs when we go undercover,' Colin grumbled.

'You really don't have to take time out to do this,' Lucy said to Famke.

'Oh I want to. You need support and we're it. Also, I am still a selfish artist. This will give me actual distance from the work; time to think about it, assess it. So believe me I'm not losing out here.'

Colin had become quite the sleuth, with the terms and planning, and Lucy worried that he had a trench coat secreted in a closet, ready to embrace his new genre and the drive south-east.

'I really appreciate all your efforts, Colin, but you have to have noticed that I'm petrified about facing my husband. I have absolutely no idea what I'll say or do.'

'Perfect,' Colin said, and he meant it. 'Spontaneity will free the truth. It will be a total success. And, for the record, I got us all single rooms. I didn't think it was that kind of jaunt.'

Mouths agape, Lucy and Famke took all of the rest of their instructions in the silence and suffering of those out of their depth. Colin outlined their car rental plans (Lucy, your car is so known to the perp we cannot risk blowing our cover with it) and where they should gather.

They sat next to and behind him the following day as he proclaimed joyfully that they had caught the worst of the traffic jams leaving London, as befitted a Friday afternoon, and that he looked like the most wholesome of family men in his four-door saloon.

'Oh, I think not,' Famke scoffed. 'But if the car suits . . . and so on.'

She pulled her sunglasses back down over her eyes and wondered was she the mum in the scenario if Colin was the dad? She gave an involuntary shiver at the notion then gave herself over to thinking about her work and where it was going.

Colin fiddled with the dial of the radio. 'If this journey is going to be in any way enjoyable for me I'll need music to drown you two drags out.' He settled on a pop station and Famke was grateful that he didn't know any of the words to the latest releases, else he would have felt obliged to 'sing' along. He began to read out all of the traffic signs aloud instead.

'You are a bona fide menace,' she told him.

Lucy had descended into a pit. She lay across the back seat wishing Jack was here to hold her and whisper comfort. He had work to do. He had remained distant since Monday but she knew they were both working things out and she didn't push for any intimacy if it was not forthcoming. They still made love, Lucy falling deeper and deeper into this man and hoping that he felt the same way. Which made this journey to see her husband surreal and undesirable. But she couldn't hide forever, and neither could Pete.

She remembered little of the hotel afterwards except that it was cosy and the walls filled with pictures in all styles. There were battle scenes, portraits and cardboard three-dimensional reproductions of the Impressionists and Van Gogh's chair. The staff were wonderful. There was an honesty bar in operation, which meant signing a notebook admitting to any drinks purchased, and a stereo played vinyl records of seventies disco and Dame Joan Sutherland arias. Colin was enthralled. He and Famke made friends with the pretty, Irish crew of a new European airline, which flew into Manston airport down the road.

'It's Kent International,' Colin corrected. 'The pilots look so young, which must mean I'm getting old.' He forgot to fret for long, however, and stayed up shrieking happily till all hours and signing the little blue notebook.

Lucy stayed to one side unable to participate. Fearful anticipation knocked her heart rudderless and she swallowed constantly at an imaginary blockage in her throat.

In a lull, while the smokers were outside, Colin crouched beside her and said, 'I know you're worried about tomorrow. That's understandable. So if you want to go to bed now, do.'

Famke held out her hand. 'I'll see you up. If you're lonely or anxious during the night remember I'm next door.'

Lucy lay on her bed trying to watch television. Eventually, she went to her en suite and threw up into the lavatory. She washed her teeth and face and made a cup of weak, sweet tea, then sat on the edge of the bed to watch the sea and the sky change, over the long hours, from darkness to light, the tiny fishing boats bobbing out of the harbour to work and the ferry lumbering back from Ostend.

She joined the others for breakfast and had trouble watching Colin tuck into the gloriously named 'Darling Jamie's Kedgeree'. She nibbled on dry toast and drank some more watery tea. Her mouth remained sandpaper dry and her head pounded as if she was hungover.

Famke smiled reassuringly. 'You're doing the right thing, Lucy,' she said.

'I know. I only wish it wasn't so hard to face.'

'There are three of us,' Colin said. 'Which means the problem is divided up.'

Lucy wanted to believe him with all her broken heart.

Colin had changed into a worn T-shirt, jeans and a beany hat. The look was styled as no-hoper but not quite dangerous, the sort of loafer one might expect to hang around a supermarket car park. Famke and Lucy wore simple tops and skirts and Lucy, at Colin's behest, had on a sun hat to disguise her head and hair. They paid their bill, thanked the staff and drove the car around the corner and down the hill to the supermarket. Lucy was stationed close to the main door by the cars but had a good view of an extra side entrance which opened onto the street. Colin sat on the boundary wall topping up his tan. Famke stayed in the car. They all had juiced-up mobiles. Lucy felt nauseous again and swigged on a litre bottle of mineral water.

'Don't go mad with that,' Colin bossed. 'If you're in the kazi when Pete arrives we're wasted.'

'Great. I can die from dehydration but I can't go to the loo.'

She saw her reflection in Colin's wraparounds, looking beaky, small and foolish; the sort of picture that looks cute and annoying on a calendar when it's made up of fluffy kittens, but also worryingly exploitative. I have become a ridiculous creature, she thought. I'm better than that. I can and I will do this.

The wait was excruciatingly painful on the limbs and boring in the extreme. Lucy had plenty of time to wonder why people brought pushchairs full of kids with them when it only added to the mayhem and grief of shopping on a Saturday. I am never having children, she resolved. A text from Famke held much the same sentiment.

Three and a half hours in, Lucy was licking an ice cream cone supplied by Colin when her skin crawled across her temples, stretching like clingfilm pulled too tight. A familiar car drew up and an equally familiar figure got out. She felt bile rise to her throat and let the ice cream fall to the ground. She fumbled for her mobile and made a hash of texting the news to the others. Pete seemed to spend a century in the supermarket then emerged with a trolley full of bags. His face was a mass of angles, light and shade masking expression in the blinding glare of the sun. He looked taller than she remembered and thinner. He loaded the bags into the boot and back seat of his car while the Farewell trio rushed to get into theirs to follow him.

They drove south from the town past derelict buildings, which had once been grand, past caravan parks and chalets.

They nearly lost him at a roundabout. The car was loud and uncomfortable with their concentration and their rasping breaths. Lucy rolled down a window and held a paper napkin to her face in case of spewing. Pete turned inland and drove down some meandering roads, which became lanes and narrowed with each furlong travelled. Colin held back in case they were spotted. They were sailing by a dirt track when Lucy spotted Pete's car parked in front of a mobile home. Colin pulled into a lay-by and killed the engine. No one spoke. A bird flew overhead and shat on the windscreen. 'Show time,' Lucy said, regretfully. When she thought she was ready she stepped from the car and barfed drily into a hedge.

'Better out than in,' Famke encouraged. 'If you need us just call. Good luck.'

Colin held up two thumbs.

She rinsed her mouth with water and went to talk to the man she had married. The cold vapour of apprehension surrounded her. Her bowels jerked painfully; she needed a pee, or release at any rate.

The plan, in as much as she had one, was to approach Pete with frost-cool composure, calmly tell him of the error of his ways, organise the return of the money and announce that she was divorcing him. Simple. But not how it panned out. She swerved and careened across a cattle grid guarding the field, almost ending up in the ditch. Look at me, she thought, stumbling towards my future. Her husband turned, stunned. She was convinced she was still at a list as she approached him. This was a conversation that was impossible to begin satisfactorily so she settled on, 'Hello, Pete.'

He was mute, at first. 'Lucy,' he said, eventually, 'you found me.' He looked relieved. 'At last,' she thought she heard him say.

The mobile home was all brown and russet and a thing she thought was velour.

'It's got its own flush loo,' Pete said, the information dying on uninterested ears. He could not meet her eyes. She was glad. If he had she'd have had to belt him one and she wanted to be sure it would hurt and not be as girly as the blow she suspected she'd deliver.

'Super.'

They sat awkwardly across a table. Pete clocked the pale indentation where her wedding ring once lived but didn't comment. His own still shone golden on his left hand. He poured tea from a pot and she stared at it, uncomprehending. Tea? Why? How was that supposed to help?

'Would you like to try to explain what's happened?' she asked, giving him his chance.

'I can't help myself,' he started. Not a good start, as she had to admit. 'It's a disease.'

Now, Lucy knew that was true. Gambling, like alcoholism, is a disease. But she found she didn't give a rattle's curse at that moment. She was furious; beyond words, beyond measure. Her hands gripped her thighs, trying to stem the rage, nails biting into her soft flesh. She exploded.

'How could you reduce our future to this?' she cried.

'You lied to me. Worse, you didn't trust me. You abandoned and degraded me. Was my future so meaningless
you could cast it aside as you did? How could I be so
worthless? You shit. You fucking utter clown of a shit.' She
quaked with after-tremors of anger and sobbed into her
hands.

He did a poor version of humility simply because he
was caught and he was weak and he almost didn't know
what he'd done wrong. 'Luce,' he pleaded.

'Don't you dare call me that,' she warned. 'You forfeited
the right to call me anything after you fucked off and abandoned me.' She hated herself for the emotional swearing
but didn't know how else to express her anger. She paused,
resting her head on her hands and giving space to her
thoughts and urges. 'How could you be so reckless?' she
asked. 'With us? You wrecked our happiness.'

'I'm sorry,' he said, in a low voice. 'I didn't know what
else to do. I owe a lot of money to some . . . criminals . . .
and once we had it from the apartment sale I thought I
could see a way out. But I hadn't told you any of the
trouble I was in by then and I couldn't, just couldn't, bring
myself to look that bad in your eyes so I ran.'

Was that the precise moment when her marriage truly
ended? In the face of this delusion, this lie? He had told
himself this version of the events so often he probably
took it for truth now. But it wasn't. Now was the time to
call it or forever live with the regret.

'That's not quite true, Pete, is it?' she asked, not bothering to hide her disappointment. 'You had to plan it all.

This was on your mind for a long time. You didn't just panic. You had to get me to sign over all of our spending power, bank accounts, the lot.'

She looked at him with new eyes. He was a mess, really. His hair was thinning, rendering his forehead too large. His blue eyes, once dancing with what she'd assumed was harmless mischief, now had a milky quality and were rimmed red with worry. Lines and dark blotches sculpted his face into a gaunt expression. His lips were thin and drawn in a tight line. They suggested a meanness she now knew him capable of. His skin shone as he tried to squirm out of trouble and back into her life.

She felt punchdrunk. The weariness it bestowed precluded vituperation, which would have been a waste of time anyway. She kept it as plain as possible. 'I'll need you to come back to London with me. We have things to clear up. And we'd better pay off the money you owe.' She paused, not wanting to know the answer to the next question but knowing that she had to ask it. 'How much are we talking about?'

'Eighty grand.'

She felt her stomach lurch. Not now, she prayed. She shook her head grimly. 'You sicken me. We'll pay this debt, then you'll give me a quick divorce and disappear from my life. Do you understand?'

He looked at her with eyes full of tears. 'I never meant for any of this to happen.'

'I'm sure.'

She felt the force of the revelations crashing in on her.

She was sitting in a tin can in a field in the middle of nowhere with her heart broken and her marriage over. A knock on the door saved her from further analysis or apportioning of blame. Famke and Colin had come to check on the meeting's progress. Lucy did cursory introductions. No one shook hands.

They let Pete gather his things and left in the rental. They didn't dare risk losing him in traffic if he drove his own car and none of them wanted to share a journey alone with him, and his whingeing self-pity, all the way back to London. As it was it blotted the air without a word spoken. Lucy sat in the front seat, avoiding his gaze but felt it burn holes in the upholstery. She couldn't bear to look at the imprint of regret on his face, painted there as a badge of his martyrdom.

But that wasn't all. She realised she was disappointed to have this weak, plain man to show for her troubles. She had imagined he would look as he did in her pared-back memory, a handsome dynamic force whom others would meet and say, 'Yes, we can see how you would fall for this man and trust him with all of your soul and earthly possessions. Who wouldn't?' Instead, he was a pale waste of space and this degraded her too. He made her feel ashamed for him, but mostly she was ashamed of herself.

Colin played a news-talk station to distract from the void in the car. They listened to woe and opinions and sometimes a feel-good item but heard none of what was said. Signposts pointed to other directions that travellers might take but the hire car had only one destination. For it, all routes led back to London. Lucy remembered the half-eaten ice cream she had dropped in the supermarket forecourt and imagined its coolness melting to liquid then disappearing into the tarmac. Had the cone wafer been cleared away, or was it still lying there, imploded and useless, a pathetic reminder of one small life passing through?

TWENTY-FIVE

Events bled one into another. Lucy walked through them as if on Valium. A lawyer ended her marriage, all that remained was to wait for a decree nisi. Stella knew some Brothers who ushered through the payment of Pete's debts without interest or physical harm accruing, then showed him the road south again. He had spent his London time in the box room of Famke's house, mostly, but Lucy chose not to see him more than was absolutely necessary. He looked every inch the penitent miscreant, wearing a mantle of suffering she found unbearable to watch. It pained her to think of the total happiness she had known and trusted with him, and so she didn't want to physically confront the man in whom so much was invested and so little returned. The connection was broken between them and neither could mend that. There were no exequies for their union. He left one day while she was at work. She found a note later, addressed to her in his hand, which she didn't read. She tore it into tiny pieces and threw it in the recycling bin, where she imagined it reinvented as further bullshit further down the line. Nothing wasted but the squeal, she thought.

She continued to live at Jack's house and, though they continued their congress, each was more subdued than initially. This seemed natural. They had both been let down and needed to help themselves up again. It deepened their affection for one another and the caution with which they pursued their romance was touching. They were careful of one another, as Lucy had said they should be, and took nothing for granted.

Jack was still haunted by his encounter with Laura but knew that he had to cut some slack or go mad. She was under his skin and might always be but he had to be rid of her. She was destructive and he didn't want her back. When he thought of his wife he shivered but Lucy made him smile and he was a better person for that.

Laura, however, had plans.

Ulrika was to be taken apart and put back together again at a rehabilitation centre in Balham. She wished her therapists luck getting to subterranean levels of her mind. She felt she should warn them that there might not be a lot to encounter there. While she appreciated that they wanted to show up her emotional blight, she also wanted some acknowledgement that she was just someone who hadn't put on the brakes in time, and that this might not mean that she was a genius trying to compensate for a fatal flaw. She had just wanted to lose some weight and if that made her vain and stupid, so be it. But no need to tart it up in psychobabble and send her back like a lunatic glossed over with a shallow cure and let out to pull the wings off flies. These were the arguments of the first days of treatment, back and forth, with Ulrika intractable in her resistance to help.

Slowly she began to look at herself in a new light. She gained a little weight and got to like how it filled out the parts of her that looked good with curves. She even grew to think that she might not be a waste of time and perhaps had some endearing qualities. This didn't make her either Einstein or Miss World and she came to the conclusion that she wanted neither of those in the long run anyhow. Her face shone with health and her body moved with purpose. She felt less hollow. She forgave herself her appetite and studied her nutrition charts in order to change her eating habits, or lack of them. She decided to alter her wardrobe. But she was most proud of the fact that she avoided picking up catchphrases or aphorisms about this new lease of energy and purpose.

She was allowed to go home.

There were other areas she wanted to address, and one of them was her job.

'I need a change,' she told Famke and Colin. She took a long breath. 'I'd like to teach something that can make a difference in the world. I don't want my old routine back. It's as if I've been reprogrammed. Now, for instance, every time I see a cream doughnut I have to go through a whole lot of steps as to why I'm walking away from it, if I am, and whether or not that's a positive decision. All very time-consuming. The rest of my life will be an eternal gradient to recovery, or that's how it looks from here at this moment in time.'

Colin was pensive. 'How would you feel about making a difference, even if it didn't involve teaching?'

'That could work,' she allowed. When he failed to elaborate she asked, 'Will I ever get to know what you meant by that?'

'All in good time, my sweet.'

Not long after rain finally came to wash the city down. It didn't stick around long on that occasion, in spite of a rapturous welcome. It returned twelve days later, having collected a few cousins and gave London a sound hosing. Vast sheets of sparkling drops thundered from the heavens, soaking the parched population and refreshing the land and buildings. Drains clogged with dust and waste prevented a run-off and mini floods sprang up throughout the boroughs.

'This is biblical,' Colin said staring out of the window. 'We should build an Ark.'

Children rushed about in wellingtons, screeching delight and drinking in the heavens as if they'd never seen showers before.

The weather drained the sun of its angry energy and left it wan and listless in the sky. The heat, when it returned, was milder, kinder, more humble.

Bill and Helen assembled their friends for a garden party. They stood before them, shy but radiant, and told of their new baby. The waterworks began again, this time human and joyful beyond what words could express. Each neighbour seemed to take a turn to approach the couple, touching them to verify the news and to share their happiness. For a while no one spoke, then Colin let out a triumphant cheer and they began to dance in celebration.

That night Ulrika dreamed of Stephen and Archie again. Their cheeks were flushed with laughter and they were running through their golden meadow. This time she heard what they had shouted to her earlier. 'Tell Mum and Dad her name is Sarah, in case they don't notice straight off.' They sped away again, playing tag, and when Ulrika woke she chided herself for such fancy and wondered why it was her mouth tasted of orange.

Evie and Lucy made plans for the gallery. After Famke's exhibition they scheduled a David Mason retrospective. Evie had kept a ledger of who had bought his work, as far as she could, and they put out feelers to borrow as much as possible. Lost works resurfaced, like old friends rediscovered, unchanged and wondrous after all the years. Lucy made a note to ask Jack for the painting of her as a baby. It would be a key piece.

She was laden with this thought and four shopping bags one evening as she approached the house. Knowing her keys were buried at the bottom of her handbag she rang the bell, in the hope that Jack was home and she wouldn't have to ruin the perfect balance of her load by poking about in search of them. The door was opened by a tall beauty, wearing a supercilious expression and a tight wrap-around sheath that left little to the imagination. The woman's clear, green eyes gazed from beneath a dark, silken fringe. She looked amused. 'What can I do for you?' she asked, as if she already knew the answer.

'I'm Lucy,' Lucy spluttered, not knowing if this made sense any more. 'I live here.'

'Ah, the lodger. I'm Laura, the wife.' She intended that last word as a dagger blow and it was.

Lucy fought for breath and eventually squeezed out a plaintive, 'Is Jack in?'

'No, dear, he's gone for some food and wine. We're having a reconciliation dinner. I'm surprised he didn't mention it.'

'No, no, he didn't.'

'He probably hasn't mentioned we've been sleeping together again either?' She cocked a perfectly plucked eyebrow.

'No.'

'Now would be a good time for you to consider your accommodation arrangements,' Laura suggested. 'I know that Jumbo hates facing such conflicts, so I usually have to.' She let a long-suffering sigh out into the world. 'Men.'

Suddenly Lucy could control herself no longer. She began to laugh, then cry, the perfect mixture of both creating rivulets of saliva, saltwater and viscosity from her mouth, eyes and nose. She wiped her face with the back of her sleeve, the plastic shopping bags banging against the door jamb, and choked on the word 'Jumbo'. She staggered back down the steps and around the corner where she collapsed against a railing breathless from her encounter. She remonstrated herself silently for not expecting this. She had relaxed and left herself unguarded. She had trusted Jack and that left a hole burnt through her. Well, I've been through worse, she thought. It's just a shame it had to end like this. She forced herself to breathe regularly to restore calm. Then she took one last look at Nicholas Farewell and the grand houses of the square, and walked away.

Jack froze to the spot when he found his wife in the conservatory enjoying a crisp gin and tonic. She adorned her face with a smile that forgot to take in her eyes and offered him a drink. He refused. The air crackled with malice.

'Really, Jackie, I am surprised at you. I thought you'd be glad to have me back. You seemed hungry enough for me that day we made love in your office building.'

He hated the way she made the word love dirty with her recollection. She was goading him as well as flexing her power, testing his resolve and her opportunities. It was imperative that he remain calm.

'Your new lodger friend was here but she's gone now, never to return, I fear.'

His pulse nudged up the speedometer.

'Interesting little thing, but harmless. Oh, come on, Jack,' she wheedled. 'Show me how glad you are that I'm home.' She opened the dress and revealed her nakedness. Then she parted her legs and let him see her sex glistening, ready. 'You can see how glad I am to see you.'

He turned his back to her. 'Get out,' he said, his words rasping. 'You disgust me.'

'Have it your way,' she said, her own voice joining his for tone and ice. 'But you have made a big mistake. I no longer want just half, I want everything.'

He didn't move again until he heard the heavy front door bang shut and reverberate through the house. Then he cut loose, bellowing like a madman. His rage burst forth in surges of malevolent energy. He ranted against the elements, an agonised human thunderstorm. He punched walls and kicked chairs.

Lucy returned to familiar territory. The cul-de-sac sat quietly waiting for her, without rancour at her absence or judgement at another lapse in her life. She opened up the red car and let it air. There was no point in trying to drive it away because the engine hadn't been turned over in many weeks. It was incapable of going further. She felt like that now too. She sat in a front seat and ate some fruit, drank some water. Then she fixed up her bed for the night and climbed into the back seat. Her mobile rang, Jack's name flashing as the caller. She ignored it and switched off the phone. Then she settled back into her old home. Her heart twisted in the throes of breaking asunder all over again and quiet tears poured forth.

The following morning a tap on the windscreen woke her. Helen stood holding a mug of coffee and a Danish pastry.

'I've got a great tree house if you're interested.'

'Thanks, but no. I'm a car woman, me.'

'Want to talk about it?'

'Nothing much to say, really. I think we've taken on too much too soon.'

Helen looked into some middle distance. 'Reality pulls you one way, the truth another. You make a decision and stick with it. You're both raw now but it might be useful to look at the bigger picture and if you like what you see you must go after it, whatever that future is. In the meantime, I'll be here for you, Lucy. Now go shower inside and leave your mug in the sink when you've finished with it.'

Later, Lucy walked along the river, keeping her mind neutral, engaging only in admiring the architecture and the act of placing one foot before the other. She propelled herself like an automaton. It was quite soothing. At Mario's, Vida gave her what she knew was 'the Look' but she pretended not to notice. She saw Vida go to the phone and talk urgently to someone on the other end. About fifteen minutes later Greta arrived, her tiny, wizened face locked into an eloquent expression of worry.

'Vida tells me you need somewhere to stay,' she said.

'How does she figure that?' Lucy asked, her brain unable to commute what she was hearing into sense. How had Vida come to such an accurate conclusion?

'I smell your car on you,' a gruff voice said.

She turned to see the Slovenian woman shrug as if this was elementary.

❊　　❊　　❊

363

Greta's house was a genuine marvel. Hidden behind a high hedge and in the shadow of tall apartment buildings it was a gem hidden from passersby.

'This used to be a small townland estate,' Greta explained to an amazed Lucy. 'The surrounding parkland required a gardener-cum-warden, my father, and this was our family home. The big house and most of the land were sold off for development and my family was left with this lodge.'

From the outside it looked like a gingerbread house and indoors was just as delicious. Lucy longed to lick the candy-coloured walls in the hallway to taste the sweetness.

'It's heaven,' Lucy said.

'Oh, heaven's everywhere, dear,' Greta said, matter-of-factly.

Through the window they saw birds swoop from the sky and hop about the garden. Shrubs bloomed pink and yellow. The walls held sweet pea and honeysuckle aloft. Roses scented the air and herbs spilled from pots and containers from many different decades.

'My son will return to live here with his family when his contract in Cape Town is up and I have a little granny flat to the side to move into. That's where I thought you might like to stay for the time being. You needn't worry that I'll be living in your ear, I have lots of outside interests, like my book club, and I play a mean hand of bridge several nights a week, not to mention the odd game of pitch and putt. Vida says you need me, so that is what our American brethren call a "deal maker", I believe.'

'Vida is a witch,' Lucy said, giving words to her theory.

'To be sure, but a white witch, don't you think?'

'If you say so.'

'I do.'

'How much and when can I move in?' Lucy asked.

The deal was done.

'I think a pale sherry is in order,' Greta announced. 'After all, it's six o'clock somewhere.'

They retired to the garden, protected by high walls and lush vegetation. A plane flew overhead.

'You can tell the time by the air traffic,' Greta said. 'We're on the Gatwick flight path.'

Lucy looked up and began to laugh, hard. Finally she lifted a weak finger and pointed at the sky. 'Jumbo,' she said, tears rolling down her face.

TWENTY-SIX

Evie and Lucy visited Famke to review the exhibition and to discuss how to hang the work to best advantage. They were in awe of what they saw before them. Here was a story of the urban landscape, and the city tribe laid bare within it. Yet it told a personal story also, of abandoned and damaged women fighting to return to trust and sanity. I am one of those women, Lucy thought, aware now of the journey she had taken.

'Does art have a redemptive power?' she wondered aloud.

'Only if you want it to,' Famke replied.

They agreed it should be laid out as if the gallery was the cul-de-sac so that the viewers could place themselves on the journey.

'I want it to mean something, anything to the people who see it,' Famke said. 'If it has the power to change the way even one person looks at life I will deem it a success. I would like it to reach everyone though. You know I read an article about high versus low art recently and some man said that gold is more valuable than water because there's less of it around, and I thought yes, but you can't live without water whereas you'll survive without gold.'

Evie found words hard to come by to describe what she was seeing. 'It hurts me,' she said. 'I want to reach out to these women. It moves me, involves me. It makes me wonder. It matters.'

Helen came to the door and hesitated on the threshold. Finally she entered and they watched her move from painting to painting. Her face went from smiling to tears and back. Sometimes she reached out as if she might touch a work, then she would withdraw the hand and place it on her swelling belly. She seemed to be showing the baby all that had happened. Finally she came to rest on the last image, her back facing the main road as she took her first steps back into the world.

Famke spoke. 'I think the cul-de-sac stands as a representative of the human paradox: it's the same way out as in.'

Helen turned. 'There's something missing. Wait here.' She returned holding the green ribbon from Archie and Stephen's simple road shrine. 'I think if you put this with Stephen's painting at the start, the story is complete.'

When they stood in the White Rooms on the night of the opening they knew she had been correct. It was momentous to see the punters move through the event, and be moved by it. They began with the tiny orange oil and green ribbon, nearly every single person touched one or both of these, and moved into the maw of the exhibition. They were no longer spectators, but participants. The muscular brushwork battered them, the bold images stunned. They journeyed through the despair and healing, most stopping to wonder halfway at a large study of Lucy, an expression of post-coital satisfaction unmistakable across her face as she leaned back remembering a pleasure. They were left exhausted at the doorway again, with Helen's back as she stepped out, sensing that happiness could be regained, against all odds, because that is what the human condition demands.

'I bought that particular painting of you,' a deep voice told Lucy. 'No one but me should see you like that.'

She turned to him. 'The news is that plenty of the British public will enjoy it when it goes on tour.'

'True. Then I'll have to make do with seeing the event live in our own home.'

'Jack, I can't move back in. I have to survive alone for a while until I'm fit to share with someone again. I suspect you need that distance too.'

He was the very definition of crestfallen.

'However, I am willing to grant you visitation rights and we'll see if you can actually achieve that expression on my face again or if you're all bluster.'

'Can I start tonight?'

'I see no reason why not. I'll meet you after work.' She walked away grinning.

She refilled glasses for stunned and delighted punters. The critics had come early and rushed away to post their copy and she was certain this augured well.

Colin explained the politics of the cul-de-sac to Evie. She could understand all stories bar one.

'So, Tony left his fiancée to run off with you?'

'Yes, briefly. I think I came along at an opportune time for him. He needed out of there. But ours was not a love affair till the end of never. Now we're friends and I'm on the hunt again. In fact, if I'm not very much mistaken that large Scot over there could be Mr Right. Do introduce me.'

Lucy joined Helen who was standing outside, her face lifted to a hazy autumn sun. Lucy wrapped her arms around her and whispered, 'We made it.'

'I think we may have, yes,' Helen said, kissing her cheek and squeezing her tight.

Colin rushed into the house in a state of hyper excitement. 'The birthing pool has arrived. I gave it a test run.'

Ulrika spat out some mangled asparagus. 'Tell me he didn't just say what I think he just said,' she implored of Tony, who sat with his mouth hanging open and dribbling hollandaise.

'You'd better run us through that,' Famke said.

'It's simple, really. The pool needed to be filled and checked for temperature and leaks and I felt it was important to give it a proper testing so I got in and thrashed around a bit. Quite a good bit, actually, in case the labour is intense.'

Ulrika pushed her plate away. 'If only we'd had that image to scare me with months ago I'd never have needed speed to lose weight, and I could have been spared a visit to the hospital and rehab.'

'I'm sure Bill and Helen are very grateful,' Famke offered.

'I may have started her off,' Colin admitted. 'She laughed so hard she wet herself a bit, but said if it was her waters breaking we'd know all about it. I left before the details got too gory.' He picked out a shard of cucumber from the salad bowl and crunched on it. 'How was saving the world today?'

Ulrika looked at Tony and rolled her eyes. 'Hackney's no Africa, I'll give it that. But as you're asking, we're doing our best with what we've been assigned.'

'Small steps, my lovelies. You knew when you started with World Hocus Pocus Focus that you would have to do your time here before you were let loose on another continent. Today London, tomorrow the universe. I'm sure you'll be exploited in some exotic location by the end of the decade.'

'He is such a help,' Tony said, sardonically, as they savoured Colin's wake.

When he reappeared he was in his best Calvin Klein jeans and a furiously casual shirt.

'Hot date?' Famke asked, on cue.

'Bob,' he confirmed. 'You met him at the private view.'

'I did?'

'Yes, Scottish chap. Fab accent, GSOH, wore a kilt.' Colin fanned his face with his hands. 'A big, hairy man in a skirt. Bliss.'

❋   ❋   ❋

371

Bill rang when the labour started and a gathering came together in Famke's kitchen to drink wine and worry and await the news of the birth and the rhapsody of a new life beginning. She didn't keep them long. Three hours later a baby girl joined the residents of Farewell Square. She weighed in at eight pounds three ounces and had Stephen's nose and Archie's curls. Her parents nuzzled and kissed her and when she had fed for a first time and lay sated at her mother's breast, Helen said to Bill, 'She is the most beautiful girl in the world.'

'Yes. And her name is Sarah.'

The Woman on the Bus

It's a typical Tuesday evening in Kilbrody.

Cathy Long is on her way to collect her drunken father from the pub. Ozzy O'Reilly is in the graveyard, watching the Dublin bus through his binoculars. Charlie Finn is pulling pints, when suddenly it hits him: he's bored. And that's when the woman from the bus walks through his door and drinks herself into oblivion.

Now the whole village wants to know, who is the woman on the bus? The question is, will she tell them?

'Pauline McLynn is still fondly remembered as her role as Mrs Doyle in the Channel 4 sitcom *Father Ted* but her career as an author may yet prove her most memorable move. A stylishly written, hugely enjoyable journey into Maeve Binchy-Marian Keyes country. Laugh-out-loud funny, *The Woman on the Bus* also packs a serious heavyweight punch. All this and a tender love story too' *Scotland on Sunday*

'A funny yet heartwarming tale about human relationships and frailties . . . the characters in her books are not only believable but extremely likeable' *Irish World*

'A deeply moving story. The Irish community is evoked in wonderfully lyrical passages . . . She is a gifted storyteller as well as an exceptional comic actress' *Sunday Express*

0 7472 6782 0

headline
review

Right on Time

Pauline McLynn

'The kind of chatty, self-deprecating humour that has seen the former *Father Ted* housekeeper likened to an Irish Bridget Jones' *Irish Times*

Every second counts for private investigator Leo Street on her latest case. She must find a missing teenager in the drug-fuelled streets of Dublin before it's too late. But with a watch that's stopped and a biological clock that's taken over, it's not going to be easy.

Leo's irrepressible sidekick Ciara, her mischievous mutt No. 4, and Ciara's gorgeous twin brother Ronan, lend a helping hand. But can they track down the missing girl and save the day, or will a case of bad timing put all their lives at risk?

Praise for Pauline McLynn:

'Fabulously funny' *Sunday Independent*

'A cracking plot with nice one-liners' *Eve*

'Funny and snappy... will sit well on a shelf next to such writers as Cathy Kelly, Morag Prunty and Marian Keyes' *Sunday Tribune*

'An amiable anti-heroine who clearly has a great deal of life in her' *The Times*

0 7472 6781 2

headline

Now you can buy any of these other bestselling books by **Pauline McLynn** from your bookshop or *direct from the publisher*.

FREE P&P AND UK DELIVERY
(Overseas and Ireland £3.50 per book)

Something for the Weekend	£6.99
Better than a Rest	£5.99
Right on Time	£6.99
The Woman on the Bus	£6.99

TO ORDER SIMPLY CALL THIS NUMBER

01235 400 414

or visit our website: www.madaboutbooks.com

Prices and availability subject to change without notice.